RJ CLARK

Lockdown

Contents

Dedication

For my father,
Chief Robert D. Clark,
who gave me my love of reading,
which turned into a love of writing.

Thanks... for everything.
I miss you, Dad.

Thank you,
Harlan Coben,

your thanks — as requested.

"All that we see or seem
   is but a dream within a dream..."
   –Edgar Allan Poe

"Life is but a dream."
   –Lewis Carroll

A "**LOCKDOWN**" is defined as:

1. A state or period in which movement within or access
   to an area is restricted in the interests of public safety or
health.

2. The forced confining of prisoners to cells,
   especially as a security measure following an incident or
disturbance.

Prologue

Something Old, Something New

The rules were simple.

    There was only one.

    Stay alive.

    Just...

    Stay.

    Alive.

It was starting all over again. The game. That game. THE game. The infamous one. The dangerous one. The game that had been banned everywhere except in Florida, the former "sunshine state," where it was openly encouraged. *Florida, "we make Mordor look like Beverly Hills."*

If history proves anything true, it is this: banning something, especially an idea, only makes it more desirable. *Here, Eve. Take a bite out of this nice, juicy, perfect apple.*

People want what they cannot have. And they wanted to play the game. They would kill to play, and they would do just that and more.

The board was ready. The pieces moved into place. The timer set.

It was almost time to play.

Strapped In

Today was the day. He had decided that morning by the dawn's early light that he was going to do it. Finally, he was going to do it—kill his daughter.

It was unavoidable. She had to die. It was her or them, or at the very least HIM. He was sure of it. Maybe his wife, her mother, would be spared. Or, more accurately put, overlooked because she seemed to be the only thing in this world their daughter shrank from, like a vampire from a crucifix.

But the rest of them were as good as dead—especially her siblings. She did little to hide her loathing of them.

There were five of them in all. Four girls, and a boy. And only one of them was not like the others, his youngest daughter. The one he decided only that fateful morning had to go.

She was different, as though underneath the skin and bones, she wasn't a kid at all but an approximation of what a child should appear to be. She seemed to him like something of an *old soul.*

And sometimes, when the light hit her face just right, he would swear that something darted and hid behind her eyes, safely tucked away in the shadows. It was not natural, whatever this dark cloud was.

He suspected it was very, very old. So old that it possibly

predated language. A thing without name. Something that was not only the very definition of evil, but so much more. He didn't have to know what to call it to know its dark light needed to be snuffed out.

He agonized over the situation for months, maybe even longer. Maybe he'd been thinking about it since the moment he'd first gazed upon her in the hospital when she'd been born. Yes, that was it. In truth, though he would never dare to say the words aloud, from day one, the child unnerved him. His own flesh and blood, if that's what she was, made his very skin crawl.

From the earliest days, she did things. Or, to say it more rationally, things just had a way of happening whenever she was around. Little things, at first. Lights that would flicker or just turn off completely for no earthly reason. Objects would go missing, only to return some weeks later from the "Greenpoint Triangle," as their home came to be known thanks to all the dematerializing and rematerializing.

Car keys. Books. Wallets. Pictures. Toys. The things had the knack for coming back from The Triangle just when they were about to be missed or forgotten about completely. Sometimes, though, the disappeared did not come back. Or they came back... different, off in just the slightest almost negligible way, like a brand-new pair of sneakers made up of two left shoes.

As she got older, it wasn't just things that went missing. Eventually she moved on to more organic things. Things with life in them.

There'd been the "incident" with the neighbor's Rottweiler, Hercules. He was a one-hundred- and fifteen-pound dog, and he'd been skinned alive in broad daylight. No one saw anything, and no one heard anything—not a trace of a howl or a whimper. Nothing.

That is, until the lady of the house came home from grocery shopping and found the miserable de-furred animal dragging itself across the front lawn as neighbors and bystanders shrieked and cried with horror. Hercules, however, never made a sound, right up until he breathed his last.

His daughter had never liked that dog. Hercules's barking kept her up at night. And she was... disagreeable when she didn't get enough sleep. The morning Hercules was separated from his skin, she had complained that the beast's barking had ruined her sleep again and wondered if someone would just silence the mutt once and for all.

As soon as he heard the news about poor, poor Hercules, he knew exactly what had happened even if he didn't know how she had done it.

Still, that hadn't been the last straw. It should have been, and maybe for a better man, it would have been. No, for him, the straw that finally broke his back was finding his son—her own brother—drowning in the bathtub; his head held under by an unseen hand.

Her hand, he knew. The claw of the old thing inside of her. He had come so close to losing it all, but right at the last minute, as his wife stormed up the stairs, the invisible hand relented and released the boy.

He almost lost him then, his beautiful baby boy. And it wasn't the first time she tried to kill her brother. Next time she might finally succeed. Because there surely would be a next time.

What if he wasn't fast enough? What if his wife wasn't home? What if... what if...

No, he decided. This had gone on too long. Too many years

living in fear, and too many sleepless nights. He was going to kill her before she did away with all of them. His wife would understand in time why he'd done it. He'd make her understand, make her see what a foul thing their daughter had been all along.

But how—how to do it? That was the only question that remained in his muddled mind.

It needed to be done in a way that would not raise the child's hackles or bring the long, inept arms of the law to their doorstep.

Drown her in the shallows of Willow Lake? Say she tripped, hit her head on a rock? Or maybe push her over the railing at the scenic overlook over by Wolfe's Point? He could say she must have climbed over while he wasn't looking and just tumbled over and down.

Of course, he could always just hold her down in the backseat of the car and stuff her mouth full of scalding hot French fries and melty spoonfuls of Rocky Road until her pipes were so clogged that not even EX-X-X-Tra Strength Drain-Oh could unclog them.

Or maybe he'd just lock her in the car and watch her bake in the sun for a few hours while she slept soundly thanks to itty bits of Ben-Ah-Drill carefully mixed into her ice cream.

Something would come to him, and if it came back to him, the deed, well... that's why god made lawyers, right? All would become clear once he got the day going. He was sure of it.

One way or another, at the end of today, only one of them would be coming home.

"Come on, Sandra. Let's go for a ride," he said, steadying his voice though he felt himself tremble on the inside. The last thing he wanted to do was tip his hand to the little monster.

"Just the two of us. We can go to the bookstore. I know how much you love the bookstore. And then we can get ice cream at Pat's. Rocky Road. It'll be… fun."

She simultaneously squinted dubiously at the word "fun" but brightened by about 600 watts at the mention of books and Rocky Road ice cream. And at the same time his daughter's world brightened for the fleetest of moments, he felt something like fingers flipping through his thoughts as though they'd been jotted on index cards.

Sure, Daddy. It'll be so much fun. Just you and me.

The thing behind her eyes, the shapeless darkness, slithered. But he didn't see.

If he had seen it—that flash of the thing that lived in her shadows, grinning out at him from the void—he never would have gotten in the car with his daughter that morning.

No, he never would have strapped her into her car seat, locked the doors and windows, or cranked up that annoying kid's music cassette that was the rage with all the kids in the neighborhood at that moment—all of the kids but her.

Old soul.

He never would have eyed his daughter in the car's mirror, noting maybe for the first time what big eyes she had.

And he never would have driven past Pat's, the best ice creamery in Brooklyn, and turned onto Park Street from Oak Drive.

He also might never have taken notice of what big teeth she had, too. Such sharp, tiny teeth. The kind made for tearing and ripping.

But he had decided that morning the deed needed to be done, and so now here he was, trapped inside the steel frame of a speeding car that was likely to be his coffin, a vehicle he no longer had control of, heading straight for the massive old elm in the square, with his daughter. A monster in human clothes.

The drive lasted only ten minutes. Six hundred seconds, and then it was all over.

It happened fast. The impact.

The car had been going a hundred and thirty when it settled on the elm. The tree ate through the car's exterior as though it had been constructed of notebook paper. Glass shattered and blew out. The exterior side mirrors took off like rockets, then rolled down the street a good fifty or sixty feet. The joints and beams of the car's solid frame bent and broke like twigs as a horrible ear-piercing screeching sound came from somewhere in the bowels of the vehicle.

He thought it sounded like a mechanical shriek, like the soul of the car was screaming.

The seatbelt, which he'd been wearing right up until moments before the collision, came unbuckled as the two objects crashed into each other. It felt like a small unseen hand had pushed on the red lock button and unbuckled it.

He shot through the windshield head-first like a bullet. Shards and pointy bits of glass tore into his delicate skin. He thought it felt like little teeth gnawing at him. Almost like baby teeth, or the teeth of a young child—like his daughter. Blood oozed from what must have been a million cuts and gashes by the time his body smacked onto the well-manicured lawn of the square—his tax dollars hard at work, and he had to admit, it did cushion the landing somewhat. He spun and rolled through the thick greenery, leaving a slick red trail in his wake.

Finally, he lay flat on his belly, arms and legs outstretched so that from above he might have appeared to be the "X" that marked the spot on a treasure map. That he was still alive and breathing was the treasure. His life was now worth more to him than a chest full of shiny gold coins.

He winced and wheezed simultaneously, as everything that already hurt suddenly hurt even more as he tried to breathe. For a small moment, he thought everything might still be fine. He might still be okay and maybe not walk away from this but crawl away at the very least.

But then he heard it, and his heart nearly stopped its rhythmic pumping right then and there. That giggle. That awful, awful giggle. It was a child's voice, HIS child's voice, but that giggle did not come from any human-born child. It sounded older, wiser than a child and with a sinister edge to it. He thought it sounded like it might have come from the depths of hell.

His blood, which had but a moment ago felt fiery, now felt cold as it painted his white skin red. He shivered, and then sharply sucked in air as the pain from the shivers hit what must have been every nerve ending in his beat-up body. Tears filled his eyes, then spilled over and made a clean path down his soiled cheeks.

As the giggling intensified to a maniacal frenzy, he knew how this game was going to end.

Suddenly, he felt his right leg twist and bend, bones snapping and crunching until his leg rested against his back. He screamed out as his left leg repeated the motion. Next, it was his arms that twisted and bent until they lay broken and limp. It was as though someone was using his body like one of those Super Stretch action figures he had when was a kid.

Miraculously, somehow, despite the pain and the state of what was left of his body, he was still alive and breathing. His breaths came in unsteady gasps while a steady river of silent tears flowed out from his bloodshot eyes. There were words he wanted to say, things he wanted her to know, but he felt her in his head, thumbing through his every thought.

He sucked in air one final time as his body quickly twisted into impossible shapes like his extremities were pieces in a puzzle cube.

Clicking. Turning.

Bones cracked, some tearing through the weak armor of skin he wore.

Turning. Clicking.

Blood spewed in all directions, spurting up and out like he was a fountain, an artistic centerpiece elevating the drab town square. Blood soiled the freshly mowed lawn and painted the pristine sidewalk crimson.

Oh, Daddy. Mama always wanted you to paint the town red. And now you have.

At last, he lay still. His body tucked together so neatly that it might slide into a medium-sized moving box with little effort. His head and upper torso were just about the only parts not obscenely twisted out of place. There was no pain now, only the bittersweet taste of surrender.

Death stood on the other side of the door now. It rapped gently, an unassuming knock. *Shave and a haircut... two bits.* As he opened the door and let Death in, he saw her exit the broken vehicle and skip over to the lawn as though she was playing a game of hopscotch in their driveway. She hopped until she stood over him, and then stopped to giggle. And in that moment, she seemed to tower over him, blanketing him in a shadow that could not have been cast by his daughter's small frame. The shadow was the thing, the evil thing.

"You were right, Daddy. That WAS fun," she squealed, lowering herself to him. "And when I get home, after I've shed a few waterless tears for dear old departed Dad, I'm going to squeeze the life out of that precious little sissy boy of yours until his eyes pop right out of his head like little green olives."

His mouth filled with blood. It dribbled out at the corners and rolled down his neck. "N-n-o, S-S-S-and-ra-a-a, d-d-don't. P-plea—"

His eyes bulged to mammoth proportions, almost cartoon-ish. Then, his jaw dropped as he took in a deep inhalation, readying in his mind for the futile protests and pleas he'd make with the monster to spare his beloved son, and the rest of his family, too.

But he wanted the chance to bestow on his only son the last life vest before the Titanic sank under the dark, frozen waters into the abyss below.

Only nothing came spilling out. No words. No sound. It was like everything had stopped, even time. But then, a slow and steady hiss of dead air slipped through the wide open mouth at the end of the dark tunnel of his insides as his face froze in a portrait of sheer terror.

It wasn't long before the wheezing wound down to a stop, and he walked off to maybe not greener pastures with Death.

At that, she leaned in and kissed her father on his cheek as someone, somewhere behind her began to scream and yell.

Someone call 9-1-1. Get help. Did anyone call an ambulance? Oh my god, is he dead? A body isn't supposed to twist like that.

Showtime, she thought to herself, scrunching up her face to approximate anguish. She held her breath in until she knew her cheeks were glowing nearly as bright as that damned reindeer's stupid nose. The crocodile tears and empty wails came next. For fun, she'd sprinkle in a "wake up, Daddy, please" here and there just to tug at the onlooker's heartstrings.

Judging from the audience response, she'd done it. Nailed it. Landed every line perfectly so there wasn't a dry eye in the house. *And the award for best actress in a leading role goes to...*

She basked in every *there, there* and *everything is going to be okay.* If anyone had looked, really looked at that young girl's face, they would have been horrified to see the proud glow coming off of it. And the more they bought her act, the brighter she glowed.

I was born for this.

There was one dissenting voice among the others that caught her ear. It was only there for a fraction of an instant before it went quiet, but she knew it didn't need more time to sow its salacious seeds. *It was her. The girl. She did this.*

On that day, the voice said nothing more.

When many years had come and gone, and some Greenpoint-ers thought about that horrible day and the terrible accident, some would think, without hesitation or guilt, that the little girl had indeed done it.

In a little while, when the roaring sound of the sirens filled the normally peaceful square, drowning out the chatter and her crocodile crying, only when she was certain no one would hear, then, and only then, would she laugh her head off.

And now that she'd finally done away with her nosey little father, she couldn't help but wonder what else she could do. It was time she found out. She was tired of hiding. The day had come for a reckoning. There was a whole lot of hell that needed raising.

Coming Around Again

The phone rang. Loud and obnoxious, sounding more like a choir of tone-deaf Karens singing Puccini than a sophisticated telecommunication device. In the pitch black, tucked under a mountain of bedding, the sleeping figure did not stir. Instead, a slow and steady symphony of resonant snores drowned out the electronic *brrrrinnng, brrriiinnng, brrrriiiinnnnnnnggggg.*

Then the room fell silent. The loud ringing had, momentarily, lulled the dreamer into a deeper, noiseless sleep. It was so quiet that a simple gust of butt wind would've sounded more like the boom of a bomb than a fart. But all good things eventually meet their end, and the momentary peace was soon once again broken by the ringing of the phone.

It rang once, then paused. And then it rang again, and then again. And again and again, somehow sounding louder with each new alert; screaming at the top of its non-existent lungs—*hey, dumbass! Wake the fuck up!*

At last, the mattress groaned as the sleeping figure rose and slept no more. A second groan escaped from his mouth as he wiped the crusty sleep from his eyes and looked at the cellphone sitting on the nightstand. It was dark and asleep. Dead quiet. Its screen painted in electric black, but the ringing persisted.

He turned to the cluttered desk in the corner, which really was more of a collection plate for dirty clothes than a work-station, and eyed the blocky red phone occupying the only free space on the fake wooden table. It was one of those old-school analog phones. Once upon a time, people called them "landlines" because they plugged into the wall, connecting to the land and not sending invisible radio waves into the ether. Our guy, now wide-as fuck-awake, called this phone the "Bat phone," as this line only rang in case of an emergency—an actual DEFCON-1 type of emergency and not some b.s. bodega hold-up that any beat cop could manage.

Before he knew it, a sort of somnambulist instinct took over and the distance between the bed and the desk was made. He pressed the receiver to his ear. The line crackled and hissed. He cleared his throat of whatever crud had taken up residence there in the four hours he lay in bed and said in a low growl of a voice that sounded far more like the late Clint Eastwood than he cared to admit, "Go for Detective Harding."

Harding coughed, turning his head away from the receiver but still keenly listening to the voice on the other end. He wiped at his mouth, fingers searching for something the cough had dislodged from his chest onto his chin.

"The Willows? Yeah, I know where it is. ETA… say fifteen minutes." He caught a whiff of his scent. "Make that twenty."

Harding sifted through the unfolded pile of clothes as he listened to the flat, nasal drone of the dispatcher on the other end of the line. He moved in a memorized rhythm, hearing the beat only others on the job can hear when their phones ring in the middle of the night.

But then he froze. The words received through the telephone wire stunned Harding into docile inaction.

He stood there, caught in imaginary headlights, as motionless as the statue of David.

Something disturbed the water in Harding's brain. A memory came loose and swirled to the surface. It was so close that Harding could almost discern it.

San—

He was sure he'd heard that wrong. What the dispatcher on the other end of the line had so calmly and matter-of-factly just said. *No, no. NO.* His ears were playing tricks on him. They had to be. There couldn't be any other explanation.

At least, Harding hoped there couldn't be. Because if he *had* heard the dispatcher correctly, Harding had just stepped out of bed and into a world of shit.

"Would you… say that again, please? No, no. That last part. Just the last part. Would you say it again?"

The dispatcher repeated the message verbatim.

Ah, fuck, Harding thought. *Not again. It's starting again.*

—dra.

Idle Hands

"Like, I'm just sooooo boreddddddddd, Imo. Bored. To. Death, for real. IRL. I feel like... like... this lockdown is never gonna end. We're just gonna be trapped inside these same four walls for the rest of our lives. OMG. My dad would just love that. No more boys ringing the bell. No more wondering if I'm gonna end up knocked up like Angela Thompson. You knew Angie, right? The tallllllllll one. They used to call her Jolly Green, like the vegetable guy? Ho, Ho, Ho! So... Jolly Green, Angie, she has like... nine brothers, I think. Nine boys and only one moderately cute one. What are the odds of that? Like one in what... a million, billion, trillion? Shit. I can't do the math. This brain wasn't wired for that shit. Jolly Green... she had to drive like eight hundred miles to get rid of it. The kid. Anyway. I'd probably be okay for, like, a week. I mean, if we never got to go out again. But then I'd miss Bobby—"

Imogen made a barfing sound, but Ally plowed on, undeterred.

"And Billy. Of course, there's Tommy Twotone. I don't think that's his actual real last name. Like, it can't be. Right? Twotone? What kind of a name is Twotone?"

"Uh—"

Imogen wanted to say *it's pronounced "Tuttone," like TWO-*

TONE-EH, but there wasn't any room to get a word in. Rarely did Ally leave space for anyone else.

Without stopping for breath, Ally went on. "Well, there's that guy Greg from last summer. Or was it two summers ago? Shit. Maybe three. Greg. You know Greg! Josie Filmore's cousin's best friend's old neighbor who used to go to Wilbur, but now I think he goes to Sanderson. Or is it Standerson? I don't know. Is that important? I'll tell you what is though. He has a biggg package. I'd be walking like old widow Castella, all hunched over and shit, but it'd be worrrth it! So worth it. Well, anyway. And then it's like... we're just never gonna go back to school, you know. Cause of this lockdown thing. I mean, it's not like that's a bad thing or anything. OMG, did I just snort? That was me, right? I think I snorted. Can you believe it? Let me find out I never have to see that creepy A-F janitor—"

"Custodial engineer," Imogen said, without sounding like she was shouting across the small bedroom. The phone sat, lit and open, on her desk five feet away. She lay on her back in the middle of the floor, staring at the glow-in-the-dark stars stuck to her ceiling. That one peeling sticker that was trying to leave Orion irritated her. When this was all over, she'd have to replace it. Even her fake constellations needed to be perfect. Or else why bother? "Was that all one breath? Damn girl. That might be a record even for you. Don't you ever stop to take a breath, Al? I swear one day you're just going to keel over, gasping your last breath just so you can have the final word. Come on, do it with me right now. Take a breath. In through the nose, out through the—"

"Was *that* all one breath, Imo?" Ally snorted again. "OMG. I can't stop doing that. Can you believe it?"

"I can," Imogen said, her voice sounding like an auditory

eye roll, if there was such a thing.

"Oh, you bitch!" On the other end, Ally laughed and snorted yet again.

Imogen thought it sounded more like the *oink, oink* of a hog than the nasal squeal of a teenage girl but kept her mouth shut and her eyes glued to the stars glowing faintly above her.

"Anyway," Ally began. "Yes, and, like, what?"

"We speak English here, Al. English, remember?"

"Huh. Whatever. Yes, that was all one breath. Namaste, motherfucker. Namaste! And what in the actual fuck is a 'custodial engineer'?"

"A janitor."

"So why don't we just call them 'janitors' then? When did this happen?"

Imogen stretched her arms to the stars and sighed. "I don't know. I guess it's kind of like how we call Native Americans... Native Americans instead of just Indians, you know?"

"Blech. I still call them Indians. It's less of a mouthful, you know? It just rolls off the tongue better."

"You're not supposed to. And I thought you *liked* having your mouth full."

Ally howled with laughter. No snort this time. "The rumor of my oral fixation has been greatly exaggerated. And, whatever. Is like the Grammar Police gonna pull up and arrest me? Noooo-body cares."

"I think *they* do, you know. The Native Americans."

There was a slight hesitation before Ally blew a raspberry and continued. "Well, I don't care. I mean, how many are left anyway? I thought we killed them all with like poisoned blankets and scurvy."

"Scurvy? Are you being serious right now?"

"What? Scurvy's a thing." Silence. "It is a thing, right?"

"Yes, it *was* a thing... for pirates and sailors in the 1500s."

"Arghhhh. Yo, ho, ho and a bottle of gum," Ally said, treating Imogen to her very best approximation of what she thought a sixteenth-century pirate sounded like. She sounded like neither a person from the sixteenth century nor a pirate. Rather, her voice reminded Imogen of her great Aunt Margie, a chain-smoker with a perpetual wet, throaty cough.

Imogen couldn't help but laugh at Ally's gaffe. "You're dumb. It's *rum*. Not *gum*."

"Wait, what?" Ally stopped long enough to presumably ponder her word selection. "Yo, ho, ho and a bottle of... Yo, ho, ho.... a bottle of... rum. Gum. Rum. Rum. REDRUM! REDRUM! Huh. Yeah, I guess that's right. Rum. Who knew?"

Imogen rolled onto her side, tickled with laughter. Her head faced away from the phone, so that when she spoke again, Imogen unconsciously raised her voice. "Like everyone. Everyone knows that, seriously." She laughed harder. Tears spilled down her cheeks. "Everyone but you. Yo, ho, ho and a bottle of gum!"

"Oh, hardy har har. I'm sure I'm not the *only* one. Wait. Am I on speaker? Did you put me on speaker? Why would you put me on speaker? You know I hate the sound of my voice."

Imogen wiped at her eyes and rolled onto her back. "Yeah, so does everyone else. Ohhh, burnnnn!"

Ally said something like *yeah, yeah* but Imogen's attention had wandered to the open laptop sitting on her bed. During her victory cheers and jeers, the computer chimed, signaling a new incoming message. Its screen slowly woke to the familiar desktop photo of Imogen on London Bridge with her parents from two summers ago when she took part in a summer abroad program.

Imogen noted how none of them had visibly changed all that much in the two years between London and now. The world outside was another story.

The familiar streets of her neighborhood, the same streets she'd mapped mentally since she could walk, felt about as familiar as a dirt road in some unpronounceable village in an unpronounceable city in a country whose name changed with every successful coup. Imogen felt as though she'd landed somewhere over the rainbow and was most definitely not in Kansas anymore. These were thoughts she pushed away. Or tried to. But like a persistent itch, they kept on coming back, needing to be scratched even harder.

"Hey, Red Beard," Imogen yelled to the phone as she got to her feet. Ally responded by starting a lively round of *yo, ho, ho and a bottle of gum.*

It was only a few short steps to the bed, so Imogen could immediately read the message on the screen. Comprehending it took longer.

"Oh, shit," she said out loud, but still more to herself. Ally, still living her best pirate life on the other end of the phone a few blocks away, heard nothing. Imogen moved a shaky hand to her chest, checking if her heart was still pumping. It was, but Imogen was sure it had stopped for a second or two when her eyes focused on her laptop's screen. "Yo, Red Beard! Give it a rest. Go... walk the plank for a second or something."

And just like that, Ally gave up her seafaring life for one of an average, maybe a little less than average, teenager. "Um, rude! And totally unnecessary. It's weird though, right? How I can hate the sound of my own voice, but damn if I don't think I can carry a tune with the best of them. Mmm, yeah! Eat your heart out, Miley."

The mattress, which hadn't been comfortable when it was new, was now very far from new and even less comfortable. Imogen wasn't sure who groaned louder whenever she lay on it, her or the bed. As she sat now, the mattress let out a long, slow sigh.

Ally, who had slept on that bed for as many years as it lived in Imogen's room, recognized the sound at once. "Are you on your bed? Why are you in your bed? And why are you quiet? What's going on with you?"

Imogen's throat suddenly felt as dry as the Eerie River. "I... uh..." As much as she tried, the words wouldn't form. There were too many of them, and Imogen had no idea where to start.

"Yeah? Speak, girl!"

The hint of a smile appeared on Imogen's face. *Was this real? Was this happening? Really happening?* All the nights she'd lain awake on her floor, staring up at the dollar store plastic stars and planets, imagining clearly in her mind this moment. *This very moment.* And now, here it was. Happening. Happening to her. And Ally. Jesus H. *Ally.* No matter how many ways Imogen pictured it, Ally was never a part of the fantasy. *And that's why it's called a fantasy*, Imogen mused.

"Hey, Earth to Imo? Earth to Imo. Come in, Imo!"

The sound of Ally's voice grew more and more distant, and the ambient white noise of the bedroom muted. The whole room seemed to be covered in a thick, fluffy quiet. The words, the message, became clearer and clearer. The words making more and more sense the longer she looked at them as though they had moments ago been hieroglyphs that were now translating themselves into English.

Greetings from Gemeo Labs and the Gemeo Project!

"No, seriously… Imo, are you there? Hello? Did you die?"

We've received the results of your familial DNA inquiry.

"Hellllllllloooooooooo?"

And we're happy to report—

"Really, Imo. This isn't funny anymore. If you don't say something, I'm just gonna hang up. Like, really hang up."

—that you have received a match on your genealogical tree.

"Okay, Imo. I'm hanging up. I'm doing it. I'm hanging up."

Click the sparkling tree graphic to see your results. We hope this will be the beginning of a very exciting journey for you.

"Um, so," Imogen finally said.

"Oh, good. You're not dead. Speak."

Click the sparkling tree graphic to see your results.

"Do you remember the, um, gene thing I was telling you about? That ad I saw before the world went to shit."

Do you ever feel you don't belong? Do you feel alone even when surrounded by friends and family? Do you ever think you were meant to be somebody else? That you are, in fact, someone else. Do you have questions, the kind that keep you up all night staring at the stars? Does your family have the answers? Any of the answers? Maybe we can help. We're Gemeo Labs. And this is the Gemeo Project. Knowledge is our business. Click the sparkling tree graphic to begin your journey.

"That, like, family tree thing, you mean? Yeah. It sounded kind of… culty. No, wait a minute. You didn't. Tell me you didn't click the tree and join a cult. Imo!"

Imogen's pointer finger hovered over the trackpad. "I clicked the tree."

"Holy shit, Imo! Are you in a cult now?"

"I got a hit." Imogen couldn't hide that her voice broke at the word "hit." A small word loaded with years of pent-up emotion.

"HOLY. FUCKING. SHIT."

Imogen giggled. "Yeah. So..."

Click the sparkling tree graphic—

Mirror, Mirror on the Wall

The sound of the permanently shit-brown stained coffee mug hitting the floor and breaking into three big, chunky pieces startled Olivia awake. Her eyes adjusted and surveyed her surroundings like a lab rat coming out of anesthesia as it lay strapped to a rat-sized gurney. A stabbing pain in her head sent shockwaves through every part of her body, jolting her awake faster than a double dose of caffeine.

Where the fuck am I? Wasn't I just in my car? What just happened? Did I fall as—

"Oh, I'm sorry, d-d-dear," the super-sized waitress stuttered, looking down at Olivia with a strange but sympathetic look on her grotesquely made-up face. She wore glasses that appeared as large and wide as her head. And worse, their tone matched her tall, coiffed purple hair.

She looks like a clown. A goddamned clown.

Olivia caught sight of the server's nametag, swallowing a laugh: "My name is... (your name goes HERE)."

Is that a joke? Is all of this just...a joke? Screw it, I'm going to just call her "Flo."

The nameless waitress jerked her head to the side three times in rapid succession, almost like she'd been seized by a mini fit of some kind. When it subsided, her head remained cocked. Her jaw dropped and hung open. The server's thick, saliva-soaked tongue wagged about in her mouth like a blood-gorged worm.

A low groan stirred from the back of her throat, eventually getting louder until it came out as, "d-d-dear." Her head snapped back to center with a click. The waitress blinked her eyes several times in rapid succession and now only stared out from behind her spectacles, looking as though she were awaiting instructions from the mothership.

"Nasty weather out there." Flo tipped her head to the steamed-up front windows. Despite being clouded over and dripping with condensation, Olivia could still make out the distinct pattern of rain pelting the glass façade. "Really, it's raining cats and dogs out there. MEOW! Ha!"

Did she just...meow at me?

Flo froze again, this time with her mouth locked mid-laugh, making it look more horrific than humorous.

"So glad you came in out of the rain. You really should dry yourself off a bit, d-d-dear. I hope you won't mind me sayin' so, but you're looking a bit like a wet pussy yourself right about now. Ha!"

Please don't meow. Please don't meow. Please don't—

Only then did Olivia realize she *was* soaking wet from head to toe. Strands of her long, thick hair stuck to the side of her face like blood-stuffed leeches while her cold, wet clothes hugged her body closer than her pervy Uncle Morris on Thanksgiving, Christmas, and twice on her birthday.

Wait...wasn't I dry a second ago, or...am I losing my mind?

"Shall I g-g-get you a towel, d-d-dear? You really should have brought a change of clothes. Always be prepared, that's what my mama used to say. My mama had a good head on her shoulders. Of course, she never saw Daddy coming with that twelve-gauge. Blew her head dang off her shoulders. *That* she wasn't prepared for, I can tell you. Ha!"

Flo's head ticked as though a sudden jolt of electricity had zapped her.

The. Fuck?

What is this place? Am I high or in the loony bin or something?

How did I get here? I don't remember...getting here. Or... anything.

Olivia surveyed her surroundings. It looked like your run-of-the-mill greasy spoon. A small box-car diner with about sixteen booths and a long counter with seating for another two-dozen people. Coffee brewed in an industrial-sized pot behind the counter, while steam puffed up in thick clouds through the two clear portholes in the dirty, food-and-sauce-splattered pair of swinging doors that presumably led to the kitchen.

Weird. It doesn't smell like a diner. It doesn't smell like anything.

Utensils clattered, and food sizzled on the grill, but save for the waitress, herself, and...*what the fuck is that...is that... an Indian sitting at the counter...or is it Native American now?* Save for Flo, herself, and the Native American at the counter—dressed in what seemed to be full traditional regalia, headdress and all—Olivia didn't see another soul in the joint. Still, it felt haunted, like there was more life in the place and Olivia just couldn't see it.

No, Olivia just couldn't see it *yet.*

Against the far wall of the diner, just before a narrow hallway that Olivia assumed led to the shit boxes—which she didn't need eyes on to guess were about as well-kept as the rest of the place—sat a massive old-timey coin-operated jukebox. A thick blanket of dust covered the unit, but it looked like it was still fully stocked with about a hundred of those small vinyl records. Olivia wondered if that old jukebox had any music left in its sleeping heart.

As if on cue, the jukebox roused from its slumbering state and whirred noisily to life. Its lights flashed and flickered. A record dropped and spun on the turntable. After a few hisses and pops, "Don't Dream It's Over" by Crowded House began to play.

Olivia continued to survey her strange surroundings. A garish neon sign caught her eye. It dangled precariously above a clunky old cash register, the manual kind with big, round push-button keys. The neon sign pulsed as light swirled through the tubes. It read: "The Greasy Spoon Diner."

The...what? Had that been there a minute ago? I was thinking it. This place is a greasy spoon. Maybe I saw the sign, and it didn't click? I don't know. I...I don't know. There's something very off here.

"It's just through there," the waitress said, pointing a finger capped with glittery purple polish to the bathrooms. "You can, you know, freshen up, d-d-dear. There's an air dryer, too."

"Jesus, fuck!"

Olivia was standing beside the waitress. Only, she didn't recall getting to her feet. One moment she was sitting in the booth, taking stock of this corner of the Twilight Zone, and then...boom, she's on her feet. She looked at the waitress in disbelief.

The waitress cocked her head, her forehead wrinkling as though she was now confused as well. "You know, for your clothes?"

Olivia gave herself a vigorous pat down. *Still soaking wet.*

Olivia was about to give her brain a pat down to see if it was still there, when the waitress planted a slap on her ass. It resounded like a thick wad of wet toilet paper being hurled at the ceiling. *SPLAT!* The unexpected contact and the surprising force the waitress put into the ass plant sent Olivia stumbling toward The Greasy Spoon's shit boxes.

"Go on now, d-d-dear. Git!"

Olivia went to take another step forward, and the next thing she knew, she was standing in front of the bathroom door. The door had seen better days and was now covered in graffiti, obscene writing, and stickers. So many stickers. *Junior Miller Eats Shit.* She shuddered.

Let's hope old Flo has a close and personal relationship with Mr. Kleen.

She pushed, and the door creaked open.

Olivia only glimpsed what lay behind the door, but it wasn't any kind of shit box she'd ever seen. It was...something else entirely. Something she didn't know if she had a name for—if *anyone, anywhere* had a name for.

"I say, do you mind?" an agitated and very proper sounding voice rebuffed.

And then the door slammed shut in Olivia's face. She gasped and then found herself sitting back at the booth where this strange dream began. A quick pat down told Olivia her clothes and her person were now very much dry.

Keep your shit together, girl. Don't react. Don't...do anything. Just breathe.

The waitress held up a pot of steaming coffee, offering to refill Olivia's already obviously full mug sitting on the table.

"I know it's hotter than Death Valley out there today, but can I top you o-o-off?"

Olivia checked the front windows. Outside was nothing but bright sunshine and a cloudless blue sky.

Broken mug. She dropped a mug.

But it wasn't on the ground in pieces where it *should* have been. All Olivia saw down there were a couple of old French fries and Flo's cheap loafers that looked about as comfortable as a Judas Cradle.

She dropped it. I know she did. I know she did. Where the fuck did that mug come from? When did she put it there? When did I dry off? What the hell was that in the bathroom that wasn't a bathroom? How the FUCCCKKKK did I get here?

"Sorry, d-d-dear. Clumsy old me," Flo said, sounding like she had not a care in the world. Her eyelids fluttered three times, then two times more, before remaining open wide. Her fixed gaze bore holes in the center of Olivia's forehead. "It's just that you look so much like her. It's downright uncanny. That's what it is. Un-canny, I'll tell you what. More coffee, d-d-dear?"

Look so much like her...who? Why does that sound familiar? It's right there, and I just can't seem to get it. FUCK.

The mug on the table bothered Olivia. It *really* bothered her. None of this made a lick of sense, but she *knew* old Flo had dropped a mug a minute ago. Now it was gone, and abracadabra, shama-lama-ding-dong there was a shiny new one in its place. Well, not new exactly. Nothing was new in The Greasy Spoon, but new to Olivia's table.

How the fuck did she do that? Did I space out again? Or is she like the Harry Houdini of hired help?

A thought came to Olivia then, something random. A thing she hadn't thought about in a long time. A very long time.

Pay no attention to the man behind the curtain.

"Off to see the wizard," Olivia said softly. "The wonderful wizard of Oz."

"Pardon? Well, I'll just come back and check on you in a few, dear. See if I can't tempt you with a slice of my a-a-apple pie. It's homemade, you know. The best you'll ever taste."

The waitress smacked her puffy lips, then not so much turned to take her leave but jerked around slowly as though she stood on a mechanized turntable that hadn't seen a spot of grease in decades.

"No, wait. Hold up a sec."

The waitress turned back to Olivia in the same jerky manner. "See? I knew I could tempt you with some pie. Pie makes everything better. You know what they say?"

Olivia stared and waited, but the waitress remained frozen in place. Stuck.

"You know what they say," Flo repeated.

This time Olivia deliberately waited, just to see what would happen. Just to see what Flo would do. Five seconds passed. Then twenty. And then thirty. It wasn't until the ticker was closing in on a minute that the waitress finally turned back on and said, with the smallest of edges in her voice that had not been there before, "You know what they say."

"No, what do they say?"

"All things are possible...with pie!" The waitress flashed a toothy smile. If this had been a cartoon or a farce, her teeth would have sparkled.

Olivia laughed. "Right. I'll, uh, keep that in mind."

"That's nice, d-d-dear."

With that, Flo turned to go. Olivia grabbed her arm. "No, wait. I want to ask you something. I want to ask—"

The waitress, her face still blazing with a smile, looked down at Olivia's fingers wrapped around her forearm. She raised her head, and the smile was gone.

Olivia let go of Flo's arm, noting that for the first time since she found herself in this...place, wherever and whatever the fuck it was, for the first time she felt afraid.

"Yes, d-d-dear?"

Flo fluttered her false lashes—*were they there before?*—as if to say, *could you hurry it up, sweetheart. I've got seven other tables and an impatient geriatric waiting on a side of slaw.*

"It's just...what you said before. Remember, Flo?"

The waitress narrowed her eyes. If looks could kill—or maim, at the very least. "Flo? Hmm. I like the sound of that. It...flows." A look of resignation came over her face. Then she continued. "Yes, d-d-dear?"

"You said I looked just like her."

"Oh, that." The waitress laughed, but it came out sounding like a poor attempt. It sounded like the sound one might make if they'd never actually heard a real live laugh, but only had one described to them. "Well, that's because you do, d-d-dear. Near spitting image, I'd say. Why, I bet it'd be like looking into a mirror."

"But, who? Who is it you think I look like?" Olivia said, masking the frustration in her voice. She half-imagined this Wacky Wanda wrapping her hands around Olivia's throat if she said anything that ruffled her pulchritudinous plume.

Something flickered in the corner booth ahead of her. Flickered like it was there for a split second, and then gone. The image jerking like a film missing frames. The overhead lighting cast long shadows over everything, impossibly long shadows. And somewhere, hiding in the shadows, something sat. Olivia was sure of it.

The waitress blinked three times. Her nametag now read "My name is FLO." The writing looked as though it had been penned by a child with a crayon.

A small gasp escaped Olivia's mouth. She hadn't wanted to react, but her mouth moved quicker than her frazzled brain. Down below, her stomach gurgled and churned. *Feed me, Seymour. Feeeeeed meeeeeeeee.*

Flo smiled, her eyes bright and buzzy. "Why, you look like the dead girl, of course."

Movement caught Olivia's attention. The thing in the corner reappeared, but only for an instant before it was gone again.

Flo blinked so many times, so fast, that all Olivia saw was motion blur. Her lids and spider-like lashes danced up and down so swiftly that they reminded Olivia of Irish step dancers she'd once seen perform on a school trip to the city. *Mickey Flatley Jr.'s Step-Dance Extravaganza!* She feared Flo's lashes might catch fire from all that friction.

"You look just like that d-d-dead girl, d-d-dear. Now, how's about some pie?"

Viva Las Vegas

"Ladies and gents, won't you please welcome to the Eden's main stage, your favorite and mine, and I mean that sincerely, I do. Let's give a real, warm Garden of Eden Casino and Nightclub style welcome to The Strip's number one rated, by your votes and mine, Seventies Elvis impersonator, the one…the only…the incomparable… Barrrrr-ry Foss!"

"Also Sprach Zarathustra," aka the theme from Stanley Kubrick's *2001: A Space Odyssey*, crackled through the casino's outdated sound system. The house lights dimmed, and a lone spotlight cut through the smokey darkness, lighting the stage. A sweaty "Elvis" doppelgänger lumbered onto the stage, curled his lip, and gave the audience an embarrassing karate kick followed by an even more embarrassing chop. The applause that followed the portly Foss's arrival was tepid at best, uninterested at worst. Nonetheless, he persisted right on into "That's All Right."

A scattering group of people walked out, heading back to the tables or the coin-hungry slot machines, desperate to find the next "hot" machine ready to pay out. It was one of these inebriated hopefuls that accidentally elbowed Joanne Garriga in the shoulder as they strode toward the din of the casino floor. She clutched the serving tray hard, practically white-knuckling it, not wanting any of the multicolored drinks sitting on the tray to spill onto a patron's head, or worse—right into their lap.

"Oh, oh, heyyy!" the elbower, a middle-aged doofus doing his best to relive his glory days, turned and raised a hand in apology. "Sorry, honey. Apologies. No harm, no foul, right?"

Joanne pursed her lips as though she'd just sucked the sourest lemon candy. That was about as much discontent as management allowed staff to show on the floor, where a billion eyeballs could see. After all, the customer was always right. *Right?*

"Here." Doofus reached into his pocket, fished around for a moment, the contents making a jingly sound, and then finally pulled a ten-dollar chip out of his pocket. He made a big show of dropping it onto the tray. "Your next one is on me, okay, babe?"

Joanne squinted her eyes in defiance, and her lips pursed even tighter. But the man and his fellow pack of revelers were gone, off to seek their fortunes in the sea of smoke and people on the casino floor.

"*Pendejo,*" Joanne said, under her breath. Even though the sound equipment was from another era, the music was loud enough to cover the insult. Just to be sure, she said it low, so she alone could savor the satisfaction of the word passing through her lips.

Still, there was a part of her that wished she'd been able to get a picture of the guy on the sly with her phone. While that might be more of a "no, no" from management than mumbling cusswords under her breath, the risk would have been worth it just to post said pic on the "Nosey Next-door Neighbors" app. Joanne was a paying platinum member on the platform, screen name "NoJo," and her sneaky pics had earned her quite a following. Or maybe she'd add it to the stockpile she kept in a hidden folder on her phone to possibly be used in her next tell-all book. Her book on the Millers, *The Evil Next Door*—she still hated the title—had sold well enough. Until…

It was a hobby, being a busybody, and it filled the time since things fell apart with her husband, Jose. Fifteen years of marriage down the drain. He didn't understand, and there was no making him understand about the voices in her head. Well, the voice, mostly just the one. Mostly. But sometimes there were two, maybe three. Joanne wasn't sure, and really, once you hear voices in your head, does it really matter how many?

Jose had been a good man and a good husband. He was no saint, but he never laid hands on her and gave her space when she needed it. Jose never approved of Joanne's busybodying, spying on their neighbors, and gossiping. It was easier to play blind, deaf, and dumb to it rather than try to get Joanne to stop her leisure-time activities. He'd stuck with her for a while after St. Augustine Place. He'd been by her side on the ill-fated book tour for a time after. A year, or was it two? *Vermont.* It was so hard to keep track of time these days. Pandemic and all.

She thought the moving around was the straw that broke his back. The constant moving. New York to Vermont. Vermont to Maine. Maine to Pennsylvania. Pennsylvania to Ohio. Ohio to…who knows. It was all in the rearview mirror now, and at that moment it was zip code 89109 that Joanne called home. It wasn't all bad. She got to eat for free in the casino's restaurant, a nice perk of the job. Maybe the only one. Rents were cheap.

Tips were decent, considering the pandemic, most of the time.

The pandemic took a big old bite of the clientele. It got the senior citizens first. And once they started dropping like flies, the rest, even the die-hard weekenders that'd been going to the casino for thirty, hell forty years, stopped coming. Nothing stirs the fear of god like being the only one left alive in your circle of friends.

Sometimes, when she dined alone at the buffet, Joanne wondered about some of those regular seniors. The ones she hadn't seen in months. The Davidsons, from Baton Rouge. The Westerlys, from Chicago. The Doyles, from Haddonfield. The Millers from—

Not *the* Millers. Not the ones from the Bronx. Certainly not the ones that ruined her life and gave her nightmares. No, simply the Millers. The ordinary Millers from Anchorage. Joanne hated that name now. *What's in a name?*

They were probably all dead now. Those seniors. Dead like the Millers from New York. At least, Joanne hoped they were. These days, six feet under was a far better place than six feet above.

She took her dinner break outside. Joanne had had her fill of people since that *pendejo* bumped her shoulder an hour ago. Since then, she'd felt amped up and ready for a fight. She needed to get some air. The air outside, whether the virus was in it or not, was easier to breathe than the smoke-filled air inside the casino. Joanne wondered if she had it. The virus. No way to tell yet. Be on the lookout for symptoms. That's all there was to do. And pray. She wanted to. Pray. But after St. Augustine and the house of horrors, Joanne had lost the faith.

It's a waste of energy. Prayer. Pfft. It's not like anyone's listening.

But someone *was* listening. They were always listening, and sometimes they talked back, too. Told Joanne what to do, where to go, who to be next. It was all part of a plan. *The* plan. And this was her part in it. Her atonement for what she'd done, and not done, back in New York. A pricey penance, but the alternative was worse.

Her appetite was gone. Joanne wrapped up the rest of her sandwich and gave it to a panhandler on the street before heading back to work. The beggar, who appeared no more than twenty years old, looked skeletal. His number would be called soon.

At least he'll have something in his belly when he meets Charon on the River Styx, she thought. *Death be not proud.*

She thought about Jose as she swiped her timecard. Where was he now? Back in the Bronx, or did he stay in Boston with that Irish bitch that lived next door? The one with the huge tits who was always flirting with him...with those grossly low-cut tops. Bending over the right amount to give her husband a free peek at her tight, young ivory-white flesh.

And sometimes, he flirted back. *Pendejo.*

Was he dead? Did the virus get him in the end, or was it something else? She wanted to see him lying there in his sickbed, coughing and gasping for breath, reaching out to her.

At first, she'd smile. A warm and tender smile. The kind they used to share before...before the Millers...before St. Augustine Place.

Then, she'd reach her hand out to his, and just as they were about to meet, at the last possible second, just as they could feel the heat coming off each other's fingers, Joanne would pull her hand back and flip him off.

Vaya con Dios, pendejo. Vaya. Con. Dios.

But maybe Jose was already dead. A lot of people were.

Joanne hoped so. It felt good to finally admit that. Say it out loud, even if she was the only one listening.

Was it true though?

She really hoped so. Otherwise, when this was all over, and her penance paid, she'd neuter the bastard and then put him down. That made her smile. Really smile. And for just a moment, Joanne Garriga felt okay, not exactly happy, but content.

Just a moment...

...and then the sensation of fingers thumbing through her brain overtook her.

She wondered which voice it would be tonight, and then everything went black.

Déjà Vu

Harding popped Tums like they were breath mints. Back in the day, his go-to was Pepp-Ah-Mint LifeSav-Ahs, but that was before the ulcers and acid reflux. Now, he was strictly a Tums guy. They kept his gut happier. His gut, which felt as though it was on fire, was never wrong.

Never.

Over the course of twenty years on the job, Harding's gut had a perfect record. It paid a price, what with the ulcers and acid reflux, but Harding knew his gut was his best asset. That was why he bought Tums by the gross at that bulk discount store in Summerlin. Once upon another life, his wife used to joke that no one ever had to wonder what to get him for his birthday.

But then she left him. Really, he did the leaving, if not physically, then mentally. Spiritually. It was possible for a person to be there physically, to be a presence, and at the same time, be completely checked out. A big part of him was caught in a loop somewhere else. Trapped in some other time. Somewhere in the far-off past. *Objects in the rearview mirror appear closer than they are.*

It was that case. That one damned case. There's always one. Everyone working in law enforcement has one. The case that digs its claws into you, rearranges your guts, and pretends to let go. His was a real horror show. That kind of depravity changes a person. Harding used to say *the guy it doesn't change is the next psycho we'll be looking for.* That was back when he gave a shit. Now there was only one goal—stay the fuck alive.

The Willows, the desert development where the emergency call had originated, was only about a ten-minute drive from Harding's house, but somehow tonight it felt like the road stretched on for miles and miles ahead of him in the dark. The bright lights of The Strip were nowhere in sight. It was like there was no destination, and no end in sight. Driving headfirst into the unknown.

Harding's gut was talking up a storm. All of his senses felt alive and on alert. There was a buzz in his head like he had OD'd on caffeine. He took a hand off the steering wheel. It shook in the dim light streaming in through the windshield. Harding pressed hard on the gas pedal. The engine roared, and the car sped on into the darkness, right for the dark itself.

This was something.

Harding knew his gut was onto something.

He was onto something.

Something big.

Something...monstrous.

A Doll's Life

"Ah, there's our girl," Oliver, Imogen's dad, said. His eyes brightened as he spied his daughter walking into the family room, where he sat reading a book as his wife, Janet, sipped a glass of red wine on the chaise. She'd nurse that one glass all night as she did most nights—and some days, too. But as soon as she was alone, Janet would down it, and then refill the glass, repeating the charade until she'd drunk her way through more bottles than she could count.

"Ugh, what are you listening to?" Imogen asked, walking over to the record player.

"Josh Groban," Janet replied.

Imogen threw her head back and groaned. "I hate that guy."

"I can't imagine why. He sings so beautifully. We had tickets to see him at the Oasis, but then..." Janet motioned about, indicating the house and the lockdown. All plans cancelled indefinitely.

"The one good thing to come out of the pandemic. And Josh Groan-ban sounds like he gargled with broken glass. Now, Elvis? *He* sang beautifully. Nobody ever gonna dethrone the King, especially not a poser like Josh Groan-ban."

Imogen reveled in how that nickname for the crooner got under her mother's thin skin.

Janet tisked. "No, he doesn't. And what do you know about Elvis Presley, anyway?"

"Plenty. He was born Elvis Aaron Presley in Tupelo, Mississippi in 1935. And that's Aaron with two As, even though it's misspelled on his gravestone. His parents were Vernon and Gladys. He was a bit of a mama's boy and bought Graceland for her in—"

"Enough, Miss Walking Wikipedia." Janet sipped her wine, resisting the urge to chug it down. "Sorry I asked."

Imogen smiled, savoring the small victory. "What's for dinner? I'm starving."

"I bet. Talking to Ally for hours on end works up an appetite," Janet said between baby sips.

"Oh, that's not fair, hun," Oliver began. He removed his eyeglasses. "It's more like listening, isn't it? To converse properly, to have a dialogue, one must stop talking long enough to listen. And it's not like Ally lets anyone get a word in, does she?"

Imogen laughed. Janet frowned, wrinkled her nose, and took a bigger sip of wine than expected.

"It's true," Oliver said to his disapproving wife. She glared at him from behind her glass, her lips stained a dark ruby red. "What were those dolls they used to sell?"

"Cabbage Patch—"

"No, not *those* abominations," Oliver cut Janet off. A devilish smile creeped onto his face. Imogen smiled back, and Oliver winked.

Janet had a "thing" for collecting vintage Cabbage Patch dolls, a hobby both husband and daughter not-so-secretly detested. The dolls, rightfully so, creeped them out. But, for Janet, they filled a void neither would ever, could ever, understand.

Oliver went on. "Even older. Your mother owned several, if I recall correctly. Or was it... your grandmother?"

Janet sat up, nearly spilling the wine. She overreacted as though she'd nearly just spilled the cure for cancer. "Oh! The Chatty Cathys. Now, those were some creepy dolls."

"Yes! The Chatty Cathys!" Oliver slapped his forehead as though he was knocking some sense back into his brain.

"They're all a little creepy, though, right?" Imogen said. "They're like...babies for kids. You're basically grooming girls to want to be mothers. And why only give them to girls? It's not like men have nothing to do with babies, from making them—"

Janet interrupted, "I played with baby dolls when I was a little girl."

"And look how you turned out," Imogen replied, not missing a beat.

"That's enough," Janet said sharply. She frowned again, this time at Imogen. And this time, with far more aggression. "Get off the soapbox."

"I'm serious," Imogen protested.

"So am I," Janet shot back before taking a bigger sip of wine.

Imogen threw up her hands, mocking defeat. "You just love being a slave to the patriarchy."

"That's exactly it." Janet's voice had the beginnings of a tone that told Imogen to back off.

"Play nice, girls," Oliver offered, returning his eyeglasses to their spot on his nose. Imogen shot daggers at him with her eyes. This time, Oliver threw his hands up. "I'm sorry. Play nice, *ladies*. Better?"

Imogen's face relaxed, and Oliver smiled.

"As I was saying," Oliver began. "Ally is like one of those Chatty Cathys. They talked non-stop until their batteries ran out. And oh, it was so creepy! When they were almost drained, the dolls started talking really slow. And their voices got deep. They sounded possessed. Dddooo youuuu wanttt tooooo plaayyyyy?"

"Hell, no." Imogen laughed. "The power of Christ compels you."

"And that's where Ally is different. At least the Chatty Cathys stopped talking eventually," Janet said. "That girl will be a pile of ash, and still somehow find a way to talk from the beyond."

Imogen smirked, not allowing Janet any more for the win.

Oliver got a serious look on his face and thought for a moment. "I stand corrected. And it was *my* grandmother that had the Chatty Cathys, not yours. I think it was a knockoff. Still might be worth something."

"Thank heavens you cleared that up, dear. It was going to keep me up all night," Janet said.

"Whatever. Guys..." Imogen pointed to her belly, which grumbled as if cued. "Dinner?"

Oliver looked at the clock on the wall. "It is nearing six, I think. Or is it five?"

"Six," Imogen said. "Feed me, Seymour! Feed me!"

Oliver laughed, pantomiming Audrey, the man-eating Venus Fly Trap from *Little of Shop of Horrors,* using his fingers to re-create the open and close motion of the plant's mouth. *Little Shop* was a father-daughter movie fest favorite.

"This pandemic. It's so hard to tell time when you're just stuck inside all day. Someday, maybe we'll all get to go outside again."

"Amen," Janet said, raising her glass.

"Probably a good idea to get something in the oven, hun."

Janet sighed, carefully setting the wine glass down on the table beside the chaise. She stretched her arms over her head and made her way to standing, albeit less than gracefully. It was the wine. "I'll see what we have. We'll need to do an order tomorrow, though."

"Running out of vino?" Imogen asked, smirking.

Janet gave Imogen a mock smile before heading out the door. "I'll be in the kitchen."

"Exactly where the patriarchy wants you," Imogen shouted.

Oliver couldn't help but laugh. "Go easy on your mom, would you? She's had it hard since they laid off her department. This damned pandemic is going to bleed us all dry."

"But you're okay, right? I mean, we're okay? Right? We're not going to have to dumpster dive or, like, eat each other or anything."

"No." Oliver chuckled. "No cannibalism for this family. Everything is fine. We're fine. Leave the worrying to me, okay?"

"But...you're *not* worried, right? About any of this?"

"No, I'm not worried in the slightest. Once the numbers come down, everything will go back to normal. We'll look back on this time and laugh. You'll see."

Imogen sat on the bench by the window and looked out, even though there was nothing to see. "When do you think that will be? They said it was just going to be for fourteen days and that came and went a while ago."

"I'm not a virologist, Imo. I don't know how long these things take. I think we're smart to be careful. If we go out there too soon, we'll just end up where we are now, and more people will have died for nothing."

"Yeah. I guess. I just…"

Oliver removed his glasses and studied his daughter's face as though by staring he could read her mind. "What?"

"I miss my life. My friends. Staring up at real stars."

Oliver smiled. "Remember when we used to drive up to Snake Hill and look for U.F.O.s with the telescope?"

"Yeah. That was fun. We never saw one, though."

"I don't know about that." Oliver put his glasses back on. "That one time in October—"

"It was a frigging drone!"

Oliver cocked his head. "A little big for a drone, don't you think? I don't know. I still say we saw *something.*"

"Whatever." Imogen smiled. "I need more stick-on stars for my ceiling. I'm losing Orion."

"I'll see what I can do." Oliver gave a wink. "We should do that again sometime. When all this craziness is over, I mean. Pack up the telescopes. Drive up the hill."

"Yeah. Who knows how many drones we're missing out on being stuck inside."

"They're here already! You're next," Oliver shouted, quoting from another of their faves—*Invasion of the Body Snatchers.* The black and white original with Kevin McCarthy. They'd probably watched it together a hundred times, if not more.

"Whatever you do—"

"Don't. Fall. Asleep." This, one of the most famous lines in *A Nightmare on Elm Street,* they said in unison.

Imogen walked over to her dad and planted a small kiss on his cheek. "Love you, Daddy."

"Love you too, pumpkin. And go easy on your mom, okay?"

"I'll try." Which really meant *yeah, right.*

"I'll see what I can do about those stars."

Imogen nodded and made her way to the door, feeling both content and a little disappointed with herself. She hadn't brought up Gemeo Labs or the Project. The results of her test. The timing just didn't feel right. Maybe later. Or tomorrow. Or the next day. Time felt limitless and, for now, they weren't going anywhere. No need to rock the boat yet. Steer clear of the proverbial iceberg, so to speak. Their family was okay. Oliver and Janet were good people. They loved her and took care of her. What more could she expect from the universe when so many others weren't as lucky?

"Oh hey, pumpkin. You knew Jemma Jones and Freddy McDonough, didn't you?"

Knew? Why did he say "knew"?

But the answer was obvious.

Without turning, she said, "Yeah. I did. Knew them both. Why?"

"I'm sorry, pumpkin."

Imogen didn't react. Jemma and Freddy weren't the first of her classmates, *former* classmates, to die in the pandemic, and they wouldn't be the last.

"How? Virus or vax?"

"The hospital didn't have enough ventilators."

Quietly, Imogen said, "Shit."

"The Kleins, too," Oliver added, his tone matching hers.

"Which one?"

There was a long silence. A heavy silence. Finally, Oliver said, "All of them."

Fuck. Fuck. Fuck. There were eight people in the Klein family. They lived, now used to live, three doors down. I've known...knew them all my life.

Imogen took a small step out of the room into the hall when she heard her dad add, "Their dog, too."

And Fido makes nine.

Fuck. My. Life.

I Can't Get No—

The Greasy Spoon's jukebox had moved on to the rockabilly stylings of the Everly Brothers and their classic hit "All I Have to Do Is Dream." *Anything but Josh Groban.*

The thing in the corner booth flickered in the dark. Despite the thing wearing the dark like an oversized coat, keeping most of its form hidden from view, Olivia knew it was there. And more, she knew it was staring right at her.

"Hey, young man!"

A single, booming voice startled her and pulled Olivia's attention to the counter, where now sat not only a Native American in full traditional regalia but a tan, muscular, denim-clad construction worker. While the Native American had his back to Olivia, the construction worker sat on the edge of the circular bar stool and peered at her over his sunglasses. Impossibly, given the distance from where she sat to the counter, Olivia saw herself mirrored in his super-reflective shades. The lightning bolt decal on his hardhat glittered and glowed. He winked, and in an instant, spun on the stool so now his back was also facing Olivia.

The strange duo sat off the stool about six inches, raised their right arms into the air, and shouted, "Young man!" Then, they sat back down as smoothly as they had risen, like they were moving as one...in synchronicity.

What the actual fuck?

The waitress appeared at the counter, smiled, and ex-changed words with the two strangers. They smiled familiarly and began conversing with the effervescent food slinger. Only Olivia noticed something odd. No, this whole fucked up scene was not merely odd. This ship flew right on past odd and landed on *unsettling*. Even though the waitress and the pair sitting at the counter appeared to be having a lively chat, no words were being spoken—not out loud, anyway. It was as if someone had muted the sound. But not all the sound in The Greasy Spoon. No, Olivia still clearly heard the percolating coffee, dishes clanking, and something sizzling on the grill in the back.

The only thing she couldn't hear was the only thing she wanted to hear—their conversation. Something muted the dialogue and kept on the background noise.

And every time Flo threw her head back to laugh, it pissed Olivia off even more.

Just then, almost as if on cue, the thing in the corner booth stirred. At least, Olivia *thought* it stirred. The faux leather upholstery squeaked as the thing adjusted itself. She couldn't deny the booths were uncomfortable. Her ass had fallen asleep some time ago, but Olivia dared not move, afraid she might fall into some new hellish version of The Greasy Spoon.

The light above the corner booth pulsed, growing in both intensity and brightness, and then falling back to the lowest brightness before it gave no light. It did this several times. And then, as the light continued its show, a set of hands pushed out of the dark.

First, the hands appeared. Then, slowly, the thing's forearms emerged from the black. Its fingers wiggled several times, then curled into a fist and released. Olivia thought it looked like the thing was warming up its digits. Stretching itself. *Preparing* itself for something. The thing continued this wiggle then curl into a fist pattern until its entire forearm poked out of the dark, stopping at what Olivia assumed were its elbows. *Does it have elbows?*

With half of its arms now visible, the thing dropped them onto the table. Olivia watched, mesmerized, as its long, slender, pointy fingertips deliberately tapped out a rhythm. It was vaguely familiar to her, but she couldn't place it.

I know this. I know I know this. What is that?

The waitress howled with laughter. Laughter Olivia could suddenly, strangely enough hear. And now, there sat not two but *three* costumed gentlemen—the Native American, the construction worker, and a Navy sailor.

"Oh, James," the waitress roared, slapping one of her substantial thighs. The flabby skin rippled. *The sound was back on.* "You just k-k-kill me!"

The trio that had been moments ago a duo, sat up on their respective stools and spun around until they faced Olivia. They pointed at her and shouted, "Young man!"

And then, just like that, they sat down and spun their stools back around until they had their backs to Olivia. Their silent dialogue with the waitress resumed. Olivia supposed they picked up right where they'd left off, but obviously had no way of being certain. She just *knew* it.

With the floorshow over, Olivia turned her attention back to the corner booth. And when she did, she gasped at what she saw. Not only were the thing's forearms and hands visible, but now its head was too. The thing's face was looking right at her.

Olivia's heart raced in her chest.

What the fuck. What the fuck. What the fuck is that?

The thing's face looked like a drawing. A child's art project. Its face was a cartoonish line drawing made up of squiggles. Olivia thought they looked like a horde of fresh bait worms squirming at the bottom of a tin can. The squiggles were in constant motion, animating it as though it was being drawn in real time.

Giving it life, she thought.

What she took for its mouth curled into a smile, while what she took for one of its beady eyes winked at her. It did neither in a threatening way, but the effect wasn't any less terrifying. Olivia dragged herself to the end of the booth and jumped to her feet, only to ricochet off Flo's formidable tower of a body like a ping-pong ball. Olivia plopped back into the booth with a squeaky *THUD*!

"M-m-more coffee, d-d-dear?"

"What the fuck is this place?"

Before the waitress could answer, the group at the counter — formerly a duo, then a trio, and now a full-on group of six oiled-up, muscular, costumed men — hopped onto the counter and shouted, "Young man!"

Besides the Native American, sailor, and construction worker were a cowboy with an oversized tan hat and a cap gun in each hand; a cop clad in a skin-tight white jumpsuit, shiny black motorcycle boots and a clunky helmet on top of his head; a furry man sporting silver chains around his chest and covered in black leather from head to toe.

Oh my god...it's...the Village People!

The actual fucking Village People.

How old are they? Are they even alive?

This can't be happening. This can't be. This can't be…

A disco ball dropped from the ceiling and shimmered in a bright white spotlight that came from nowhere. The jukebox hummed to life. A record dropped onto the turntable, and a second later the needle found its groove. The funky brass opening to "Y.M.C.A." hissed over the jukebox's old speakers as The Not Dead Yet Village People shimmied, clapped, and then right on time, sang out in one voice the opening line of their classic dance hit.

Olivia, momentarily distracted by the enthusiastic gyrations of The Village People, turned back to Flo, who was now using her flabby arms to spell out Y-M-C-A. It was a sight Olivia hoped she'd be able to scrub from her memory at a later date.

"What the fuck is this place?" Olivia repeated.

"Why, it's whatever you want it to be, d–d–dear," Flo said, keeping perfect rhythm with the song. "Y-M-C-A!"

The thing in the corner booth grinned with what Olivia took to be strange satisfaction.

Papa, Can You Hear Me?

Joanne Garriga sat in the dark of her small one-bedroom Vegas pad. It was "small" even by Vegas housing standards. Back home, in New York City, the joint would be palatial. The place was the definition of "no frills," but it suited her needs and those of the complex's other transient tenants just fine. It came furnished with tacky furniture that smelt of cigarettes and liquor. She guessed they once lived in a casino a lifetime ago. The wallpaper, a nauseating floral print leftover from the sixties, made her dizzy.

The dark was better. She could block everything out, from the wallpaper to the world outside of the four walls of her temporary home. Tune out and tune in to the voices in her head. Really, it was the *one* voice she was listening for. It was the loudest of them, and the one that scared her the most. This was the voice that gave her instructions, told her what to do, when, and where to do it. Joanne never questioned it. She wouldn't dare. So far, it had been right about everything it told her. Everything it had shown her. *Everything.* She didn't know how it knew things, maybe everything, but it did. And if it knew all, there was no telling what else it could do.

Joanne had gotten a small taste of its power in Montpelier. *Vermont.* A small taste, she guessed. The things it showed her. The things it said and did. Until Vermont, she considered herself a believer. Joanne believed there was a place reserved just for her in heaven, despite the busybodying. Now, she wondered a bit if she'd taken a wrong turn and ended up in the suburbs of hell. The Las Vegas landscape nearly indistinguishable from that of Hades.

If it could do...all *that*...what else was it capable of? Joanne couldn't imagine where its power began and where it ended. Its limits, if it had any. It was a thought that was beyond her comprehension of the universe. Her head ached every time she dared to ponder any of these questions. It was better to just sit quietly in the dark and wait. Just wait.

A short time ago, before the Millers and the house of horrors, you never could have convinced Joanne Garriga that she'd be sitting in basically a flop house, in the dark, in Sin City, waiting to hear from a voice in her head.

But that's exactly what she'd continue to do. Eat. Sleep. Work. And wait.

Any day now. I can feel it. It's getting closer.

Until then, until it told her what to do next, where to move next, the emergency to-go bag would sit, useless, beside the front door. And like Joanne, waiting to serve its greater purpose. Its *only* purpose.

Yes. Soon. I can feel it.

Joanne sighed, feeling somewhere between exasperated and anxious. And maybe a little tired. She'd need to sleep soon. It was already late. It always felt late in Vegas. They don't let you see the sun. They wanted to keep you stashed away inside like Rapunzel, inside where you could throw your money into the hungry machines and onto the tables for as long as you were physically able. It was better to die at a machine than to walk out a winner. The house always wins. Always.

So, tomorrow she'd throw on that ridiculous uniform, show far too much skin for a reserved woman of her age, and serve drink after drink with a fantastic smile glued to her face. Suck up and kiss ass. That was the way, the only way to get decent tips. Since the pay was less than stellar, tips were necessary if you wanted to eat and keep the roof over your head, no matter how shitty a roof it was.

Soon.

Joanne would laugh at their inane racist Mexican jokes and wisecracks. Act as though she'd never heard similar words pass through the lips of a racist gringo.

ICE, ICE baby. You got a green card hiding under that skirt, mamacita?

The high rollers always thought they were just so funny.

Oh, sí, sí, señor! Green Card.

Why did they think winning a little money at a table transformed them into a stand-up comic or something? Why did throwing down some green make them feel entitled to say whatever they wanted to anyone they wanted without reproach? Imagine, the entitled needing an excuse to feel even *more* entitled. *Pendejos.*

And why?

Because...

Joanne said, "Money makes the world go round and round and round and..."

She hummed the old *Cabaret* show tune. The hairs on the back of her neck rose as a sea of gooseflesh swam the length of her arms. She wrapped herself up in a fluffy blanket and smiled, a real one because Joanne Garriga knew something no one else in the world did—it would all be over soon. All of it.

Everything. Everywhere.
Yes. Soon...

The First Interlude: Bostonians Do It Better

Jose Garriga did not like Boston. Everybody talked funny—
who the fuck says "cah?"

Where did the "r" go? Some place warmer, he thought.

It was ball-freezing cold in Boston. Colder than a Kar-
dashian. And it was only mid-December, for fuck's sake, and
already it felt like the Arctic Circle outside their front door.
He was hot-blooded, not made for this bone-cutting weather.
Heck, was anyone?

They'd lived through their fair share of New York winters,
record-setting blizzards, sub-zero windchills. That was cold,
but it wasn't Boston cold. Jose wondered why the voice
couldn't send them south for the winter with the birds and
senior citizens. He was a card-carrying AARP member. He
practically *was* a senior. This freezing cold shit was for the
birds and the gringos.

Jose wondered the point of it all. The moving. The transient
lifestyle.

What are we doing? he often wondered.

He didn't know. The voice—voices—didn't speak to *him*.
That honor belonged to Joanne and only Joanne. A few hundred
miles back, Jose Garriga wondered if his wife hadn't gone a

little loco.

I mean, hearing voices? That's crazy talk, sí?

They put people away for less than that, or they used to anyway. Hell, Jose's own abuela had been sent away for "nerves."

"Ha, nerves," his abuela used to say. Very quietly. "I just liked to read, is all."

Locked in an institution for a month because she liked to read. Crazy.

But Jose couldn't help wonder what might become of his wife if anyone got wind of her talking about the voices. They'd put her away for sure. Throw away the key, too. Ain't nobody gonna care about a crazy Mexican woman, anyway.

There was a moment somewhere between New York and Montpelier, Vermont, that Jose wondered if his wife hadn't blown a fuse. He'd understand if she did, after everything that happened at the Miller house on St. Augustine Place. Hell, he'd almost lost his shit back there, too. That was some real fucked up shit. It changes a person. Scars their insides...their psyche. Ain't no way something like that doesn't leave a mark somewhere. Jose wondered if this voice, or *legion* of voices, was somehow the manifestation of her mark. Stranger things have happened. Hell, just look at the Millers. Shit didn't come any stranger than that.

But then they arrived in Montpelier, and he saw for himself that it was real, this main voice. And more, he saw what it could do. *All of those people.* A glimpse of its power. *Gone.* That was all it had been. A peek behind the curtain. And that had been more than enough to convince him that his wife was not only *not* crazy, but they were knee-deep in some serious shit. And if they weren't smart, if they weren't careful, they'd drown in that shit like it was quicksand. That thought shook Jose Garriga deeper than the thought that what happened in Montpelier could happen again. It *would* happen again. It chilled him worse than the Boston winter.

After Vermont, Jose Garriga *knew* it was for real. All of it. Any doubts he may have had about Joanne's sanity, or the power, were erased in the blink of an eye. *All those people. Dead.*

And now they were in Boston, freezing cold Boston, and he wondered how many more miles lay ahead for them, for her, for him. He was nothing more than a chauffeur, a shopper, and occasionally a triage doctor, stitching her up in the trenches. That was his purpose. His *only* purpose in all of this. A supporting player.

And Jose Garriga was growing tired of it. He wanted to be a headliner, just once. Have the spotlight shone on him for a change. He wanted something more. Something that could belong to only him. Be his, not hers or theirs. *His.*

It was right around this time, the middle of December, three days into a Boston freeze, that the Garrigas got themselves a new neighbor. An attractive thirty-something redhead with big tits.

That'll do. I'd say I've earned a little...something, something.

The first time their paths crossed—the red-headed neighbor and Jose—he swore she winked at him. Suggestively. *Oh, so suggestively.* Just as he fantasized she would. Undressed him with her icy green eyes. *She eye-fucked me.* The playful expression on her pale face told him plainly that she liked what she saw. A lot.

Yes, that'll do just fine.

Mirage

Harding stopped the car about one-hundred feet from the front gates of The Willows. That was as close as he could get—even with the red and blue siren flashing on the dash. The scene at the gates was pandemonium. The night sky was ablaze with the red, blue, and white lights from the various vehicles. Harding counted nearly a dozen ambulances, eight fire trucks, and more squad cars and unmarked cruisers as far as his eyes could see. Some were from Summerlin, others Henderson. They were from all over. Hell, some had even come from as far as Boulder City, some thirty-odd miles away.

Harding expected the scene to be a bad one, but this was some next-level shit. He hadn't seen this many first responders since—

No. Don't go there. Do. Not. Go. There. Lock that shit back up in your memory box.

He steered his mind back to the present and willed it to stay. Whether it did as it was told was another story. Harding's mind had a will of its own with some things. The ghosts he tried to keep buried somehow kept coming back like zombies from a C-grade horror flick.

Fuck this.

Harding grabbed the pandemic mask and considered it. He

tossed it in the backseat, took a deep breath, and exited the cruiser. The wailing sirens and excited radio chatter drowned out the sound of the cruiser door slamming shut. He took a few steps toward the gates, popped a Tums into his mouth, and heard a familiar voice above the cacophony of the scene.

"Harding! Hey, Harding! We're over here," his partner, Detective Vincente Vallance, called, waving a hand up just in case Harding couldn't hear him calling over all that noise or through the pandemic mask covering most of his face.

Harding flashed Vallance a patented professional smile. He wanted to frown but kept his face stoically cool and unemotional. *Ah, fuck. Why is he still wearing that?* The "to mask" or "not to mask" debate divided officers almost evenly. Harding and Vallance landed on opposing teams but kept things civil. The rules changed daily as the scientists at the top learned more about the virus. He made his way through the bustling sea of first responders, who, for the moment, looked more like chickens running in circles without their heads.

The two veteran officers shook hands and exchanged pleasantries before getting to business.

"You might want to mask up," Vallance offered with audible hesitation in his voice. "It's like a loony bin back there."

Harding shook his head and pointed to his right arm. "I'm good. I got the shot."

The vaccine. Effective, but—

"It's not one hundred percent, Harding." Vallance was breathing heavily behind the mask. The mask fogged up almost instantly.

"Is anything a hundred percent these days? I'll take my chances with ninety-seven percent. Come on, let's go," Harding said, extending an arm as if to say *lead on, my good man. Lead on.* Vallance walked ahead, and Harding trailed. "And take that off. You're liable to trip on your own two feet and break your pencil neck."

Vallance held up a hand, a placating peace offering. A second later, he stumbled but did not fall. Harding said nothing, and Vallance dared not look back.

They walked fifty feet, then a hundred. Then two hundred, then three. Vallance stopped to take off the pandemic mask. His face dripped with sweat, and he panted as though he'd just run a 5K through Red Rock Canyon in a hundred-degree heat.

The partners stood dead center in the street, in the heart of the small unfinished housing development. Between the housing market crash and the pandemic, there was a record number of abandoned housing projects in and around Las Vegas. The Willows, sadly, was just one of many. A semi-circle of a dozen ranch-style homes rose out of the dark ahead of them, looking more like gravestones than houses. The multitude of emergency lights flickered on the façades and reflected off the front windows, creating even longer shadows in the ghost town.

What the fuck?

Harding thought the scene outside the gates to The Willows was chaotic enough, but he was not prepared for the scene that greeted him behind the gates. It was beyond horrific, and yet, somehow, *familiar.*

No. Stop it. Don't go there. Stay here. Stay. The. Fuck. Here.

Body bags littered the front lawns like holiday decorations that fell over during a storm. They were everywhere, as far as the eyes could see. Harding couldn't count them all. He didn't *want* to count them all.

"I don't understand," Harding began, but cut himself off.

His throat closed up on him, burying the words deep inside. He scanned the houses with his eyes. "Which...which one is it? Which house? Where did they play the game?"

Somewhere, someone retched violently. Somewhere, someone screamed. Somewhere, someone sobbed.

Vallance said nothing at first, only stared at Harding looking as though he was trying to find the words in a language Harding and he alone were fluent in to put a name to this vile scene, but none came. Harding studied Vallance's face. Peered deep into his partner's eyes. The answer was there before the words finally came out of his mouth.

"It's...all of them, Harding."

Harding moved his eyes from one home to the next. Every door stood open. On every porch was a flurry of activity. And sitting at the end of every drive—*no, nearly every one*—sat a lone blood-soaked person wrapped in a blanket, staring into the nothingness with wide eyes. He noticed that only one house was different from the others, and only subtly. But he saw it right away, and it triggered a reaction in his gut.

One of these is not like the others.

"Every house, Joe. Every damned house," Vallance said, his voice finally breaking. "I'm sorry."

"What?"

Jesus Christ.

Harding looked back to the lone house that called to him like the sweet song of the siren. *That one.*

"Have tech sweep for cameras. Make it a priority," Harding barked.

Vallance appeared stunned and confused. "All of them, Joe? That'll take time to get IT—"

Harding shook his head. "No, just that one."

Fuck. Sandra. I can feel her.

He pointed out the house in question to Vallance, who nodded.

"Alright, Joe. I'll call Sy. He's the best we got in the dugout. What do I tell him?"

"Tell him I think his day just got a lot more interesting."

Vallance nodded and then placed a shaky hand on Harding's shoulder. It felt as though it weighed a ton. He held it there a long moment, squeezed, and then walked a good distance away from his partner. When there was some distance between them, Vallance fell to his knees and sobbed. Harding couldn't hear the sounds coming out of his partner's mouth, somewhere from the depths of his soul, but he recognized the jerky shoulder shrugs to know the man had fallen apart. And Harding didn't yet know if all the king's horses and all the king's men could ever put his partner back together again.

Harding forced himself to walk deeper into The Willows. It felt like he was wearing cement shoes. Every small step took an enormous amount of will and strength.

You know this.

A paramedic hurried past Harding; their shoulders tapped each other. For a moment, their eyes met. Harding observed a steady trail of tears rolling down the young paramedic's dirty cheeks, and there was a far-off, distant look in his eyes—like the lights were on, but no one was home. It was an expression photographers often caught in the battlefields and trenches. The look of trauma. PTSD and dull, dead eyes.

Harding nodded, as though saying—*hang in there, mate. It'll be okay.*

But even Harding doubted his own sincerity. The sleep-walking paramedic returned an almost imperceptible nod, then wandered off. Harding lost sight of him in the ocean of uniformed personnel flooding the scene.

You've seen this before.

No, shut up!

You have.

No, be quiet, I said.

The dam in Harding's mind cracked, and one by one, images and memories came spilling out. He placed both of his hands on either side of his head and squeezed hard, as though by doing so, Harding could stop the dam from cracking further. But he knew, deep down, nothing could stop it now. Come hell or highwater, it was all going to come rushing back whether he wanted it to or not.

He screamed, guttural and primordial. Harding was aware he was screaming but felt as though his mind and body were separating. He was no longer in control. His screams continued, joining the others, coming from all sides and everywhere, creating a melancholy symphony in his ears.

Harding closed his eyes, focusing his internal eye on the past. On the memories rushing through his fevered brain.

Remember.

One by one, the sickening slideshow flashed before his mind's eye.

Remember...

It was all coming back, unearthing itself from its grave. The monster would have life.

Remember...

And then, as Detective Joseph P. Harding remembered what was now past, a voice slightly louder than the rest, louder than his own screams, which had not faltered one bit, brushed past his ear.

"I won. I did it. I won. I won the game."

The voice, a female, trailed off into tears.

Harding silenced his scream and opened his eyes. And there, just for a moment, hovering like a macabre mirage, he saw it—

The house of horrors. St. Augustine Place. The Miller House.

One of these is not like the others.

And then, it was gone.

It's time, Detective Harding. Time to go back. Time to go home. You need to remember...remember everything. It's coming.

Remember... now.

Dream Lover, Part One

It took Imogen longer to drift off to sleep than normal. By the time her eyelids went down for the count, it was nearing three o'clock. Ironically, the last time she'd stayed up this late was when she debated ordering that testing kit from Gemeo Labs a few months back. Then it had been a lively internal debate that kept her brain from unplugging.

To test, or not to test, that was the question.

Do you ever feel like you don't belong? Feel alone even when surrounded by friends and family? Do you ever think that you were meant to be somebody else? That you are, in fact, someone else. Do you have questions, the kind that keep you up all night staring at the stars? Does your family have the answers? Any of the answers? Maybe we can help. We're Gemeo Labs. And this is the Gemeo Project. Knowledge is our business. Click the sparkling tree graphic to begin your journey.

Imogen decided to test because that was *exactly* how Imogen felt. All of it. Every word, like all the time, since as far back as she could remember. She just felt...*different.* It was like the ad was written for her. Most of the time, she felt like the proverbial fish out of water, thrashing about, trying to fit in. She was smart enough and a good enough actress to keep the best of them fooled, sometimes beguiled, by her performance.

Few suspected how Imogen really felt in her own skin, or what her face really looked like behind the mask.

Janet, her mom, had her suspicions, as mothers do.

Mothers always know. They're like fucking Santa Claus. They know if you've been bad or good, so fuck it all and just be bad and die happy for fuck's sake...

But then the virus came to the States for a visit, soon followed by a full-blown pandemic and house arrest for everyone but essential personnel. Most people were anything but essential. The cost-cutting and downsizing came next, and that went through her mom's company like a tornado. Half her department was cut, a devastating blow, but then a quarter of the entire payroll saw the axe as well. Her job was really all she had of her own, something Imogen thought gave her mom a sense of identity. Without work, her mom said she felt like she'd woken up with amnesia. Most of the time now, all her mom saw clearly was the bottom of a wine bottle, and even that she didn't see too clearly. This made it even easier for Imogen to hide in plain sight.

Tonight, Imogen felt restless, fidgety. She contemplated sneaking downstairs and pilfering some of her mom's wine but thought better of it. *She knows exactly how much wine is in the house down to the last drop. Fucking Santa Claus.* Imogen sighed. No matter how she positioned herself on her bed, she just could not get comfortable. It felt like she was sleeping on a bed of very dull nails, but nails, nonetheless. After hours of tossing, then turning, and then tossing some more, Imogen gave up and surrendered, winding up flat on her back as she had begun hours earlier, only now she was utterly exasperated.

Her mind raced with thoughts of her latest dead classmates—*former* classmates. She was getting more accustomed to saying that the longer the lockdown went on. But not only that, her head was filled with creepy as fuck talking baby dolls and those nine ordinary yet exciting words: "*You have received a match on your genealogical tree.*"

What the fuck does it all mean?

As much as Gemeo Labs promised answers, Imogen found herself stuck somehow with only more questions. A lot more questions. She hadn't expected a hit, let alone prepared herself for the possibility her DNA might find a match in their database. She knew Janet and Oliver didn't hold much stock in those "do-it-yourself" test kits. Janet thought they were about as reliable as the new at-home virus test strips—

I'm sorry, but most people are stupid. Incredibly stupid. They have to be told not to iron in the bathtub for Christ's sake. How can you expect them to follow directions on one of those self-test kits? I imagine all the results are pretty unreliable.

There she'd been talking about the DNA kits, not the virus test strips. Imogen was sure of it.

I bet there are a lot of false hits out there. Getting people's hopes up only to pull the carpet out from under them later. Rug, Imogen wanted to correct, but bit her tongue and let the offense pass this one time.

Huh.

A thought fired up in her brain, lighting up like a thousand-watt bulb. It was more of a revelation, and it made her sit straight up in bed.

Janet and Oliver were *very* anti-DNA testing, like absurdly vocal about it, and poo-pooing the idea anytime Imogen tossed it out there like chum in the water.

Me thinks they doth protest too much.

She processed the idea slowly, drawing out a myriad of

conclusions that brought only questions. More questions. *Fuck. My Life.*

Imogen clicked on her bedside lamp and fired up her laptop. She read and re-read the email from Gemeo Labs a dozen more times. She could almost recite it from memory. Unsatisfied, she clicked the sparkling tree icon and waited for the result page to load. The tree sparkled and glowed, but the page did not load. Imogen checked her Wi-Fi connection and then clicked over the "reload page" icon a dozen times. But still, *nada.* Just the same damned sparkling Gemeo Labs tree stared back at her. Then, a red "X" appeared over her Wi-Fi connection icon.

Fucking hell. Perfect timing, as always.

Imogen tapped the Wi-Fi icon one final time, hoping against hope the red "X" would turn into a green check mark. When it did not, she slammed her laptop's lid closed.

Outages were happening more and more since everyone was home and online nearly 24/7 now. Every social media platform's servers crashed at least twice the first week of the lockdowns. Folks bugged out of their minds because they couldn't share how bored or how freaked out they were or how it was all a hoax. They felt like they were on the Titanic without a life vest. Whatever its problems during its long lifespan, social media became for some their only lifeline beyond their own four walls during lockdowns. Being cut off so abruptly only reminded those isolating on their own how truly alone they were.

Later, the platforms served a grislier function—providing real-time death notifications. It hadn't been uncommon to see someone go "LIVE" to broadcast their final moments. Nothing like starting your day watching Penelope from second grade gasping her last awful breaths. There were suicides too. Eventually, AI could censor the gorier of the content, but something always slipped through. In the game of man versus machine, man would always win. And it was the darker side of human nature that glued eyeballs to screens to watch the "death-casts," as they became known.

Imogen saw part of one, and only by mistake. As soon as she realized what was happening, she slammed her laptop shut, much like she had just now. Even though it had only been seconds, a few dozen frames of pristine 12K video, the images haunted her. But Imogen supposed in a society so hellbent on capturing every single second of their living hours, it was inevitable people would want to capture their deaths as well, when death was the foremost thing on nearly everyone's mind since the virus crossed the Atlantic.

Luckily, Imogen had something of a magic charm to ward off the bad thoughts, the creeping dread, and most important of all, the nightmares. She had her *Dream Lover*—the moniker Ally bestowed on Imogen's nocturnal Casanova. But to Imogen, the name was hardly the best fit. He did so much more than simply take her away to exotic places, make her laugh, or make her feel less alone in her slumbering hours. He kept her safe from the night terrors and all those terrifying things that creeped, lurked, and slithered in the darkness and still went bump in the nighttime.

Her Dream Lover was more Lancelot than Romeo, but these were the kinds of things Imogen kept to herself, not because she wanted to, but because she had to. Ally would never understand this, any of it. There were limits to the friendship with Ally, and this was one of them. Ally's brain hardly wrapped itself around the idea that there was an invisible pathogen in the air that could kill them all. Imogen knew her friend would never comprehend the things Imogen felt somewhere deep down. These were not the things she *knew* for certain, like Josh Groban should have hung up his pipes before she was born, but these were the things she *suspected*.

There was more to this. So much more. The dreams were so...*real.* Hell, *he* was so real. Sometimes it was like Imogen felt his breath on her neck or the light touch of his fingers on her shoulder inside of her dreaming. It wasn't in a creepy, stalker-y way. Despite the moniker, he failed to live up to the name in the romance department. It was all business with Mr. Lover. He was more like a friend. A strange, yet wonderful friend.

Imogen couldn't recall the first time he showed up. Maybe two years ago...*three? Who knows what the fuck time is anymore? Time lost all of its meaning.* The pandemic made it harder for everyone to recall the days, months, even years before the virus and the lockdowns interrupted everyone's regularly scheduled programming. But she knew he'd been there in the pre-virus days and was still there now.

At first, he visited Imogen's dreams once or twice a month. Then, gradually, his visits became once or twice a week until around the time the virus landed Stateside, Imogen had a permanent place setting ready for her Dream Lover every night of the week. And, like clockwork, he came. He always came, even if there were nights where she could only recall snippets of her dreams. Impressions, vague images without context. The only thing that connected them was him. Her ever-faithful Dream Lover.

As she clicked off the light and watched the blanket of black cover her bedroom, the tick on stars slowly twinkling back to life, Imogen wondered how he'd call on her tonight. Would she play the damsel and he the dashing hero arriving seconds before the bomb exploded? Or would they be tourists in some strange new world, exploring every nook and cranny, every street and avenue, together?

In the end, it didn't matter. Imogen knew as long as he was there, she'd feel better. All the real-world stress would melt away—the results from Gemeo Labs, her classmates... no, *former* classmates dropping off one by one—and she could lose herself in a fantasy for just a little while.

Still, underneath it all, Imogen felt something bad was out there, getting closer. She didn't know *how* she knew. She just knew it was out there. Something not fully formed.

Yet.

But becoming. Yes, it was *becoming*. One thing, becoming another thing. And whatever it was, this thing, it was coming for *her*.

Unless...

... her Dream Lover got to her first.

The Dead Girl, Part One

You look just like that d-d-dead girl, d-d-dear.

That was what Flo had said just before the floor show started and weird got weirder. That was *all* the old gal had said about it, too. *For a Chatty Cathy, Flo sure clammed up when it came to "the dead girl."*

Now the floor show was over, The Village People were somewhere out back on a smoke break, "Get outta My Dreams, Get into My Car" hummed on the jukebox, and Flo was chatting up the latest additions to The Greasy Spoon's roster of peculiar patrons—an annoyingly perky and oily-slick tween couple who had taken up residence in a booth at the other end of the diner.

Olivia was hardly a prude or disapproved of PDAs, but watching the pimply-faced, wide-eyed couple paw at each other in front of everyone—*all, what, three of them?*—made her want to shout *get a room.* Seriously, they were basically dry fucking.

Who does that? In public, no less. Christ, when did I get so old? Next thing you know, I'll be listening to Josh Groban in the car. No, fuck that. I'll kill myself first before I listen to that crappy old crooner.

Olivia heard the chirping of the trio's chatter but strangely couldn't make out any of the words. Their exchange sounded like they were speaking in Pygmy Goat, or some dialect of bird, rather than the bargain brand American English.

She bit her tongue and eyed the never-empty cup of coffee on her table. In all the time she'd been holed up in The Greasy Spoon, she'd never seen her gal Flo refill her coffee—not once—and yet, Olivia's cup ranneth over with dark, steaming, caffeinated goodness. She wasn't complaining, exactly. Hell, Olivia's blood was ninety-eight percent coffee, so she'd happily keep drinking it as long as Flo was serving it.

But it was *odd*. Extremely odd, which Olivia suspected was "normal" at this greasy spoon.

The thing in the other corner booth, the one not presently occupied by sexed-up hormonal tweens, sat patiently. Silent and still. Olivia only saw a glint of it out of the corner of her eye. That was as much eye contact as she was willing to make. Every few minutes, she forced herself to gaze in its direction, just to see if it was still there, performing a sort of roll call for the odd and peculiar.

Fuck. One peculiar thing in the corner booth, present and accounted for. One wildly eccentric waitress, present. And one confused patron questioning her sanity, present.

The dead girl. Flo said it so casually, like Olivia was supposed to know who she was. Olivia wondered if another pseudo-celebrity got the virus and passed on and she'd somehow missed news of it. Reality stars, pseudo-celebrities, and worst of all—influencers—were so not her thing.

Olivia felt left out when everyone else was going on about some dipshit on the TV acting like a fool, but really, what the hell made those "stars" so damned special? Nothing. Trained monkeys could act like fools. It wasn't a talent for a human being. Olivia refused to be a part of the cult of celebrity.

So, who was she then? This dead girl. Her dead doppelgänger. If not a person of note, then who? A local? Did they call them "townies" out here too? Flo was being icy cool with the deets so far, divulging nothing substantial about the corpse in question. Not even something basic like a name. And now it felt like Flo was willfully avoiding her table. *She knows I'm going to press her about the dead girl.*

Olivia cradled the hot, impossibly fresh cup of coffee between her fingers. An idea came to her. A good one, too. In an instant, she moved the mug to her lips and downed it all. The coffee wasn't as hot as it felt in the mug, but it was warm enough going down to make her face wrinkle and wince.

Second-degree throat burn? It'll be worth it if this works.

Olivia wiped a dribble of java from her chin and waved the empty Greasy Spoon mug high in the air like she was Lady Liberty waving her torch. *Come on, Flo...come on...take the bait.* But Flo paid Olivia and her empty mug no mind. She merely kept on chatting with the sexed-up tweens with the biggest shit-eating grin Olivia had ever seen in her life.

Getting thirsty here. So very thirsty. Must. Have. Coffee. Come on, Flo. Do your thing. I've got an empty. Could really use a refill here. Getting parched...

Olivia wanted to throw the mug right at Flo's face. Break those stupid glasses of hers and get that stupid grin off her face. In her mind, she played and replayed the scene, relishing Flo's look of surprise at the precise moment when the mug and her face met.

That would surely get the old gal's attention.

For a moment, she debated what might happen if she really threw the mug at the waitress. *What's the worst thing that could happen? I break her nose? Hell, with my aim, I'll probably end up hitting the jukebox instead. Then again, in this fucking place, I'll wind up having perfect aim and kill the poor old thing. Maybe even lop off her head just like her papa did to her mama with that twelve-gauge.*

Olivia eyed the mug. It could do some damage if thrown at a decent speed, and it probably wouldn't even need too much of a wind up. Hell, toddlers had maimed their mommies with bowls of pureed peas. Surely, she could do better than a toddler.

Fuck it. I'm going for it—

Before Olivia could even move a muscle to wind up her throwing arm, Flo snapped her head in Olivia's direction, narrowed her eyes a bit, and then shook her head slowly. Olivia smiled nervously and returned the mug back ever so gently to the table. It was then she realized that not only was Flo staring daggers at her, but so was everyone else in The Greasy Spoon. Even the Village People, who had their angry faces pressed up against the front windows. She didn't have to look to know the thing in the corner was staring. That's all the thing did—stare at her.

Shit.

"This is a family restaurant, d-d-dear." Flo was suddenly beside Olivia's table, holding up a full steaming pot of dark brown coffee. "You best remember that, you h-h-hear?"

Olivia found herself at a loss for words, surprised by Flo's materialization. The only words coming to her were *yes, ma'am*, but she got nothing but air out.

Flo leaned in close to her and whispered, her voice dripping with equal parts menace and malice, "Trust me, d-d-dear. You don't want to get thrown out. It's a cold, dark, d-d-dangerous world out there. Lots of p-p-predators that would like nothing more than to eat you alive."

Between the lines, she really said *you don't want to fuck with me, girlie.*

Olivia picked up what Flo was putting down, loud and clear. Flo's sudden change in temperament and temperature sent a shiver up her spine and caused the fine spattering of hairs on the back of her neck to stand upright and salute.

Flo smiled, the kind of smile one gives when they've eaten the last slice of chocolate cake, and someone else immediately asks if there's more. It's known as the 'fuck you' smile. "Now, what can I do for *you*, d-d-dear?" she asked with a tiny twinkle in her eyes.

"It's just..." Olivia felt her throat betray her, closing up so she choked on her words.

"Yes, d-d-dear?" The twinkle was fading. Flo's eyes took on a more maniacal gaze.

"The, uh..."

Flo huffed, and then she puffed, but Olivia's booth did not fall down. Flo's patience tank was empty. "Maybe I should come b-b-back. When you're ready."

The wide waitress made to spin on her heels, but somehow Olivia found her voice.

"NO!"

She released it in one booming exclamation that appeared to rattle not only old Flo in her loafers, but the concrete foundation of The Greasy Spoon itself. It felt as though they were under the dome of a recently shook snow globe.

What was...THAT?! Did I do that?

"Come back here, Flo!"

In an instant, Flo once again stood beside Olivia's booth.

And although the waitress had previously been presentable, Olivia saw now that Flo's oversized specs had fallen so far down her nose that now only the broccoli-like bulbous tip kept them from sliding off her face completely. Stray strands of hair poked in all directions, rising and hissing like mini serpents on a Medusa mane. Olivia couldn't be positive, but she thought she saw a shimmering bead of sweat rappelling down Flo's Everest-sized forehead.

What just happened? It was like...a seismic bomb went off in the joint. It passed right through me. I felt it...in my bones.

Around them, the diner had gone quiet. The jovial, light atmosphere had taken a turn. The joint wasn't entirely silent though—for the first time since she found herself in The Greasy Spoon, Olivia heard the loud inhalations and exhalations from Flo, who sounded like she'd just wandered in for her shift after running the Boston Marathon.

Olivia's eyes searched the diner to confirm that all eyes were on her and Flo, and they were indeed. All that was missing was the disco ball and spotlight for Olivia to feel more on the spot.

"I want to know," Olivia began, but stopped herself to adjust her volume and tone. The one being too loud and the other harsher than she'd intended. "I'm sorry. I want to know about the dead girl. I want *you* to tell me about the dead girl."

"M-m-me?" Flo stammered. Her tongue poked out of her mouth, sliding over lips that had gone dry. "But I...I mean, I don't really...oh, d-d-dear. Isn't this just a pickle? Ha!"

"Tell me," Olivia said with just the perfect amount of gusto. Flo appeared as surprised at its sound as Olivia had been, only Olivia held her poker face firm and Flo all but signaled she had a bum hand with hers.

Flo swallowed hard. "It's just—"

"Tell. Me." Olivia's voice rose, and this time she didn't adjust her volume. "Tell me about the dead girl. NOW!"

"Which one, d-d-dear? They're have been so many since the pandemic. So many foxes in the henhouse nowadays." Flo tisked so loudly it sounded as though she dislodged and swallowed one of her chicklet teeth.

Olivia waited a moment, and then satisfied she wouldn't have to perform the Heimlich on Flo, she said, with a dry laugh, "Which one?"

Flo's only recognizable response was a fluttering of her eyelids.

"Which one? The one you said looked like me!" Olivia wanted to close with *you stupid, fat hick* but buried the thought under a mountain of more pressing matters, like the dead girl.

"Oh, *that* girl." Flo waved it off like yesterday's special. Beef goulash, in case you were wondering. "That girl…"

Flo cocked her head to the right, and it locked in place. Then, as before, the rest of her froze as well. Olivia hoped Flo's reboot would be a quick one. And it was. A second or so later, Flo's head whipped back into place with a crack that sounded like someone taking a bite out of an apple, and she went on as if nothing peculiar had just occurred. And Olivia had to admit, the more it happened, the less odd it became.

"She had an odd name, that girl."

"Odd…how? Like, Susquehanna or Elvira or Rosalita or something more exotic sounding?"

The waitress laughed, and her belly shook like a bowlful of grape jelly. "Oh, you kidder! Susquehanna!" Flo continued to laugh as though she were the only one in the room in on the gag. "No, no. It was just something you don't hear every day is all I meant. At least, not every day around these parts."

These parts? Where does she think we are? In West Virginia or worse, Staten Island?

"What was it?" Olivia was inching closer and closer to losing what little patience she had left. She fought hard to stifle the thoughts of throttling Flo's thick neck until she gave up the weird name.

Flo placed her hands on her hips and, oddly, looked more like she was about to draw guns at high noon than she was about to think really hard on something. "What was that girl's name again? Omaha? No, why silly me. That's the steak company, isn't it? Oooh...prah? No, that's that old lady from the TV. No...what the heck was it? It's right there on the tip of my—"

Olivia knew before Flo even said the word, what it would be. It was almost like the lightbulb went off over both their heads at the same instant. They even said it at the same time, Olivia speaking just above a whisper.

"Olivia."

Flo clapped her hands together triumphantly. "Yes, that's it, d-d-dear. Olivia."

The name coming off Flo's lips, *her name*, sounded as appealing as arsenic to Olivia.

"But...that's my name."

Flo's hands went to the sides of her face, pantomiming surprise. "Well, if that isn't a co-ink-a-dink. What a small, small world it is." She held up a coffee pot that was filled to the very top with steaming coffee. "Do you need a top off, d-d-dear? Or would you like something stronger?"

"Something stronger, I think. Much stronger. The strongest you got."

Flo smiled and put a heavy hand on one of Olivia's tight shoulders.

"I got just what you need. Have something in the back that'll clean you out better than Drain-Oh. Comin' right up, Oh-liv-ia."

She didn't like how Flo said her name—over-exaggerating the "Oh." It stung her ears like fingernails scraping a chalkboard. A cutting chill moved through Olivia, as if someone—

—how does that expression go?

As if...someone just walked across my grave.

Time Flies When—

Joanne Garriga was most definitely not having fun. She was over Sin City. The glitter and the glitz, the dazzling lights on The Strip, the synchronized fountain shows, not to mention the abundant supply of kitsch, had grown mundane. Worse than mundane. Las Vegas had become boring. Predictable. Whatever charm the city had when Joanne arrived had faded.

But the debt was looming overhead. Always.

Her gaze cut through the thick clouds of cigarette smoke and the endless bullshit, and she saw it for what it was, or what it had become—a sad and desperate place, inhabited by sad and desperate people. It was past its prime, much like the show girls who should have hung up their garter belts and stockings a decade ago. All the smart, younger girls were home shaking their titties on FantastyFans for dollars.

Mucho dinero. If Joanne hadn't been past her expiration date, she might have considered doing the same. Hell, she figured there *was* a market for sexy sixties out there somewhere. There was a niche for everything, the weirder the better. *Bratty barely legal preggo dwarves from the hood with vitiligo into pegging.*

But she wasn't that desperate, *yet*, and still had a debt to repay.

Las Vegas was just another holding pen, just as good and just as bad as every other place she'd been to since St. Augustine Place. She'd been holed up in some dive in the middle of nowhere, Minnesota, when the first signs of the virus hit. Bustling metropolises like Boston and San Diego were hit hard. But Bumblefuck, Minnesota, had been on life support long before the virus sunk its teeth into the local population and sucked the life out of smaller cities and towns from one coast to the other. What little commerce these places had pre-pandemic died quickly and everything around them for miles became a ghost town overnight.

Euthanasia, Joanne thought.

But things were good in Sin City. Pandemic? What pandemic? When everyone else shuttered up their doors, Vegas opened theirs wide and said *yippee ki-yay, mother fuckers. Enter freely of your own will and leave some of the happiness you bring.* Hell, a month into this thing, even Florida said *nah, bruh, we're good. Come back later. Much later.*

No doubt, Vegas was bustling. Thriving even. Who doesn't love a little vice at the end of the world?

But like all good things, it came at a steep cost. Nothing's free in this world. No one really knew what the body count was in Las Vegas. After one month, they'd surpassed New York and California combined. Two months into the pandemic, they had more bodies than the entire East Coast. Now? God only knew, if the big guy even had a clue. Once they ran out of places to store the dead, converted buses called "Death Chariots" drove them out to the desert where they were dumped and served up to the coyotes like roadkill.

No one went that far into the desert anymore. The smell of all that rotting flesh was enough of a deterrent. And if it wasn't, the hundreds of carnivores that claimed that stretch of desert were. After a few days baking in the sun, the dead all looked the same. They were all just sacks of meat in the end.

Joanne figured no one would ever really know how many of the post-pandemic missing people were dragged off and eaten by those beasts, ended up in the back of a van and sold, or just breathed the wrong air. One thing Joanne noticed...the city had run out of places to put up new "Missing" or "Have You Seen Me?" posters. Now, the new ones just got pasted up over the older ones. Every now and then, Joanne thought she recognized one of the thousands of faces staring back at her. She'd almost remember, and then a new face would come to cover up the old. Joanne wondered how many faces she'd seen come and go in Sin City just in the short time she'd been there.

So many missing girls. So many dead girls.

The pandemic was keeping the cops busy, making it even easier for the predators to do their thing. *What kind of world do we live in*, Joanne wondered, *where evil such as this can flourish?*

How many dead girls did it take to equal the life of a single unextraordinary male?

Too many.

Maybe this world wasn't worth saving after all. Maybe it would be better to let it burn, leave it to the beasts and let the earth reclaim itself. The voice could do it, end everything everywhere. One of the voices, anyway. She knew it could.

Montpelier, Vermont.

Maybe they were too late already, and the virus would claim them all. How funny would that be? All this work for nothing. They'd all die anyway, just like those missing girls.

Joanne knew the luckier ones were dead already. And the unlucky ones? She tried not to think about it, but it was like a scab she had to keep picking at until it opened and bled all over again. Those unlucky girls were likely stolen for slavery, prostitution, torture...or, maybe even worst of all, forced to play the game somewhere. *That damned game.*

Many a sleepless night Joanne wondered if one day soon her face might wind up among her missing sisters out there, and would anyone even notice? Would anyone care? Jose? *Pendejo.* No, Jose wouldn't care. His head would be buried between the ample bosom of that Irish bitch back in Boston. *Puta.*

She'd rather endure a million sleepless nights, staring at the ceiling in the dark, than dream. All dreams led to St. Augustine Place and the Millers. At least she didn't have to play the game. *Not yet, anyway.*

Joanne Garriga slipped into her uniform, sighed as something somewhere in her leg cracked, and headed out to "slot machine alley," her assigned section for the day. Despite the casino being packed, she knew her tips would amount to nearly nothing at the end of the day. The slot machine whores, the specific breed of gambler that takes up residence at the slots and thinks "big money" is a quarter machine, were notoriously bad tippers. A dime on a dozen "free" cocktails? What year did they think this was? 1965?

Joanne was not having fun. But, it really didn't matter. The job was something to do. Something to keep her mind from dwelling on things for a few hours a day. *Jose. All those dead girls. The Millers. The game. The voices.* And while occasionally the job provided her with some interesting fodder for the Nosey Next-door Neighbors app, she still had an image to maintain. The job wasn't there to amuse or delight her. *Penance.* It was meant to be hard, sometimes grueling. And always unrewarding.

"Drink," Joanne said to no one in particular as she strode

through the sea of slot machine whores, parading like a worm on a hook. But none of the fish were biting today. The machines weren't paying out. The fish were more apt to drink—and tip—when the machines were looser than the showgirls.

Today was not a good day.

"Drink?"

She glanced at her watch. Three hours into her shift and Joanne had barely made pocket change. *Only six more hours to go.*

"Drink?"

Five more hours.

"Drink?"

Four hours.

"Drink?"

Three.

"Dri—"

The tray slipped from her hands. The sound of breaking glass stirred several of the slot machine whores, only for a moment. The blinking lights and mechanized music quickly sucked them back in. No one actually *saw* the tray hit the ground, or the dozen glasses breaking, spilling their watered-down contents onto the sixty-year-old shag carpet. No, they just continued to fish coins from their buckets and play their games. Hook, line, and sinker. Later, much later, no one would ever recall seeing Joanne Garriga at all.

Joanne hit the floor, her head landing beside a broken turquoise cocktail umbrella. She convulsed, arms and legs flailing as though they were performing a ritualistic dance. Foamy saliva oozed and dribbled out of the corners of her mouth like a rabid dog.

Enter freely…

Cha ching. Cha ching. Ding. Ding. Ding. Cherry. Cherry. Pineapple. Please try again.

Jo-annnnnnnnnnnnnne. It's time to p-p-play.

Ding. Ding. Ding. Jackpot! We have a winner! Winner, winner, chicken dinner.

No, Joanne Garriga was definitely not having fun in Sin City.

Strolling Down Memory Lane

The smell hit Harding like a prizefighter. Hard and fast. How had the neighbors not smelled that? He steadied himself from the blow, wishing now he had taken up the medical examiner, M.E. for short, on her suggestion to "generously apply" the Vicks under his nostrils. Three guys had puked on the front lawn already. A female neighbor, too. Slightly older looking gal. *Older than him, anyway.* Harding noticed a chunky trail led out of the house and down the porch steps. *Rookies.*

The burning and wailing sounds coming from his belly told Harding he might add to the puke pile before the day was over. That would be a career first. He popped a Pepp-Ah-Mint LifeSav-Ahs into his mouth, sucked hard, and hoped for the best. While pleasant going down, Harding imagined the liver and onions lunch special from the Second Ave Diner might not be as pleasant tasting on a return trip.

Harding waved a hand under his nose, knowing it was a futile action. In all his days on the job, he'd never smelled the rot of death as pungent as this. He ascended the porch slowly, letting himself get used to the stink, careful not to step in any of the fresh vomit.

"Welcome to the fun house, Harding," a familiar voice called out from inside the front room.

"Jesus, Pete," Harding said to Detective Pete Hollinger, homicide division, as he snapped on a pair of latex gloves. "What do we got? Where's the victim?"

Harding took a step forward and crossed the threshold, entering the house, the scene of the crime. And somehow, even then, he knew nothing would ever again be the same. This was the line in the sand.

"You mean *VICs*. Got multiples. Some fresh, some…not so fresh."

"How many?"

Harding surveyed the front room. A spacious if not a little sparse living room. The windows were covered up with what looked like newspaper. A door in the corner, open, led to a staircase. *Basement.* No visible bodies in the front room.

"It's hard to tell, given the state of them," Hollinger said.

"Best guess?"

Hollinger rubbed at his chin, clamming up even more.

"What's Dr. Sun got to say?" Yu Sun was the county M.E. Thorough and tenacious, Harding respected Yu Sun. This was not their first rodeo together, but it would be their last.

"She won't say definitively until she's had a chance to inspect all the remains at the lab. Put them together like a jigsaw. But…"

"But," Harding pressed.

Hollinger took a long, deep breath and exhaled slowly. "Based on the cursory exam of the scene? Dr. Sun thinks we got at least four."

"Four?"

"At least."

Harding moved to the open door in the corner, glancing down at the steps. The smell was even riper down there. In the basement. *The heart of the scene.*

"Why is she hesitating to give a definitive number? Either we got a body, or we don't got a body. Simple math."

Hollinger's cherubic face lost what little color it had. Large, round beads of sweat formed at his hairline and prepared themselves for the journey down his forehead and cheeks.

"What? We got parts? Pieces of parts? Is that it?"

Hollinger shook his head.

"Come on, Pete. Give me something. I'm drowning over here. Throw me a vest."

"Dr. Sun can't say how many VICs we got, Harding, because—" Hollinger began, stopping to take a deep breath and steady himself for the words that were about to pass through his lips. "Because some of the VICs have been partially eaten."

Harding rounded on Hollinger. "What are you saying?"

"Some of the VICs were eaten, Harding. Dahmer-style. And..."

Harding saw something in Hollinger's stare. His eyes said, *but wait, there's more,* even if his mouth couldn't form the words. He popped another LifeSav-Ahs in his mouth, which had become dry.

"And?"

"We got one in a crate."

Harding unconsciously inched back. His legs deciding for his brain not to venture into the heart of the house, the basement.

"A crate? Is that what you said?"

Hollinger nodded, his face twisting into an expression of horror and grief.

"Like, a shipping crate? Is that what you're talking about?" Harding asked, his impatience showing.

"No. A dog crate. A big one."

Harding shrugged it off as nothing, because it *was* nothing. Hollinger tended to make mountains out of molehills.

"So, they had a dog? Half the neighborhood has dogs. You can hear them all day and all night. This neighborhood isn't known for peace and quiet."

Then, something unusual happened; something Harding had never seen before, not with seasoned officers. Hollinger's eyes grew wet as the veteran detective struggled to contain his composure, like the reality of the scene suddenly hit him.

"No, they didn't have a dog. It's..." Hollinger broke off, unable to continue. The horrors just too unspeakable.

An idea came to Harding. Something far out, extreme. *No, it can't be. It's just a dog. Maybe they ate Fido, too. It can't be—*

Hollinger's head bobbed up and down so slowly that if you blinked, you might have missed the movement. It was as though he was now in Harding's head, reading his thoughts, and confirming his worst imagined scenario.

Harding's eyes widened as he bit down on the peppermint in his mouth. It boomed like an atom bomb in his brain. "Sweet Jesus. What the hell happened here? How did no one know what was going on?"

"There's a postal worker downstairs. I guess...he figured it out, somehow." Hollinger hesitated, cleared his throat, and then spoke gently, as though he was making a confession to Father O'Rourke at St. John's. "It's like...he was supposed to be the family dog, or something. I don't know, Harding. I've never seen anything like this. I doubt anyone's seen anything like this. Ever."

"Fuck," was all Harding could come up with.

Hollinger held up a hand, and an unusually tall, uniformed

officer with a tight crewcut and a face that looked as though it hadn't as much as sprouted a single hair of peach fuzz ran over, holding a plastic bag tagged as "EVIDENCE." The young officer nodded gravely to Hollinger, who took possession of the bag. He held it out for Harding as the uniformed officer disappeared deeper into what was left of the house that had once been a family home.

"What's this?" Harding asked, taking the bag from Hollinger. He thought he saw a tremor in the detective's hand.

"A game."

Harding studied the contents of the bag: a single piece of ordinary white paper with a few of what looked like hastily written sentences on it. The first few words jumped out at him. *STAYCATION. The rules...*

"It's like they were playing a game. They were playing house," Hollinger said, again in a hushed tone. "And it just went wrong. Horribly, awfully wrong."

Harding turned and eyed the dark basement with suspicious dread. His chest tightened, and he wondered why Hollinger had called the scene a "fun house" and not what it was.

A house of horrors.

The Second Interlude: Just a Gigolo

Nothing ever came easy to Jose Garriga. Nothing. *Life is work, and work is life.*

And if anything could be said of Jose, it was that he was a worker. Always had been. His elder family members used to say he took after his paternal grandfather, Miguel, in that regard, but Jose never met the man so he could neither agree nor disagree. Miguel lived long enough to sire a couple of kids before he died, unsurprisingly, in an accident at work. But much like his grandfather, Jose had been told time and again that he'd been born with two things—the patience of Saint Monica and a solid work ethic. Jose had some doubts about the former.

Everything he had in this life, which wasn't substantial by any measure, he worked his ass off to get. It wasn't much, but it was *his* and no one could take that away from him. They could try, but they'd have to pry it out of his cold, calloused hands. Jose didn't look formidable, but back in his army days, he'd been a boxer. Impressive track record, too. He had big hands. Oversized hands. Hands that could do damage, should they ever choose to.

Working man's hands.

Those hands helped Jose buy a home, a car, go to school, and keep a roof over his head—and later, over Joanne's head, as well. The one thing those hands couldn't do was give them the one thing they both wanted the most. A child. That was not in the cards, and given how things turned out later, after St. Augustine Place, Jose would be grateful they didn't have a child to worry about on top of everything else.

Before the Millers, the only thing that frightened Jose was idleness. *Idle hands are the devil's playthings.* Not that Jose was a religious man. Joanne was the believer, and she had faith enough in the Almighty for them both, until she didn't. *The fucking Millers.*

But he agreed with the sentiment. Jose liked to be busy, to always have a project or two, sometimes three or four, to keep his mind and his hands occupied. His mind was really the problem, not his hands. Never once did Jose's hands get him into a lick of trouble. They got him out of trouble if it ever came to it. And it often did when you looked like Jose, sounded like Jose, and had a name like Jose. God bless America.

Jose's mind liked to wander. Think, and over-think. Imagine. Fantasize. And that was what sometimes got him into trouble, or nearly got him into trouble. The fantasies. Jose had the hands of Ali, the patience of a saint, and the wild imagination of Tim Burton, if Tim Burton made *those* kinds of films. Naughty films. *Dirty.*

These were thoughts Jose kept to himself. Shame was the only leftover on his plate from a strict Catholic upbringing. *Thank you, sir, may I have another?* Purity. *Cleanliness is next to godliness.* He didn't want to be unclean. Moreover, he didn't want to be seen as dirty. The red hats didn't need any more ammo. His being Mexican gave them plenty already. *No good worthless stinking illegal Mexican. Go back to your country.*

Jose didn't see the need to add "dirty" to what was already a ponderous string of offensive and inaccurate adjectives.

Jose knew most of the red hats who slung such shit hadn't worked a day in their privileged lives. Never broken a sweat. Never worked beyond the point of exhaustion. Never bothered to learn a language other than English. Jose spoke three. They thought they were better, but Jose knew the truth. They were nothing more than gum on the bottom of his shoe. But he smiled, laughed, kept his hands to himself, and played the part of a stupid Mexican because it was easier. *Life is work, and work is life.*

And Jose always had his imagination to lessen the sting of some off-handed racist comment or tired-ass joke. After a hard day, he liked nothing more than to retreat into the world of his imagination while whittling away at one of his projects. His lascivious and wonderful imagination. It was a secret, the only secret, Jose kept from his wife. She wouldn't understand. She couldn't understand the need, his needs. If Joanne had her way, they'd make love with a sheet between them. They already "did it" in the dark. What was next? Sex stand-ins?

Joanne always said she wasn't a puritan, but Jose noted there was always a "but" after her declaration. *I'm not a puritan, but...* She wasn't a prude, per se, but her on/off switch was perpetually in the "off" position. Sex wasn't part of her basic programming. She didn't mind other people having sex, talking about sex, or just being sexy, but it wasn't "for her." She'd listen, nod, and laugh when appropriate, so no one was the wiser. No one but her husband, who was likely day-creaming at the same time his wife was nodding and laughing.

When they'd first met all those years ago, Jose thought she was inexperienced, maybe even saving herself for their wedding night. But that wasn't it at all. It went deeper than that, much deeper.

For Joanne Garriga, sex was a wife's duty. *Life is work, and work is life.* A chore, or a household task to be crossed off an endless list of tasks. It became even more of a chore after it was clear they wouldn't be having children. *I just don't need it, but do what you have to, and then let's go get some lunch, okay,* Joanne used to say. She didn't see the point of having sex with her husband. There was no way Jose could make her understand, and he wasn't going to use his hands to explain it to her, either. That would never happen. Jose would leave before he'd ever raise a fist to his wife. *Don't do what you can't take back.*

For too many years to count, sex was work, and work was hard for Jose Manuel Garriga.

And maybe that was why he didn't trust this thing that was happening with his new neighbor in Boston. *Their* new neighbor. Their new, sexy scarlet-haired Irish neighbor with the big tits, wickedly devilish smile, and those icy green eyes that seemed to wink knowingly without ever actually winking.

This was all...*too easy.*

Jose didn't have to work for it. *Don't look a gift horse in the mouth.* She came to him. She teased him. *Wanted* him.

And oh, how he wanted her, too. The *things* he wanted to do to her, and the things he wanted her to do to him. Satan would blush. It was like she stepped out of his imagination, rose off the slab, and became flesh. *Became.* A part of him wondered, hoped, that she had been made for him. *Just* for him.

Jose Manuel Garriga may not have trusted it, but he was going to enjoy it, enjoy her, if it was the last thing he ever did. He may not have strayed, he *wouldn't* have strayed, if the thing with the Millers hadn't happened. If the Millers hadn't happened, *the fucking Millers*, then Joanne wouldn't be hearing voices, and they wouldn't be moving around all the time like fugitives. *Vermont.* He wouldn't know the things he knew; the things he knew he shouldn't know. And Jose Garriga wouldn't have seen the things he'd seen. *Behind the curtain.*

The first time they met, the fIrst moment he felt her insides, everything else went away. Melted like butter in a pan. The doubt, the worry that this was all too easy, whatever trepidation...all gone. Poof!

Talk about a magic pussy. I could live in there. Fuck it all.

The second time they met, she seemed to anticipate his every wanton desire. She even wore black lace and stilettos like he'd imagined. Exactly like he imagined. But he didn't see, couldn't see. Jose was too enamored with her, with her body, with their sexing, to see.

The third time they met, he should have seen. Jose should have known. But he couldn't stop caressing her perfect breasts, savoring the curves and tightness of her body long enough to look at her, really look at her. Look *into* her. He should have seen.

The fourth time they met, he saw glimpses of her, but she had her ways to ensnare and beguile and she used them all. And he was beguiled...several times.

The fifth time they met, somewhere between cuddling and a shower, she ran her fingers through his damp hair and said, "Tell me about your wife."

Before they began this, Jose had only one rule. He didn't want to talk about Joanne. Ever. This was for him, only for him. The mere mention of her name tainted it. Ruined it. He wouldn't be able to...perform.

And she had agreed. Or had she? Jose couldn't remember.

There was a lot he couldn't remember, not about everything, just about *her*. The details were slipping away from him, getting cloudier by the second. *What was her name?*

"Hey, what's your name again? I can't seem to—"

"Don't you remember?" She threw her head back, her long red hair falling against her pale back, and then laughed and laughed. But it wasn't a normal laugh. It was the kind of sound you heard just before you died. A death rattle. "Don't you know who I am?"

Jose saw. Finally, he saw it. For the first time in weeks, he saw what hid beneath the ivory skin and those perfectly sculpted breasts. He saw what wore this woman's skin like a custom-tailored suit. And then Jose wanted to scream, run right out of the tacky pay-by-hour motel off the Mass Turnpike, buck naked, but he didn't move a muscle. Couldn't move a muscle, like he was frozen in place. Nothing passed through his quivering lips. Not a sound nor a puff of air.

The sound of her sultry, silky voice soothed him when it should have unnerved him. Jose was calmed instantly. Doors that had been closed, opened. He opened up for her like a flower, blossoming at her whim. For a moment, Jose thought he could feel her fingers flipping through the pages of his brain, scanning, and searching for...something.

But that was crazy, right? How could she do that?

Finally, he lay there, a lump, a mass on the bed. Putty in her hands.

"What do you...want to know?" Jose heard himself ask, sounding as though he was half-asleep, just waking up from a nap, or about to go lights out thanks to funny gas.

"I want to know..."

She's scanning me...deeper...deeper...deep—
"Everything."
Forgive me, Lord. I've been idle. So very idle.

Wild Horses

Imogen knew it was not a good idea, nor did it fall under the blanket of her proverbial favorite—*welp, it seemed like a good idea at the time.* Adding a bloody nose to an already blackened eye, metaphorically, even dim-witted Ally thought it was a bad idea. She called it—

"A terrible idea, Imo. That's a terrible idea. If all the terrible ideas got together, this idea would be the terriblest of them all."

"That's not even a word."

Ally tisked. "I know. I'm not, like, stupid, you know. It was for dramatic effect."

"Dramatic effect? Who taught you to say words like that?" Imogen said, trying to sound stern, but her laughter broke through.

Ally recalled a popular, but now all but forgotten—except for the occasional viral rounds on socials—anti-drug commercial. It last resurfaced not long before the first lockdown. "I learned it from *you*, okay! I learned it from *you*!"

The girls laughed together. It felt good to laugh.

As the joviality died down, Ally was the first to speak. "Can I ask you something, Imo?"

"Yep." Imogen popped her lips harder than necessary on

the "p" in "yep," for dramatic effect.

"Um, okay. So, what word were you talking about?"

That set Imogen off on another fit of spirited laughter. Ally, who did not join in the revelry, did her best to stifle the flame of Imogen's funny fire with half-empty pleads of *oh, come on* and *it's not that funny, Imo,* which only made Imogen laugh louder and harder.

Imogen stopped laughing long enough to say, "Girl, you dumb."

"It's a gift."

"I'll say. It's the gift that keeps on giving."

Ally sighed. "Oh, hardy, har, har. Riddle me this, Batman. If I'm supposed to be the dumb one—"

"Supposed to be?"

Ally spoke louder, drowning out Imogen. "If I'm supposed to be the dumb one, why are you the one talking about breaking into the Coffee Cavern? Huh?"

Imogen knew Ally had a point but dodged and weaved, trying her best to avoid giving Ally the win. "I need to jump on their Wi-Fi. And I have a key, dummy. It's not breaking in if you have a key. Technically. I still work there. I guess."

"Breaking and entering does not look good on a college application, Imo. They're gonna look at your grades, all your boring ass activities—"

"Hey!"

"And wonder how this otherwise full scholarship brainiac served three to five for B & E…for breaking into her place of employment during a lockdown! Kiss Princeton and all those fine Ivy-League boys goodbye. I was so looking forward to visiting them…you at Princeton."

"First of all, B & E?"

"What? They're like showing nothing but *Law and Order: Cyber Division* on TV. Seriously. It's on like 24-7. I've been picking up a lot of the lingo. Ten-four. Over. I've watched so much *L and O,* I could probably be a cop, you know. Work a scene. Freeze, you turkey! Bam! Bam! Bam!"

"Moving on. And second, I probably don't even need to go inside the Coffee Cavern. Just be close by, you know? Jump on, jump off, go home."

"Hmmm."

Imogen waited, but nothing else came from Ally. "What?"

"Nothing. I mean, I guess it makes sense. Kinda, sorta. But how do you know their internet isn't down too? Last time ours went down, it was out for like what? Three days?"

"Four, and it's not. I checked. We use a different provider at the Coffee Cavern."

"Okay, I know I'm dumb, but like...how did you check if their internet is out if *our* internet is out?"

Imogen laughed. For an intellectually challenged individual, Ally was being unusually logical and thoughtful about this. "I used cellular to check their website. 'No outages reported.' Okay, Sherlock?"

"Verrrry interesting, doctor. Verrry interesting, indeed."

Imogen had no idea what TV character Ally was channeling now, but she laughed at the absurdity of it.

"So, what if, like, you get there and it goes out while you're, wait for it, on the way? Did you think of that, huh?"

"I did. It's a chance I'm willing to take. The Wi-Fi at the Coffee Cavern is so much more reliable than the crap signals we get on this side of town. You know that."

"Yeah, G-Mobile Wi-Fi does kinda suck. You got me there."

"I'm not so sure I want you."

"Funnn-nyyyyy. You've been stuck with me since kinder-garten."

"And here I thought I was unlucky."

"Just unlucky at love, biii-tttch."

Imogen did not care for this topic. "Not unlucky, just...picky. Some of us have standards."

"And some of us will die a virgin with nothing but their standards to hold their hand." Ally pretended to sob and wail, as though at a funeral. "It's just...so...sad."

"Alright, I get it. But I don't think 'massive whore' will look good on my transcript, either."

"Who knows? Maybe it'll help. Some decrepit fifty-year-old Dean of Admissions will see that and BOOM! Insta-hard-on. He'll call you in for an interview..."

Imogen pictured Ally making air quotes as she said the word "interview."

"But really, it's just an excuse to call you in so he can bend you over his knee and spank that firm booty of yours right there in the office at P-U."

"Oh, my god. That's so gross. I think I need a shower."

"Holy shit, is it really P-U? That's hella funny. Where do you go to school? P-U. Excuse me? Do I smell?"

Ally laughed at her own joke. Imogen did not. P-U had been her dream school since second grade.

"Anyway, I think I need a hit from my vape pen and a drink after picturing that." Ally laughed. "That'd be so hot. Tell me again why you want to *come* to P-U... BAM! Spank, right on the ass."

"You need help, Al."

"Seriously, I do. But I'm not the one thinking of going out into the toxic air to check her emails."

Imogen huffed. "You know that's not what I'm doing." She stopped for a moment and considered who she was talking to. "Right?"

"Yes, I know! It's this stupid Gemeo cult thing."

"It's not a cult!"

"Can't you just, I don't know, go to your cult meeting on your phone? Like, virtually attend using cellular. I know your phone is like ancient, but why do you have to be on Wi-Fi? That sounds both fishy *and* culty."

"Seriously?"

"What?" Ally sounded genuinely dumbfounded.

"You don't think I tried that as soon as the internet went out? How stupid do you think I am—"

"Well—"

"Don't answer that. It was rhetorical. Only one of us has a four-point-oh GPA and it's not you, darling. No offense."

Ally smacked her lips. "None taken, lover. But that is weird, isn't it?"

"What? You mean the website not loading?"

"Well, yeah," Ally agreed. "And that's just for starters."

Imogen, who had been asking herself the same question all day, wouldn't give an inch. That was all the room Ally needed to talk her out of going out. "I don't know. It could just be that their server is down. That sparkly tree just keeps spinning, and it says 'loading, please be patient.' I just want to check. That's all. Pop over, see if I can load the site, and then come home. An hour. Two, tops."

"It's real sketch, Imo."

"This is important to me. You know that."

Ally groaned. "Just promise me you'll be careful. Like, wear a mask and shit."

"Obvs. I don't want to end up like Jemma and Freddy."

"R.I.P. Or, Steven West."

Imogen gasped. "No! What? When?"

"I don't know. Found out this morning. Chelly texted me."

"Fuck."

"I know. He was kind of cute, too. What a waste."

"Al!"

Ally laughed into the phone. "What? For real, I'm just bein' honest."

"We've known him since the third grade."

"Yep, back when he was just Little Stevie. Now, he's Sayonara Stevie."

"Oh my god, Al!" The line went quiet. "Is this what we've come to? Are we already so used to our friends and classmates—" *former classmates*, "dying, that we joke about it? Text about it, not even call to relay the news? Just *clack, clack clack*, send. 'Steven's dead. L-O-L.'"

"It's not like that."

"Isn't it, though? We're getting used to this. All of this. And, honestly, it hasn't even been that long. I can't anymore with this lockdown shit. By the time it's over, there won't be enough of us left to fill a single classroom."

There was a long silence on the other end of the phone. Long by normal standards, and incredibly long by Ally standards. Then, Imogen heard Ally crying into the phone.

"It sucks, Imo. It fucking sucks."

"I know. It does."

"Promise me you'll be careful out there. Promise me!"

"I promise!"

"Cross your non-existent breasts and your heart?"

Imogen sighed. "I cross my—no, I'm not saying that! I have

boobs. Cross my heart."

"Cross your heart. Good."

"Good," Imogen agreed. "You're stuck with me, remember? Wild horses couldn't drag me away from you."

Neither spoke again for a while. They just sat there, listening to the sound of each other breathing. This wasn't something they normally did, but since the virus arrived, it happened more often. Just listening to each other breathing, as though they were in the same place, gave each of them a great deal of comfort. Since they could not be together in person—still too risky, for now—this was an okay consolation prize. But even Imogen knew nothing beat the real thing. She just missed seeing and touching her friend in the flesh—touching *all* of her friends, however few of them were left.

Finally, Ally spoke, and it was so low, so gentle, that Imogen almost missed it.

"Until death do us part."

Yeah. Cross my heart and hope to...

Stranger Strange Things

That was it, the final strange straw that broke Olivia's back.

The dead girl had my name, and I have the dead girl's name. Well, ain't that just a co-ink-a-dink? That's what Flo called it. A *co-ink-a-dink.* And she'd had that stupid *I know something you don't know* look on her face. If Olivia wasn't so freaked out by the scene, she would have rolled her eyes and wiped the look right off old Flo's face.

But Olivia didn't think it was that simple. This wasn't just a mere co-ink-a-dink. None of it. She didn't know what it was, though, and that irked her more than all the weird shit going on at the diner combined.

The air in The Greasy Spoon suddenly felt stifling, like it had grown hands and now had those hands wrapped around her neck, squeezing. Olivia, try as she might, couldn't seem to take in any air. It felt like there was something over her head, like an old-timey plastic grocery bag, and someone had taped it shut around her neck so she couldn't get any air into her lungs. This was *crazy.*

Her hands went to her face in a flurry, swatting, but found nothing that didn't belong. *It's in your head, girl. It's all in your head.*

Olivia didn't know if it was all in her head or not, but she was certain that she had to get out of The Greasy Spoon. She rummaged through her purse, feeling her wallet and cell phone, and continued until her fingers wrapped around her car key fob. Olivia hoped when she finally went outside that her little yellow solar sedan would be there waiting for her, charged up and ready to blow this crazy joint.

Flo was there, *of course she was,* standing beside the booth, blocking the path to the front door, as Olivia swung around and planted her feet on the ground.

"Going somewhere, d-d-dear?"

Even though she should have anticipated this move, Olivia did not and gasped.

Flo laughed, strangely and loudly, and threw her head back. Her entire body appeared to ripple with each stomach-clenching guffaw. The bespectacled waitress laughed so fitfully, so heartily, that her puffy nostrils flared wildly, and her glasses nearly jumped right off her nose to take up residence beside the stale, lonely French fry on the floor.

"Oh, my! I must look a real fright to have s-s-startled you like that!"

Think, stupid. Think! Use that Ivy-League brain of yours and get the hell out of here.

"No, um. My bad. I wasn't paying attention. You look great, Flo. You do."

Really? You look great? That's all you could come up with?

Flo stopped laughing and reset her head to its normal, upright position. Her fingers moved through her mane like a comb. "Not too shabby for a girl doing a double. Thank you for saying, d-d-dear."

"Don't mention it."

No, really, don't.

Olivia smiled so weakly that it barely registered. She felt it, so she quickly added a small nod as though to say, *well, I'll be getting the fuck out of here now. See ya around, Flo.* She went to move around the giantess, but Flo had other ideas. Before Olivia took a single step, the waitress seized her arm and clamped down tightly.

"You aren't l–l–leaving, are you, d–d–dear?"

Olivia turned and looked up at Flo's flustered face. The waitress somehow seemed even taller and wider than before, and her face was speckled with red splotches, seething with fury. Even Flo's eyes seemed to radiate red. Olivia thought the waitress looked a bit like a bull staring down a red cape. All that was missing from the image was angry steam coming out of her nose.

Say something before the bull, er cow, charges.

"What? Leaving? Me?" Again, Olivia smiled weakly, punctuating it with a nervous laugh. "No, Flo. I was just... just..."

Flo's eyes fixed on Olivia and became impossibly redder until they looked like a pair of backlit rubies. Her grip on Olivia's arm tightened. "Just what, d–d–dear?"

Olivia's mind went blank. In that moment, she wouldn't have recalled her name if you asked her. She was transfixed by Flo's furious flabby face and found herself utterly at a loss for words.

Flo leaned in until her mouth was beside Olivia's ear. Olivia felt the waitress's fiery breath whip through her hair. For a moment, Flo said nothing. She just lingered there, breathing. But then, when it felt to Olivia that the moment had stretched to the point of breaking her, a sound passed the waitress's lips.

"Mooooooooooooo!"

It wasn't a bad rendition, either. Quite realistic given that the woman's laughter sounded akin to a bad laugh track on a dated sitcom.

Olivia didn't know how she did, but she wrangled her arm free from Flo's firm grasp and squeezed her more compact body through the narrow crevasse that lay between Flo's sturdier frame and the booth. It wasn't much, but Olivia took it. An instant later, she pushed the doors open, aware Flo was calling to her.

"Do try the pie next time you're in these parts, d-d-dear."

The bell above the door dinged, and Olivia was through the opening faster than she ever ran the fifty-yard dash. *If Coach Alves could see me now.* Coach Alves. Her track coach for like thirty seconds in her freshman year. On her way out, Olivia caught sight of something hastily taped to the door. It was a generic, homemade missing-style poster.

Wait. Is that my face?

She didn't stop to look any closer, but she moved forward like a ghost, more floating than walking. At least, that was how it felt. More like an out-of-body experience. First, she had managed the three steps at the diner doors. Then, the short distance from the diner to the parking lot. And finally, with the key fob in hand, Olivia made it to her small, eco-friendly vehicle.

She stood in the utter blackness of the outside and pressed down firmly on one of the fob's buttons. Her eyes were momentarily blinded by the rapid flash of her little car's headlights burning to life. *Talk about a deer in headlights.* She inched closer to her car, reaching for the door handle on the driver's side. It felt good in her hand. It felt *real*, sturdy.

Tangible. Finally, something tangible. It felt like salvation.

A sense of relief washed over her in an instant. *I'm getting out of here.* She tugged at the handle and the car door popped open. The sweet scent of cold mocha lattes and her favorite perfume, TK-1, assaulted her senses, catching her off-guard, putting her at ease.

It smells like home.

She sat behind the wheel, sighed a breath of relief, and tapped the ignition button. She hadn't realized her hands were shaking. But nothing happened. The engine remained fast asleep. *Come on. Come on. Come on.*

Olivia tapped it again, more forcefully, as though she were repeatedly ringing the doorbell at her near stone-deaf great Auntie Gertie's house. Wait...something happened that time. It just wasn't what Olivia had been expecting.

"Now, how's about that pie, d-d-dear?"

Olivia was back inside the diner. "Dream Police" by Cheap Trick was on the juke, and she was again sitting at the same booth she'd fled minutes ago. *The fuck?* Outside, it was snowing. A real blizzard, the kind that indiscriminately closed schools and roads. Inside, everything looked the same. Almost everything. The sexed-up tweens were gone. In their place sat a weathered-looking gentleman wearing blues. *A cop.* He slurped at his coffee loudly, and after he'd done that, he set the mug down and slurped at the steaming bowl of soup that sat on his table.

And there in the corner, still, the thing patiently sat.

Flo looked at her over the rim of her glasses.

"Best in the county." Flo tapped her pen on her order pad. "You know what they say?"

It's like déjà vu.

"Pie makes everything better," Olivia said. Her voice sounded to her like it was a million miles away. "Sure."

Flo scribbled something onto the pad and tucked it away in her apron pocket before sliding the pen somewhere into her nest of hair.

"I kn-kn-knew you couldn't pass up pie. Coming right up, d-d-dear. More coffee?"

Coffee? Where's my strong drink? Flo said she had something stronger than Drain-Oh, but now it's just—

Flo held up the coffee pot. She didn't have that in her hands a moment ago. It was full, and steam rose out of the top.

Olivia could only nod, feeling more and more like she'd fallen back asleep and picked up in this strange dream almost where she'd left off. She didn't even want to imagine what was coming around the corner next. In a way, it reminded Olivia of that song by that bird band her father loved. *The Condors? Vultures? Eagles?* It was the song about the hotel. Something about checking in and never being able to leave. *Roaches check in, but they don't check out. Raid.*

"You know something, d-d-dear," Flo said as she topped off Olivia's cup of Joe. "Old Herb over yonder—"

"That's...Officer...Hunt," the cop said between sloppy soupy slurps.

"You'll always be little Herbie Hunt to m-m-me, Officer Hunt," Flo said jovially.

Herbie Hunt groaned and went back to slurping what Olivia thought was chicken noodle soup.

"As I was saying, d-d-dear. You might ask Herbie—I mean, Officer Hunt—about that dead girl. I bet he could tell you something, I'll tell you what. Ain't that right, Herbie—Officer Hunt?"

"What are you on about now?"

"I was just saying to our wayward guest here that you'd be the proper one to ask about that dead girl. Wouldn't you agree?"

Herbie Hunt looked up and dropped his spoon into the cavernous soup bowl. Stringy bits of chicken and broth splashed onto his blue chambray uniform shirt. He grabbed a flimsy paper napkin from the dispenser and dabbed around his mouth.

"Looks just like her, wouldn't you say, Herb?"

He produced a pair of glasses and plopped them into place. "Why, I'll be dipped in some kind of shit if you don't look *just* like her, that dead girl. A real dead-ringer. Near spitting image. Uncanny."

"Why, that's just what I said, Herbie. It is downright un-canny."

"I'll remind you," Herbie Hunt began, removing his glasses and tucking them back into a shirt pocket. "You are to refer to me as Officer Hunt. Not Herbie. Not Herb. Just Officer Hunt, whether I am in uniform or not."

Flo leaned down to Olivia. "He's always on duty. Least, that's what his wife used to say before she left him for a swarmy solar salesman. Said he'd give her the sun and stars. Ha!"

"Listen here now," Herbie Hunt said, slamming a fist onto the table. "You best not be talking about Lulu. I kicked *her* out. Everyone knows that. Should be a law against gossip."

Slurrrrp. Slurrrp. Slurrrp.

"Best leave old Herbie alone for a bit. Let him simmer, d-d-dear. I'll get you that pie."

Flo retreated her head, gave Olivia a wink, and then waddled back into the kitchen. Seconds later, something smashed onto the kitchen floor. Olivia thought it sounded like a plate. It didn't ring like a drinking glass or one of The Greasy Spoon's weighty coffee mugs.

"Oh my. I think my fingers must be made of butter," Flo said from somewhere in the belly of the kitchen.

Olivia couldn't think about it, *the whole dead girl thing.* Sure, maybe Herbie could fill her in on some of the deets, but did she really want to go over and slide up next to Officer Slurpy? *Not really, no.* And old Herbie seemed nearly as *off* as old Flo. Nearly. Olivia didn't know if anyone else *could* be as off as Flo.

She wouldn't think about it. The dead girl. Not now, not while that thing in the corner booth was staring at her. Olivia knew it was. She didn't have to look to know—she felt its gaze boring right through her. There was a strange electricity in the air. The place felt extra-charged, even more than when the sexed-up tweens had been in earlier. Olivia felt her bones rattle and her skin ripple with ample supplies of gooseflesh and raised hairs.

I can't think in here. I feel like I'm losing it.

She fished out her cell phone. It was a brick—zero bars, no service, and "critically low" battery level.

Fuck.

She hadn't expected the phone to work. It was a pipe dream. Olivia had the vaguest of recollections. It was more like the hazy fragment of a dream. Sometime since she'd arrived, hours ago, maybe, Olivia remembered asking Flo if there was an outlet she could commandeer to charge up her phone. She'd even held it up, charger attached, showing it off proudly like a cat shows off a mouse caught in its mouth.

Flo had looked at the phone all wild-eyed, like kids looked at the barely passable strip mall Santas. It was almost as if the old gal had never seen a cell phone before, *which was impossible, right?* Then Flo shook her head and trotted off, mumbling something about not knowing jack about these "newfangled things."

New? Jesus H. Tap Dancing Christ, Flo. Cellular phones have been around for sixty years, at least. Where have you been living, d-d-dear?

Olivia also noticed that The Greasy Spoon didn't appear to have a phone anywhere in sight, neither a hard-wired old-school business line nor a pay phone plastered to a back wall in the joint for careless customers—like Olivia—who'd let their cellular phones run out of juice.

Okay, so I guess I can scratch calling anybody for help off the short-list of ideas.

Olivia sat for a while, trying not to hyper-focus on the chain of events that had unfolded since she got to The Greasy Spoon. In her experience, her best ideas, the best solutions, came to her when she cleared her mind of everything else. It was a very Zen-like practice, she thought.

Then, an idea came to her.

If the mountain won't go to Mohammed, then Mohammed must go to the mountain.

And for the first time since she found herself parked in The Greasy Spoon, Olivia felt like she'd stepped back into her own clothes. She felt like her old pre-diner self again. The smart, resourceful, Ivy-League-bound girl, not the hesitant mouse she'd become at The Greasy Spoon. This place, that thing in the corner, the bathroom that wasn't a bathroom, and Flo— mostly Flo—had Olivia unnerved and off her A-game. She didn't know why she hadn't thought of it sooner. The idea was so simple, so obvious. Practically slapping her in the face. For a nerd who sat alone at the top of her class, Olivia was the first one to admit that sometimes she could be pretty dumb about common sense things. Sometimes calculus was easier for her to decipher than the mundane toilings of human teenage existence.

But Olivia reminded herself that she'd been too distracted to problem solve all of this properly. From the moment she found herself in The Greasy Spoon, everything was a distraction. *But a distraction from what?*

The test, obviously, another voice came into her head.

All she had to do was *switch seats.* She didn't even have to switch booths, just swap over to the other side, so she wasn't looking dead on at the thing in the corner. She wanted to see if it liked the view of the back of her head as much as it seemed to enjoy the front. *Take that!*

Olivia looked around, running recon. Flo was moving about the diner like a guppy, coffee pot in hand and at the ready. *Where was my pie? Did she forget?* Olivia hadn't noticed it before, but Flo's every movement, every step was unnaturally awkward, like she'd either just learned to walk earlier in the day or recently had a cast removed from one of her trunky legs.

Everything about Flo was kind of jerky and strange, but this was stranger than strange. Her movements reminded Olivia of one of those old-school video arcade games, like Pac-Man—an action maze chaser. Low-res graphics. Choppy animation. And a fixed setting or environment, *like The Greasy Spoon*. It was one of those things that were virtually impossible to unsee once you've seen them, like it was seared right into her brain. Just something else that tickled Olivia's funny bone. Laughing, she guessed, was a lot better than screaming.

Olivia felt uneasy, but she didn't know why, other than the myriad of oddities to which she was strangely becoming accustomed that had presented themselves since she found herself at the diner—and there had been a truckload of them, to be sure. There was nothing inherently dangerous or wrong about what she wanted to do—swap seats—but it still felt risky. Dangerous, even, like a game of Russian Roulette. Would there be a bullet in the chamber when she swapped seats, or would she escape with her life? Only time would tell.

This is stupid. Why am I hung up on this? I'm just moving over to the other side of the booth. That's all. I'm sure people do it all the time. If she asks, I'll tell Flo the sun was in my eyes. Yeah, the sun. Swarmy solar salesman. *Wait, was it snowing? I don't remember. I can't remember.*

Olivia peered through the grease-coated blinds that covered up the windows beside her booth. *These have seen better days.* Her fingers stuck to the blind's sticky surface as though they were used to trap flies. *When was the last time someone, looking right at ya, Flo, took a duster to these things? How the fuck do they pass inspection?*

Olivia winced as she pushed down on the flimsy vinyl sunshine buster, seeing at once that it was now dark outside. Very dark. Full dark. No moon. No stars. No lights from the highway. No...anything. It looked and felt like all life outside of the diner had ceased to exist. And there were no traces of snow or lingering dirty snow piles in the corner of the parking lot.

I could have sworn.

Fuck, now what? Even old Flo isn't dim enough to buy that there was sun in my eyes when it's pitch-black outside. Olivia searched her memory. She had no recollection if it had just been snowing out, sunny out, or raining cats and dogs. Time, and the weather, seemed to change on a dime at The Greasy Spoon. Up was down, and down was up. But one way or another, Olivia was swapping seats. She couldn't stand to see that thing anymore, the weird thing in the corner booth. She didn't want to feel its squiggly eyes on her or its hands menacingly reaching out to her.

Her heart raced in her chest. Olivia's palms felt clammy and wet. Her whole body oozed nervous perspiration; even her ankle-cut sports socks began clinging to the dampening skin of her feet. *This is stupid. I don't need a reason. It's not a big deal. Screw this. I'm doing it.*

Olivia reassured herself, repeating the words like a mantra or a lame-ass pep-talk from Coach Alves. *Man, he was a prick.* She wondered for a moment if her former coach was still out there somewhere, or if the virus had gotten to him, too. *That feels like a lifetime ago now.* And maybe it was.

Okay, this is ridiculous. Quit stalling. Put your big girl panties on and let's do this. What's the absolute worst thing that could happen? You end up in the bathroom again or in the kitchen? Ugh. As the late, great Arnold once said—do itttttt, do it nowwwww!

Okay. I'm doing it.

I'm really doing it.

On three.

She took in a deep inhalation of the diner's funky air, then let it out quickly. Olivia did this several times, looking more like she was in a pre-natal class for preggos than pumping herself up for action. *Action? That's a laugh.*

One.

She ignored the line of sweat dripping down her back along her spine.

Two.

Olivia ignored the thunderous sound of the rapid *lub dub, lub dub* of her heartbeat ringing inside of her head.

And...on...

Olivia sucked in one last desperate gulp of air. This was it. Go time. And—

Three!

She exhaled and jumped to her feet in a flash. *Coach Alves would be proud.* And before anyone was the wiser, or so she thought, Olivia slid herself into the booth. This time, she was sitting on the opposite side. She felt a momentary sense of relief, believing that thing was now staring at the back of her head. And at least now she wouldn't have to see Herbie Hunt slurping at what had to be a bottomless bowl of soup.

Olivia slid the mug of fresh coffee over to her new side of the booth and raised it to her mouth. The hot liquid was teasing at her lips when Olivia froze. The wind quickly fell out of her sails. The thing hiding in the shadows had switched seats too. It was now on the other side of the diner, tucked away in a different corner booth, eyes still staring right at her. The squiggly lines that made up its face squirmed. Olivia thought it looked sort of like a grin or *a sneer.*

This is it. This is how I...

It's just like that damned Eagles song. I'm never getting out of here.

Jesus, Take the Wheel!

The very first thing Joanne Garriga did when she came back to herself, as she called it, was slam her foot onto her car's brakes. Outside the car, the brakes wailed and howled like a banshee in heat. *Screeeeecccch!*

Instantly, the car's worn rear tires were a smokey blur, the smell of burnt rubber flooding in through the vents. With one hand, Joanne closed the air vents, the smell sickening her, and with the other she steadied the wheel as best she could. *Jesus, take the wheel!* Her body jerked forward as the car skidded several feet and then slid several more until it finally came to a full stop, ending up at an acute angle on the road's shoulder.

"*¡Dios mío!*" Joanne gasped as she tapped on her hazards. *Another blackout.* The jabbing pain in her head confirmed it. She wrapped both of her trembling hands around the steering wheel and squeezed down with the ferocity of a patient biting down on a stick during surgery in the days before anesthesia. "*Di-os, mí-o.*"

She rolled down the window. That sickening burnt rubber smell hit her instantly. Joanne coughed and waved it off as best she could, but it lingered and slowly seeped into the car. *Carajo.* She coughed again, unclicked her safety belt, and made her way out of the car.

It was a lonely stretch of road made even lonelier thanks to the lockdowns. Joanne didn't see another car for miles in either direction. She was alone wherever she'd wound up this time.

Her somnambulistic activities rarely took her more than a few miles from wherever she was holed up, except for the one time she had driven from Portland, Maine, to Athens, Vermont, while entranced. Joanne recognized the scenery as belonging to Nevada but couldn't pinpoint her location on a map if her life depended on it. Her phone was just as useless. There were no bars to be found out in the scorching Nevada sands. Wasn't much life, either. The sun had become unforgiving even for the animals that had evolved to live in the extreme heat. They either died off or packed their bags and moved elsewhere, like everyone else.

Joanne threw her hands up. "I don't suppose you're going to tell me where I am? Or where I'm supposed to go?"

She looked around, not sure what she expected to find or see. Some kind of directive would have been nice, but nothing came. *Nada.* Zilch. Joanne sighed and kicked at the desert sands.

"What do you want from me?"

This wasn't the first time the voice had left her stranded, and Joanne knew it wouldn't be the last. It was like something blocked the *signal*, interrupted their connection. She didn't know if it was the physical distance between them, or something deeper. One of the other voices, maybe. Putting up a wall. Blocking the signal. The voices certainly seemed to be at odds with each other more often than not. Sometimes it felt like a party line in her head, the voices talking over each other, demanding her attention, and calling her into action.

Sometimes it was frustrating, but Joanne knew what the alternative was. She'd seen it in Vermont. *Jesucristo. All those people.* And Jose had seen it, too. His eyes nearly bugged right out of his head. *Pendejo.* Joanne knew that was it for him. That Irish bitch in Boston was just an excuse to cut and run. A consolation prize stuffed into double-Ds. But deep down, she knew Jose had checked out after the things they saw in Vermont.

Vermont. I don't want to end up like...no. No.

Joanne gave the desert and the lonely highway one last look before returning to her car. *Aye!* The car still reeked. She rolled up the window and turned on the air, ensuring all the vents were open and pointing right at her. Even though she hated the cold, she'd endure it if it meant she didn't have to take another whiff of that awful smell.

The car groaned back to life. Joanne steered back onto the highway and drove. She had no plan, no directive. The best thing she could do was drive until either she recognized something or encountered some sign of life. Even in the middle of the pandemic and the lockdown, there had to be something out here, wherever *here* was.

She cruised down the highway, seeming not to have a care in the world, humming a tune that had just come to her. One she hadn't thought about in years. Many years. She'd been wearing a plaid skirt, knee-high socks, and shiny patent leather shoes the last time she sang it at St. Albert's Elementary School in the Bronx. Now, a lifetime later, the words came back surprisingly easy to her, easier than Joanne could recall what she had for breakfast yesterday.

Jesus loves me, this I know, for the Bible tells me so.

Little ones to him belong. They are weak, but he is strong.

She didn't have a good voice, but merely an inoffensively pleasant one that was mostly in tune. At least, that was what Father Michaels used to tell her. *You'll burn in hell if you lie, girl.* Joanne wondered now if she was singing about her former lord and savior, or the voice inside of her head. She also wondered if it mattered one bit in the end. A smile came to her face as she thought about Father Michaels with the wandering hands. *Maybe the virus got him. He was old enough now that a good sneeze would probably do the man in.*

One could hope.

The song kept her attention so Joanne didn't see the electronic billboard flash:

MISSING! Have You Seen Me? Imogen Rockwell

Behind the words, Imogen Rockwell's face came into view, millions of pixels combining at once to bring the image out of nothing and into something.

Jesus loves me, this I know...

And she certainly did not see the faded welcome sign that once belonged to The Greasy Spoon diner that now read:

CLOSED. Thanks for 57 fabulous food-filled years!

The place looked like it had been closed for fifty years, at least.

... for the Bible tells me so.

Nor did she see the little yellow sedan parked in the lonely, otherwise empty, parking lot.

Little ones to him belong...

Oblivious to everything else, the song now the only thing on her mind, Joanne Garriga definitely did not notice the lights inside The Greasy Spoon were turned on, or—

...they are weak, but he is strong.

—the dark figure of a man standing at the diner's boarded-up doors.

Harding and the Whale

Harding took in the scene, the sheer depravity of it. He stood like Jonah on uncertain, rubbery legs in the belly of the house—the basement—but steadied himself as he felt the eyes of his fellow officers on him, as well as a superior or two, including the big cheese himself, Chief Randall Peters. This was the kind of case that brought everyone, especially the old-timers who were a breath away from their pensions, like Chief Peters, out of the woodwork, trying to attach themselves to it by proxy. Guys like Peters were about as useful in the field as the pope at a swinger's party.

Hell, over a century later, and Harding wondered how many nobodies still got mentioned in the same breath as London's infamous Jack the Ripper. Cases like this meant press, and lots of it—not even taking into account all the cell phones blasting the inter-webs about it. Media coverage meant celebrity. Book deals. Talk shows. Interviews on cable news programs with clueless pundits, one side blaming the other for creating an environment where *this* could happen.

THIS is what happens when we take God out of the classroom.

THIS is what happens when you let kids read To Kill a Mocking-bird.

THIS is what happens when we allow women to make their own decisions.

THIS is what happens when we tax the rich.

THIS is what happens when we go green.

THIS is what happens when we let drag queens read to our kids.

And when all else fails, just place the blame squarely on migrant workers, everyone's favorite scapegoat for unthinkable crimes.

Harding had no use for celebrity, book tours, or bleached-blonde Wonder-Bread-looking pundits who had as much interest in getting to the truth as O.J. Simpson had in looking for "the real killer." That's to say, less than none. Pundits had only one job—to create chaos and diversion, whether through their angry monologues or badly ghostwritten "real" exposés. Harding's grandfather, who had thirty years on the job himself, used to say *beware the fool who peddles the truth.* It was advice that stuck with Harding and had served him well, along with *always trust your gut.* The guys round the precinct got the latter plastered on a coffee mug when Harding celebrated his tenth year on the job.

He was a simple guy who didn't need to see his name in lights, have a *New York Times* bestseller, or get a six-figure book deal. Harding lived for getting the job done. Closing a case. Putting the right people away. Keeping the streets where he grew up and still called home safe. That was the notoriety Harding needed to sleep at night, if he did actually sleep at night. It was the cases that kept him up. Some haunted you longer than others, became impossible to compartmentalize. Every detective and beat cop will tell you they've lost sleep over a case, and this one, Harding knew, would keep him up for many a night to come.

Surveying the bloody scene sprawled before him, Harding

wondered if he'd ever sleep again. He pointed to a pile of blood and gore in the middle of the floor. "That's a person, right?"

Andy West, the coroner, nodded. "Was a person."

"Got a theory on COD?" *Cause of Death, not Cash on Delivery.*

West frowned. "Well, the VIC was torn apart, that's clear. But by what? Too early to say, I'm afraid."

"Well, which one is it? Can you determine? And are we sure that's just one person in that pile of muck?"

"Let me see here." West pulled a long silver pair of tweezers out of the pocket protector that lived in the chest pocket of his blue chambray work shirt. Carefully, with the grace of a surgeon, he fished out a patch of long hair still attached to a bloodied bit of scalp skin. "Female, most likely. And yes, just one individual. Hard to believe, right? There'd be more goo if it'd been more than one VIC."

"I see. Listen, West. Can you give me an idea how old? Approximately? Ballpark figure. No one is going to quote you on this."

Harding knew this was an impossible task, but he had to ask. He had to know.

"What's Dr. Sun said on the topic?"

Harding rolled his eyes.

"I see," West said, motioning to the pile of mush and goo that had once been a person but now looked more like regurgitated Taco Bell. "Let me just look into my crystal ball."

"Would you just humor me? Please?"

Harding knelt beside West, careful not to let any part of his body touch the splattered remains. "Look, West. I know it's not mama bear. What's left of her and papa bear are over yonder in the freezer. We got one male, likely a juvenile, in the crate. Another male, also juvenile, upstairs. Grandma is...there."

"Vlad Dracula would be proud."

Harding rolled his eyes. "Holy Christmas. And the mailman, sliced and diced, there. That leaves only two options if you're thinking this one is...was...a female."

"What was it Luke said to Yoda?" West asked with genuine sincerity.

"You being serious right now? Look around. And you're coming back at me with this Dungeons & Dragons shit. Did you have any friends in high school?"

"Yes, plenty. I was President of the Debate Team. And it's *Star Wars*, not D&D." West smiled. "Humor me."

"Humor you?" Harding sighed, visibly frustrated. West always pulled crap like this. It was like the guy couldn't answer a single question without nerding out first. "I don't know. Use the force, you ugly little lizard?"

West gasped, appalled. "Lizard! Ugly! You're just being mean, Harding."

"And you're about ten seconds away from feeling my hands around your throat."

West gasped again, softer this time, and then rubbed at his neck with a gloved hand. "I swear, Harding, if I looked up 'no fun' in the dictionary, there'd be a picture of you."

"I don't know, West. Your boyfriend thought I was a lot of fun last night."

Harding's face eased into a smile and both men relaxed, the testosterone in the air dissipating. West held up a soiled gloved hand, expecting a high-five. Harding looked at the glove and said, without saying, *I'll pass.*

"Good burn, Harding. I didn't think you had it in you. Mother jokes are usually your go-to."

"Yeah, well." Harding laughed. *Okay, West isn't that bad.* "Just don't report me to the diversity police."

"Scout's honor." West held up two bloodied fingers. "Anyway, as young Luke Skywalker said to Yoda, you want the impossible, Harding. This is...mush. People soup. I'm only guessing it was female because of the hair. The length and apparent styling. It could have been...I don't know, an artsy male. Or a hippie."

West held up the bit of scalp and examined the soiled hairs.

"Too clean for your average hippie."

Harding got back to his feet. "Can you just tell me one thing?"

"Possibly." West let go of the bloodied remains. They splatted on the slick, wet ground.

"Can you tell me please, if you can," Harding began. As he spoke, his gaze locked on the sight of the dead grandmother impaled on Christmas reindeer antlers. "Tell me what it was I did to deserve this."

West motioned to the surrounding room. "This, or me?"

"Both." Harding stepped toward the gored-out granny. "What makes a person do this? What kind of person could do this?"

"Drugs? And a person on drugs, I guess."

Harding stared into the granny's dull, lifeless eyes. "Let's hope that's what it was. A bad strain of weed."

"Could have been a bad trip. I heard about this one case in Alberta—"

Harding cut him off. "Cool story, bro."

West gasped. "Who taught you the cool kid lingo?"

"Everything I know, I learned from the internet."

"Ah."

From upstairs, at the top of the landing, a voice called out. "Harding?"

"Yeah, down here."

"Uh oh. Looks like someone called the diversity police," West joked, softly, so just Harding could be in on the joke.

Harding flipped him the bird.

"Chief Peters wants you upstairs," said the voice, which Harding now placed as belonging to Officer Ken Williams. "He's pretty adamant about it, sir."

"I'm kind of in the middle of something down here. Do you know what it's about?"

"Yeah," Williams called back flatly.

Harding waited, and when nothing came, he shouted up to Williams, who was not blessed in the brains department. "Yeah? And?"

"Oh, right. Chief says we got a relative of one of the VICs upstairs. He wants you to talk to her."

"Of course he does," Harding muttered under his breath. A relative? *They're all related, except the mailman, I think. He did not belong.*

"Yeah, the VIC's sister, I think," Williams said, the uncertainty clear in his voice.

Harding's eyes lit up like Ted Bundy's last sitting chair, Old Sparky. He turned to West. "Sister? It could be the little girl. Alex."

"Possible. Definitely possible," West said, agreeably enough but not sounding convinced.

"Which one?"

A longer pause than Harding expected, then Williams said, "Sir?"

Harding exhaled. *Am I the only one capable of doing my job here?* "Which VIC is she related to? Who is she?"

"Ah, right. Says she's William's sister."

William Miller. Aged forty-two. Married to Denise Miller, forty-one. The couple, what was left of them, formerly of St. Augustine Place, the Bronx, New York, now resided in their meat freezer.

"Tell the chief I'm on my way."

"Right. Thank you, sir."

Harding listened as Williams' footsteps receded and then he heard muffled voices, likely Williams telling Chief Peters and William Miller's sister that Harding was en route. *To be a fly on that wall and watch that fat pig Peters squirm, having to do something for himself for a change.* Harding buttoned his sport coat and ran his fingers through his hair, although it made little difference.

"What do you think, West? Think he's sweating bullets up there?"

West laughed, glancing down at his watch. "Oh, definitely. He's had to deal with the public for three whole minutes."

"Better get up there and let the worm off the hook and find out what this sister knows. How do I look?"

West considered Harding for a moment. "Like you are in desperate need of a fashion intervention."

"I'll tell you what, West. You tell me which Miller girl that pile of goo is, or likely is, and I'll let you update my wardrobe. What do you say?"

"Deal," West said without hesitation.

Harding went for the stairs. He popped a LifeSav-Ahs into his mouth and didn't look back.

"It's the older one. Mary."

"Mary," Harding repeated.

"How does Wednesday night work for you, Harding? Armani, Saks. Dinner at Tavern—"

"Call my secretary."

"You don't have a secretary, Harding!"

"You have the makings of a great detective, Dr. Watson."

Harding was near the top when West called up to him.

"Hey, Harding!"

Harding stopped but did not look back.

"May the force be with you," West said as he made the sign of the cross.

Operation Break into Work

It was still dark when Imogen slipped out of her house. The morning sun was still two hours away from making its regularly scheduled appearance. She reasoned that was more than enough time to dodge and weave her way the half a mile across town to the Coffee Cavern, do her thing, and be back long before Janet stirred from her previous night's drunken stupor to burn breakfast.

Imogen and Oliver would exchange knowing glances as Janet teetered on her feet, wondering out loud for the third time if she turned on the coffeemaker—usually, she hadn't, and just looked dazed while the bacon sizzled and burned beyond recognition on the stove. They'd learned a long time ago to leave Janet be in the kitchen. Janet always said the kitchen was her ship, and she was the captain. *Yeah, captain of the S.S. Titanic.* Janet didn't want any first mates or deck hands on her ship. She'd seen *Mutiny on the Bounty* enough times to know how that story ended.

Offering an assist, or worse, offering to step in and cook the entire meal for her, was like poking a sleeping grizzly with a very short stick. And, most times, the coffee was at least drinkable—when Janet remembered to click on the mechanical marvel that was the Java Joe's Brewster 5K.

Imogen hadn't snuck out of the house since…she couldn't recall, exactly. But she knew it was before the London trip, and that was just over two years ago. After that summer, Oliver had pushed Janet to loosen Imogen's reins. *If she can travel to London, I think we can trust her to stay out until 11.*

Janet fought back, as expected, talking about propriety and staying on course to get into P-U. Although Janet never came right out and said it, Imogen was sure her mother was more concerned about Ally's influence than she was about Imogen's behavior, which was model and exemplary in all regards.

Ally needled Imogen about her piety every time the weekend rolled around, and they debated which social gathering to grace with their presence. *Jesus, Imo. You're trying to get into Princeton, not a convent. Lighten up! Live a little! We're only this young once.*

Even a broken clock is right twice a day.

Imogen always took it in stride—Ally's poking. It was, she knew, just good-natured chiding. Ally would never and had never forced Imogen to do anything she didn't want to do herself. She'd never bend the knee for peer pressure, and she knew Ally just wanted her to have a more varied teenage experience before going off to college, where Imogen wouldn't be under Ally's ever-watchful eye. *Imo, I love you, girl, but you're not going to Princeton a virgin.*

Oliver trusted his daughter. Janet did, too, in her own way. But where Oliver saw Imogen as David taking on Goliath, Janet saw the world as a bomb and her daughter as Hiroshima—and that was pre-pandemic.

Since then, it was an unspoken rule that the world outside of the house was out of bounds. And, besides the house rules, venturing out into public was against the emergency state law unless you were considered "essential personnel," which Imogen was not, and there were strict limitations imposed there, too—when you could go out, how many hours per shift, per day and per week you could be outside. And always, no matter what, anyone venturing out into the wild had to wear a medically approved plague mask unless they'd received "the shot," and even then, a mask was still "strongly encouraged" but no longer required by law. For now, the vax was only being rolled out to medical personnel, police, and other first responders who needed it the most.

Imogen hated the plague mask. The eye slats fogged up, and it was front heavy—because of the mask's long, bird-like beak, which held air filters. She'd only worn it once, and that was when it had been form-fitted to her face. The most effective masks were all custom fit to each individual face, allowing for an airtight seal. Generics left gaps between the mask and the skin where the tainted air could still seep in, rendering the cheap DIY jobs and knock-off masks useless for anything but wall decor. After enduring the mask fitting, Imogen swore she'd never leave the house even if it caught fire because she'd rather die of smoke inhalation than ever put that mask on again.

Imogen hadn't forgotten the plague mask intentionally. It had innocently slipped her mind as she talked herself into violating her parents' trust. That hadn't been an easy internal debate, and Imogen almost called "Operation Break into Work" off several times, but she had to know everything Gemeo Labs had on her. She had to find out who she was. That was more important than everything else, even violating her parents' trust. *And if they've been lying to me, they violated my trust first. All's fair in love and war.*

She'd barely walked fifty feet from the house when Imogen realized the plague mask was still inside, sitting in its carry case on her bed. But she couldn't stop then. How could she? Turning back meant postponing her mission at least another day or two, maybe more. It might take her another week to talk herself back into it, even longer if Ally kept up her incessant pummeling.

For a dimwit, Ally could be very persuasive when she needed to be, in ways that didn't involve using her mouth for sexual stuff. No, for someone who slung guilt as expertly as Ally did, Imogen joked she should have been raised Catholic. It was not only possible, but likely, that if Imogen stalled the stealthy sneak-out plan for even a day, it would be enough time for Ally to weave a tapestry of guilt so heavy that Imogen would have to cave.

No, Imogen would proceed with "Operation Break into Work" tonight, mask or no mask. It wasn't that she didn't fear the virus or potentially dying; she did. But Imogen figured if she got it, at least she'd die knowing the truth. There were a million ways to weave that web of guilt, dangle it over her parents' heads like an anvil until her last wheezing breath.

You did this, not me. If you'd been honest with me, none of this would have happened.

Imogen hoped it would never come to that—blaming her parents for her mistakes. And even if it ever went there, she knew she'd never go through with blaming Oliver and Janet for her opening a Pandora's Box. And that's exactly what Gemeo Labs and the Gemeo Project were—a Pandora's Box. What hell would be released on her when she did a deep dive on her results and the Project itself at the Coffee Cavern? She couldn't imagine and didn't want to. In the days following the onslaught of the pandemic, it required little in the way of imagination to picture a good scenario turning into a nightmare.

The neighborhood looked much as it had when the lockdowns began. But the grass was now taller, and there were thick, winding clusters of weeds sprouting up on nearly everyone's once perfectly manicured patches of green. Imogen shuddered to think how long it would be before mother nature reclaimed it all, took back all that was hers and man became nothing but a sour aftertaste.

Nothing stirred as Imogen crept through the shadows of Main Street South. The vibe was stereotypical neo-apocalyptic. It felt like a video game, not that Imogen was a gamer, but she'd seen enough zombie shooters to know what the terrain looked like. And it looked exactly like this. It surprised her how many houses were boarded up, abandoned entirely. *Where did everyone go?* And those that weren't closed up appeared as dark and quiet as a grave. No visible signs of life showed on the outside.

The more she walked, the more Imogen wished she had taken Ally up on her offer to keep her company via cell phone. Imogen figured the way Ally talked, the trip was likely to take twice as long and somebody, somewhere along the planned route, was bound to overhear their chatter. The dynamic duo had been kicked out of a funeral once because their chatter and laughter from the back of the cathedral nearly drowned out the low-talking, quick-tempered Father Richards at the altar. Not their proudest moment but ranked high as one of their favorites.

It was unnaturally quiet. Imogen wondered if everyone else was dead. Maybe it was all a hoax after all, but not the kind of hoax the red hatters thought it was. Maybe the truth was something much, much worse; something…unbelievably extraordinary. It could happen. Stranger things had happened.

Hell, in the last few years, the U.S. government came clean on U.F.O.s, J.F.K., and President Clinton. And that was just round one. The appetizer before the first course. More came out later. Much more.

They washed their hands like Pilate, as though they knew everything was coming to an end. Best to die with a clean conscience, having confessed all your sins. Just in case…

The latter, the bit about the disappearance of the president, surprised and disappointed Imogen the most. Like many others, she'd had high hopes for President Chelsea Clinton and her vision of the new America. What we could be again, and how we could rise above the wedge that divided neighbors. She had a plan, and what seemed like a sound one, too. But Imogen knew better than to believe for a single second that one person had the power to change the world. Disrupt the status quo. And not even change the whole world, just their tiny part of it. The powers that be, the omnipresent "they" that ran things from behind a curtain, would never let anyone take away what was theirs. They would die before giving an inch when they should have been giving miles.

Fuckers. Eat the rich.

Still, change would have been nice. And besides, since Roswell, everyone knew aliens were out there and that there was zero chance Oswald did Kennedy.

That was just common sense, man.

Crossing Richmond Avenue, continuing to walk up Main Street North, Imogen spied no visible signs of life. Not even the scattering of rodents or the lonely meowing of a stray. It was so strange to be crossing what was typically such a busy road and see not a single car in motion. Traffic lights and walk/don't walk signs felt the very definition of "superfluous," but for a few blocks, Imogen paused when DON'T WALK flashed in red. Then, she felt like an idiot, only pausing at each intersection to check for any oncoming vehicles—of which there were none.

Imogen laughed louder than she thought was prudent, given the stealthy nature of her mission, as two thoughts popped into her head.

One: *Wouldn't that just be a hoot if she, Janet, Oliver, and Ally were the last people standing?* And then, followed immediately by thought number two: *Fucccckkk. If we were the last ones left, then Ally would be right. Imma die a virgin.*

A little further down Main Street North, close to where Imogen would need to hang a right onto Spring Hill Road, which led to the backdoor of the Coffee Cavern, Imogen came upon a pack of abandoned homes. Save for the broken second-story windows, each was sealed up tighter than Mickey Rourke's skin after his last face-lift—excluding the one that killed him. You can't get any tighter than that.

Imogen stopped in front of the last house in the pack. Something on the door caught her eye. *Huh, that's weird.* There was something spray-painted in red on the sheet of plywood covering up the front door. At first, Imogen assumed it was "DANGER" or "CAUTION" or something similar in the warning vein. However, the more she looked at it, the clearer it became that the word was not like that at all. She blamed it on the dark, or a trick of the little light there was, and the general malaise of her still sleepy eyes, because surely there was no way she was reading it right. What kind of graffiti was that? Imogen was definitely getting neo-apocalyptic vibes from that house and its mysterious scrawl.

She glanced at her watch. There was time. How long could it take to walk up to the door to make sure she was reading that right and then be on her merry way? After all, the Coffee Cavern was less than a block away now. A one-minute walk, tops. Two if she lollygagged.

Yeah, I got time for this. I have to see.

Imogen headed toward the porch. The closer she got, the more she had this funny feeling like she was being watched, which was stupid because there wasn't anyone around, any-where. There hadn't been a single light on in a single house or store. The essential businesses weren't allowed to open for another four hours, and she'd been careful to avoid any on the trek, crossing when she had to or ducking out of sight behind parked cars in the street. She was sure there hadn't been anyone, so sure that she'd bet her life on it. So why did she feel like someone was out there in the shadows watching her every move?

A part of her wanted to turn back, get away from the house and back on track. *I've got a bad feeling about this.* But the more persistent part of her had to know if the writing spelled out what she thought it did. If she didn't look now, she'd never know. She had mapped out a different route for the way back— just in case anyone had spotted her on the first leg of the trip.

Fuck it. A quick look. I won't even go up the stairs. I'll just stand right here.

Then, two things happened at once.

Imogen gasped as her suspicion was confirmed. The word was not "caution" but something older. Much older. The spray-painted letters spelled out "C-R-O-A-T-O-A-N."

Roanoke, VA. "The lost colony." One-hundred-seventeen

colonists disappeared without a trace. Only one thing was left behind. A warning? A farewell? Its true meaning remains a mystery. A single word hastily carved into the trunk of a tree— CROATOAN.

And then everything went black as a sack was pulled over Imogen's head. She went to scream but had no voice. It was just gone. Dead air.

The last thing Imogen heard before something hard struck her in the back of her head and she went out for a long, long sleep was the sound of a cold, shrill voice. It had the tiniest trace of an accent she couldn't place as it exclaimed—

There... you... are!

GOTCHA!

Buffering

Olivia sat, deflated, in her booth at The Greasy Spoon. The world of the diner slipped into the background of her mind as her own thoughts swirled and took center stage, minus the disco ball.

So, that's it. I can't leave. And I can't leave because...I'm dead. I'm the dead girl.

She pondered the possibility, staring down the thing with the squiggly face. They'd played musical chairs about a hundred times, and each time, no matter where Olivia sat, the thing was across from her. During one lively round, it had ended up in the booth beside her. Out of the corner of her eye, Olivia saw it turn its formless head to her. There it remained and considered her. Sizing her up.

And then another thought came right to her—

*Or the thing is estimating my size and weight for a recipe. Today's hot-plate special: Olivia Lovejoy, baked with a side of mashed potato, vegetable of the day. Soup or salad. Dessert included. *Premium desserts incur a $4.00 surcharge. NO substitutions.*

This wool-gathering session brought on a fit of laughter.

Olivia swore she saw the thing's squiggly mouth form a smile. At one point, Olivia imagined herself naked atop a shining silver serving platter, skin basted in oil and special seasonings, her hands and feet bound, and a delicious-looking apple stuffed into her mouth. She screamed into the apple as unseen hands slid her into the oven to bake for three hours, her skin sizzling and blistering.

The daydream had turned, and Olivia had no humor left for it or The Greasy Spoon—

"C-c-coffee, d-d-dear?"

—Or for Flo.

Olivia was determined to give old Flo the silent treatment until she stuttered herself to death. She wanted to smile as her latest musing threatened to form a picture in her head, but Olivia pushed it away. But the thing smiled. Olivia was sure of it that time.

Is it in my head? Reading my thoughts like Flo? Or are we, like, on the same frequency? No, that can't be it. If that were true, wouldn't I be able to read its thoughts?

Then, an idea swirled in the juices of her cranial cavity. Olivia's back straightened, and she sat up stiffly, just as she had in the third grade every time Sister Mary Margaret slapped her desk with a foot-long wooden blood-stained ruler.

I haven't tried to read its mind though, so how can I know if I can or if I can't do it?

Simple enough question for sure, but there was only one small, teensy weensy, almost negligible problem. Really, it was barely worth considering in the grander scheme of things. Nothing more than a pebble in the Birkenstock, really.

But there it was all the same—Olivia Lovejoy was not a mind reader, and she had no idea where or how to start.

Or did she?

This is only a test.

There had been a moment when it seemed like she was in control. When she was pressing Flo to tell her about the dead girl. Olivia had demanded it. No, *commanded* it. And Flo, despite looking as though she'd been out all night on a bender, followed the instructions. For once, the woman obeyed.

That was something. It was a start, and more than Olivia had a minute ago. Now if she could just figure out how to get inside—

Do you ever feel like you don't belong? Do you feel alone even when surrounded by friends and family? Do you ever think that you were meant to be somebody else? That you are, in fact, someone else. Do you have questions, the kind that keep you up all night staring at the stars? Does your family have the answers? Any of the answers? Maybe we can help. We're Gemeo Labs. And this is the Gemeo Project. Knowledge is our business. Visit us online today to begin your journey.

Olivia jumped to her feet. Rattled. Something new stirred within her she didn't yet understand.

Where the fuck is that coming from?

It didn't take long for Olivia to zero in on the source—a small television mounted above the counter. *Was that there before? I don't remember seeing it there earlier. No, I know it wasn't there earlier.*

"Everything alright, d-d-dear?"

Flo stood beside Olivia. Right beside Olivia, shoulders practically touching.

"I could ch-ch-change the channel if you'd prefer to watch something else. I'm not terribly picky, you know."

Olivia didn't look at Flo. *Gemeo Labs.* Instead, she kept her gaze locked on the thing in the booth across from her. *The Gemeo Project.* She couldn't be entirely sure, but from where she stood, the thing looked pleased with itself.

Why was that so familiar? Gemeo Labs and the Gemeo Project.

"No, it's fine, Flo. It's okay," Olivia said as she climbed back into her squeaky booth. She smirked at the thing. "I'm not picky either."

Click the sparkling tree graphic to begin your journey.

"Alright, d–d–dear. You just let me know if you'd like me to change it. I think there's some figure sk–sk–skating on. I love to see all them sparkly costumes. They remind me of Elvis."

"I like it when the skaters fall onto the ice, Flo. That's my favorite part. Especially if they get hurt. Bonus points for blood on the ice."

The thing in the booth opposite Olivia did not react.

"Oh. Well, I guess that's n–n–nice, too." Flo almost sounded sincere. *Almost.* "C–c–coffee?"

And then, as though it was super–glued to her mitts, Flo held up a piping hot fresh pot of joe. *Where did all these coffee pots come from? Who was drinking all that coffee?*

"No." This Olivia said to the thing in the booth, continuing the informal staring contest. She said to Flo, "Thank you."

Flo clumsily retreated, clutching her trusty coffee pot as though it was Excalibur. And then, in the blink of an eye, Flo was once again parked at the counter, her eyes glued to the television. Only, Olivia noticed there was nothing playing on the small screen; that is, nothing but static.

Flo spasmodically cranked her head toward Olivia. "I do love to watch ice skating."

And then, just as mechanically, just as oddly, Flo turned back to the TV set.

Olivia scanned the diner. Herbie Hunt, *Officer Herbie,* was gone. The booth where he sat was vacant, but the bottomless soup bowl sat untouched on the table beside a steaming cup of coffee. His eyeglasses and open case lay in the space between the cutlery and a perfectly folded cloth napkin.

Also MIA were the Village People—*no doubt out on their pandemic tour. And where were the sexed-up tweens? Maybe they finally got a room somewhere. Were they even old enough? To get a room? Did they rent rooms to minors here?*

Save for good old Flo, Olivia and the thing in the opposite booth were now the only ones in The Greasy Spoon.

There has to be a way to get into its head. Figure this out. Figure all of this out. There has to be. There has to be. There has to—

But the longer Olivia pondered the problem, the more she felt like she was hitting her head against a brick wall. Her scalp tingled. It felt like her brain was on fire. And a very real pain lurked behind her right eye but was not quite ready to come out and introduce itself.

This is how I felt when I came to in The Greasy Spoon. Exactly how I felt.

For the moment, the pain was more of a dull ache, but Olivia knew that soon enough it would explode into a full-on throbbing, stabbing discomfort. There was a chance the episode would pass. A small one. Sometimes they did. Most times, they did not. And once they moved in, they were difficult to evict. *Thank god for coffee.*

Olivia was an expert on headaches. She suffered from them as long as she could remember. If she hadn't been so intellectually gifted, Olivia would have probably been held back a grade, maybe even two, given how many schooldays she missed due to the chronic cranial pain.

Caffeine. Caffeine helps. Narrows the blood vessels in my head.

Olivia looked down and found, as expected, a hot, fresh,

delicious-looking cup of joe. That was why she'd become a coff-a-holic in the first place—it kept the headaches under control. Most of the time.

Thank you, Flo.

"Don't mention it, d-d-dear," Flo said from the counter, without turning back.

Olivia brought the mug to her lips, tilted her head back, and downed every drop in one giant, painful gulp. *G-g-g-gulp!* She set the mug on the table and closed her eyes. A few seconds later, she opened them and *voila!* Like magic, the mug was full again. *How do you do it, Flo? We all want to know. What's your secret?* Olivia repeated this sequence almost a dozen times before she threw in the towel. Her insides burned down at the core. She felt like a volcano about to erupt, but the soreness in her head was slowly subsiding, thanks to the miracle elixir that was diner coffee.

As the tenderness wore off, Olivia gradually could think straight again.

Things to consider:

1-How the fuck did I get here?

2-On a related note, when *did I get here?*

3-Who is this dead girl? Olivia who? *Is it me? (Note: talk to Herbie, if he reappears.)*

4-What's that thing over in the booth?

5-And...can I talk to it? Read its mind?

6-Worth considering, but not a priority—is Flo ever bringing me that slice of pie?

Now that she'd mentioned it, Olivia couldn't even remember the last time she'd eaten anything. She'd been consuming nothing but coffee for what felt like hours—*days.* But her belly stopped rumbling some time ago, and lord knew she didn't feel the need to pee. That was no less than a miracle, given the gallons of coffee sitting in her stomach.

Still, food might not be a bad idea. Might clear the brain even more. Protein. The gears in Olivia's brain always turned better after loading up on protein. *There must be food here. I can hear the grill sizzling. Something is cooking. Maybe it's the tweens.*

Olivia laughed out loud, then quickly brought a hand to her face as though she'd just broken wind in a sardine-style packed elevator.

But I still can't smell any food. Not on the grill, not in the air... nothing. Herbie ate that soup, though. Slurrrrppppp! There has to be something cooking. Let me just get Flo's—

Something derailed Olivia's train of thought, threw it right off the track. It was the voice coming from the staticky TV. A commercial, from the sound of it. There was still no discernable picture showing on the decades-old, clunky, square idiot box.

I know that voice.

It was so familiar. She knew that she'd heard it before, but *where?*

−Has anything strange ever happened in your presence?

Yes. This Olivia said so low only the dogs could hear it.

−Have you ever been able to move objects simply by thinking about moving them?

Yes.

Olivia's eyes traveled from the boxy TV set to the squiggly line thing that now sat directly opposite her—in the same booth... in *her* booth. She drew in what felt like all the air in the room, nearly choking on it. But strangely, somehow Olivia was not afraid.

The thing's hastily drawn mouth opened, its thin, uneven lips moved, as though it were speaking. Then, a voice, *the voice from the commercial—commercials—*came forward. *It's the same voice. The one from the Gemeo Labs ads.*

But this wasn't an ad she could recall ever hearing.

–Have you ever made things disappear?

Yes.

A tear rolled down Olivia's cheek.

–Have you ever brought them back?

Yes.

–Have you ever made things happen? Things you wanted to happen.

Yes.

More tears. Both eyes were wet and red, stinging from the salt. For the first time, maybe in the entirety of her life, Olivia Christine Lovejoy felt seen. *Understood.*

The thing now spoke in her mind, but its lips continued to move anyway, even though nothing came out, not even a hiss of air.

–Have you ever taken life from a thing?

The tears spilled like a waterfall onto her lap and onto the table. Snot slithered out of one of her nostrils, but Olivia dared not wipe at it. She couldn't even if she had wanted to. The thing had her entranced.

Yes.

–Intentionally or unintentionally?

Olivia held her breath. *No use lying. It's in my head already.*

Both.

The thing seemed to nod, as though it understood far more than just the answer Olivia had given.

–Last question, Olivia. This is the most important one of all.

Okay?

Olivia couldn't speak. She slowly nodded her head.

–Have you ever brought something back?

Back? What do you mean...back?

–Yes, back. Gave it life after it had none left.

Olivia bit her lip fiercely. She winced as an image flashed before her mind, just for the briefest of moments. *Mahalo.* Then, the bug-eyed, smiling puggle from her childhood retreated into her memories. A thin, neat line of blood dribbled down her chin.

–Olivia? Please answer me. This is more important than you could ever imagine.

A fresh pool of tears filled her eyes, blurring her vision. Now it looked as though there were four, maybe five, of those things sitting in the booth.

–Have you ever brought something back...back from the dead?

An unfathomable weight lifted as she said, as she *confessed*—

Yes. Yes, I have.

The image came and went again in a flash—Mahalo.

The thing smiled. A big one, too. It stretched beyond the drawn confines of its face.

And then suddenly, thanks to a river of tears backed-up in her eyes, the thing's face became clearer, and clearer, and clearer still, until Olivia finally saw it. Really saw it. Saw its face, its true face.

"It's you," Olivia shrieked in surprise, but she felt absolutely no fear. She knew that face; she knew him. She knew him well.

"Welcome to the Gemeo Project, Olivia Christine Lovejoy."

The lines that made up the thing's face, the thing's entire form, swirled about rapidly. Each bit of line slowly settled into a fixed position until, when they'd all stopped moving and the thing was finally human-looking, Olivia's suspicions were confirmed.

"It *is* you. My Dream Lover!"

The thing smiled, something flashed in its eyes, and then it whispered, "My name is Toby. Toby Miller."

And just as it all came flooding back to Olivia—taking the DNA test, *you look just like her*, getting into her car and driving, Gemeo Labs, and the Gemeo Project—

Toby mouthed the word "CROATOAN"

—and the world around her disappeared as though it was nothing more than dirty bath water swirling down the drain. Then everything was gone, and there was nothing but black.

The Third Interlude: Miller Time

Up until the day Billy "Junior" Miller shish kabobbed his grandmother using Christmas decoration reindeer antlers, "Cast-Iron Cassie" aka Cassandra Miller, had been the last of the original Java Street Millers. When news broke of the formidable Miller's passing, no one from the old Greenpoint neighborhood was surprised she had outlived them all— her parents, her three brothers—Joseph, Stephen, and her favorite, John, as well as her four sisters—Eunice, Janet, and the twins, Melodie and Melanie.

Cast-Iron Cassie had never been sick a day in her long, long life. Blessed with ninety-four mostly good years, she almost made it to ninety-five until Junior came along and did what he did. The few remaining old-timers left of the Java Street crew who knew Cassie Miller, and had grown up alongside the Miller clan, joked behind closed doors, because they wouldn't chance to say so openly, that death must have come as quite a shock to the woman who survived New York City's infamous "winter of blood" in 1934.

Folks around Java Street used to say the Miller clan was cursed. They had bad luck in their blood and set a place for Death regularly at their table. Suicide, boating accident, house fire, cancer, casualty of war, and the most unexpected of them all—death by Christmas decoration. No one who knew the old gal had that one on their bingo cards, that's for certain.

Cast-Iron Cassie's sudden death by misadventure did little to dissuade gossip among the old-timers. They all thought she was going to outlive Death itself. There was no way the old gal was going to go quietly into that gentle good night with the Reaper, and if push came to shove, and one of them had to go, money was on the Reaper biting the bullet. They didn't call her "Cast-Iron" Cassie for nothing.

But then the massacre in her son's home on St. Augustine Place in the Bronx occurred, and the old Brooklyn biddies dusted off their talk of the Miller curse because *things like that didn't just happen*. No, they didn't happen to *normal* families, and the Millers were anything but. They weren't "off" like the Liparis or recluses like the Gorceys, but they were different somehow. And no one could ever quite pin the tail on that donkey. It was like things just *happened* around the Millers— unnatural things, some said.

They were feared and revered in equal measure, so when the procession of deaths in the family began in the early 1900s, the "Miller curse" was born. It didn't help their cause that many of the deaths were questionable, like Eunice's supposed drowning, and others—like Janet and John's—were outright bizarre. Janet was not one prone to fits of hysteria, so it was highly out of character for her to have hanged herself in her bedroom closet. And John? John Boy? He was an expert marksman. Highly skilled with firearms. And yet, the legend was that he died in a "shooting accident" while cleaning his sidearm.

If the Millers weren't cursed, then it was something else; something vile and profane.

Despite the dark cloud that seemingly hung over their house, the Millers had been more successful than most at the rigged game of life. They lived comfortably, but never garishly. They wanted little, if anything, and always said whatever they had, they earned with a heck of a lot of spit and elbow grease. And since the Millers were by all outward accounts a family of hard workers, no one ever questioned their monetary gains. Common sense said it was the reward for jobs well done. Keener minds said it came too easily to the Millers.

Their lifestyle didn't sit right with some in the neighborhood. Maybe it came down to the green-eyed monster, envy, but some of the Millers' friends and neighbors saw what all the others couldn't see beneath the glamour—the sinister secrets the Millers would take to the grave, one by one by one.

The Millers were not your typical all-American family. No. They were an old family. An original family. And they were special. *Extraordinarily special.* Chosen for a higher purpose. Destined for greater things, the greatest of things. And that *greatness* came at a heavy price, and it would be paid. It would *always* be paid.

Cast-Iron Cassie and her husband Maurice had been gifted four children. Three girls— Agnes, Julie Anne, and Sandra— and a lone boy, William. Like her siblings, Melodie and Melanie, two of Cassie and Maurice's offspring were twins, Sandra and William. Sandra was the elder by five and a half minutes. William had almost been still born on account of his umbilical cord getting wrapped around his tiny neck. However, he eventually clawed his way out and despite not breathing initially on his arrival, William "Billy" Miller would end up screaming for a full forty-seven minutes. But how *exactly* the cord had been so expertly wrapped around his neck was a mystery, seeing as Sandra emerged from the womb without incident.

It's not like Sandra tried to kill her twin intentionally, right?

Unlike her twin brother, who had a lot to say, Sandra was quiet. Watching. Taking it all in. The first time he held her, Maurice called Sandra an "old soul." Minutes old, and her eyes told a long story, he later said. But Maurice never told anyone how much his daughter's gaze unnerved him, like there was something else lurking behind those innocent-looking eyes. It didn't help that when he was alone with her, things just... happened. Something always *happened*, whether his keys went missing for three hours, or one of the other children, usually Billy, somehow found themselves locked in the attic. The latter was particularly vexing since none of the kids could reach the string to pull down the attic stairs, let alone have the strength to pull them back up once in the attic.

Yes, things just had a way of happening around Sandra, like Maurice's accident. She'd been the only one in the car with him when it happened, securely strapped into her car seat. Though she said she didn't recall it, Sandra had seen her father go through the windshield and break his neck. Along with every other bone in his body. The seatbelt, which he'd been wearing at the time the car collided with that massive elm tree on Park Street, hadn't saved Maurice. And yet, Sandra emerged with not so much as a bruise to be found on her person.

Billy was devastated. He'd been close with Maurice, closer than any of the other Miller kids. There was something in Billy that said he needed protecting, Maurice said. At first, Cast-Iron Cassie assumed this had more to do with Billy's difficult birth than run-of-the-mill father-son bonding. The boy had come within an inch of death, and somehow seemed frail as a result—even though Billy had clawed his way back from death to life. He fought to be here. Later, of course, Cast-Iron Cassie saw first-hand why Billy needed protecting, and from whom, and she kept him under lock and key until his future wife, Denise, entered the picture. Then, and only then, she reluctantly let him go. But she kept both eyes on her Billy, even from the other coast. Mama was watching. Mama was always watching.

Billy and Denise had quite a brood of their own. Five in all. Justin, *poor, poor Justin.* William "Junior." *The bad man.* Toby. Alex. *The Bobbsey Twins.* And Mary. *Mary. The little actress. The little Greta. Greta Garbo.*

Cast-Iron Cassie adored Mary. She had since the day the girl was born, and she did little to hide her feelings nor did she attempt to conceal her utter disgust for Junior. Cast-Iron Cassie often called Junior a "rotten apple" or a "bad seed." Sometimes she said this to Junior's face or would be certain to say it loud enough if she knew Junior was within earshot. And the old gal could be loud.

That Junior was tainted, as Cassie believed, wasn't the real problem. No, it was her persistent fear that somehow Junior's corruption would rub off or even pass on to her precious Mary, jump right into her soul like a virus.

But Mary had another suitor in the family, her Aunt Sandra. And she could be oh so persuasive, buying Mary's trust with lavish and exotic gifts, working her poison into Mary's head, and subtly molding the young girl as though she were born from clay and not flesh and blood. *Her* flesh and blood.

It was a losing battle for the old gal, and eventually Cast-Iron Cassie raised a white flag and admitted defeat. Sandra's will was just too strong, and Cassie's own influence continued to wane as the years piled on her. Whatever it was she had inside of her, whatever it was *they* had inside of them, it was shriveling away like a piece of rotten fruit in the summer sun. And soon, she too would be nothing more than a decayed meat sack six feet under the cold, hard earth.

Until then, she would wage her war of wills with Sandra, whose own magic seemed to grow incrementally the more Cassie's faded. From day one, in all regards Sandra and Cast-Iron Cassie were like yin and yang. Polar opposites, and yet irrevocably drawn to the other. Somehow, some way, in her secret heart, Cast-Iron Cassie knew they would be each other's destruction.

And so, while Sandra worked her will on her niece, Cast-Iron Cassie instead honed in on Junior; determined to convince her son to ship the vile little thing off to military school, far away from her precious Mary. Sandra all but ignored the other Miller kids—although she sometimes liked to tease Junior a lewd look, a sexy stare. He liked it, too. Boy, did he like it. And this only enraged Cassie even more.

But Mary was the special one. Mary was the chosen one.

Or so Sandra thought. They both thought. She was the one who would carry on the Miller Family Business. *She had to be the one.*

No, no, no. It just will not do, Cast-Iron Cassie used to say, shaking her formidable head.

She had to remove Junior from the board, and then she could deal with Sandra, try to counteract her growing sway. But her pleas on Junior's fate swayed none on the jury of two. Neither her precious Billy nor Denise would even consider sending Junior away. *Home is the best place for him. Home is where the heart is.*

No, come hell or high water, Cast-Iron Cassie vowed to put a stop to Sandra's shenanigans. She pointed out the inappropriate way Junior followed Mary around everywhere, wagging his tongue like a lovesick puppy. And if Junior didn't follow her physically, his eyes sure did. They never left his sister.

The way he looks at her. It's not natural. Cast-Iron Cassie did not approve. It *just will not do.* But by then, something had changed in her innocent Mary. She saw it, even if Billy and Denise buried their heads in the sand. Mary was not only enjoying Junior's advances, but actively encouraging them. Just as Sandra had tempted Junior with her looks and stares and poses stolen from those dirty men's magazines.

Mary was playing her, playing them all. She was delivering the performance of a life-time.

Little Garbo has them all fooled. But they'll see.

And one day, they did.

Denise sure got an eyeful of Junior sticking it to Mary on the living room floor one day when they were supposed to still be in school. That certainly changed things. A ticking clock was set in motion, and the game was born. *Staycation.*

But that idea, the game, had not been the fruit of Mary's own loin. No, the seed was planted in her brain by another. Someone on the outside. Someone *devoted.* A silent mentor. One who was curious to *test* the power of the young Miller girl, to see how far she could go. How far she *would* go. And she had gone further than her mentor had expected, but the game failed. Mary had failed. The test was unsuccessful. The outcome was not one the game's inventor had been prepared for, and that complicated things. She had been wrong, and she didn't like to be wrong.

Billy was Cast-Iron Cassie's favorite.

If only he'd listened. If only he saw for himself. Mama knows best. Mama knows...

Family secrets.

But Cassie knew it wasn't him, it wasn't *in* him.

The Miller Curse.

He didn't have the power.

Mama knows best.

She knew he didn't have it because *she* did. She was part of the family's secret business, and for a time she was its CEO, so to speak. That's how Cast-Iron Cassie had done it. That's how she survived the winter of blood. That's how she never so much as had a sniffle in her life. And that's how she'd outlived them all, the original Greenpoint Millers. Her parents. Eunice. Janet. John. Melodie. Melanie. Joseph. Stephen.

Cast-Iron Cassie outlived them all because she killed them all—even her favorite brother, John. BANG!

But she had made a critical mistake. She'd underestimated Sandra. And that proved to be fatal.

What goes around...

Family Reunion

Harding found her, the VIC's alleged relative, a few minutes later out on the front porch smoking a cigarette. It wasn't a modern-day cigarette, but one held with a long flapper-era style shiny black holder. *A fancy way to get cancer*, Harding thought.

He held out a hand. "Detective Joe Harding. Are you the relative?"

Harding asked, even though the answer was obvious to a blind man. She was the only thing out of place at the crime scene. The only thing that did not belong, a vintage pristine Rolls Royce in a lot of KIAs. The lady was smartly dressed in an ensemble that likely cost more than Harding made in a year, maybe even two. The fancy coat alone probably amounted to a down payment on a better-than-average home in the good part of town, maybe even more. Her skin was tight and clear and had a natural radiance to it. If skin could sparkle, hers would.

"I am, and hopefully you're more useful than that awful Chief Peters," she said, blowing out smoke. "He's about as useful as sneakers for a snake."

Harding's poker face waned, and the trace of a smile became discernible.

She smiled back, more than politely. Then she studied Harding's outstretched hand for a moment and finally accepted it. "Sandra Miller. William...Bill is—*was*—my twin brother."

Harding released her hand, noting the woman had one of the firmest grips he'd ever encountered. "I'm sorry for your loss, ma'am."

"Ugh. Please dispense with the 'ma'am' and we'll get on just fine."

"Okay." Harding laughed. "How do you prefer I address you?"

Sandra Miller took a long drag as she appeared to be considering the question, but Harding guessed she already knew the answer before he even asked it. She was the kind of woman who always knew the answer, was always three or four steps ahead. He'd be wise to remember that.

"I believe," Sandra said, pausing long enough to exhale, "I have a god-given name. I've been known to answer to it...from time to time." She winked and flashed Harding a million-dollar smile. "Am I right to assume the worst about Bill?"

The atmosphere changed. The front porch suddenly felt like winter in the Arctic Circle.

"I'm afraid so."

Sandra closed her eyes, her body trembling. "The kids. Is anyone..."

She didn't need to finish the sentence, and you didn't need to be a detective to deduce where it was going. Harding took a deep breath and braced for her on-coming reaction.

"I can't say for certain. The investigation is on—"

Sandra's eyes flew open faster than a bat out of hell. "What do you mean you can't say for certain?"

Harding took a step back. This was not the reaction he'd

been prepared for, and the force of her delivery triggered his fight-or-flight instinct. *Run, fool. Run.*

"I'm not sure you want to hear this, Sandra."

"I'm a grown woman. However bad it is, I can take it, I assure you."

Harding had no doubt. Sandra appeared more than capable of scaling Mount Everest with nothing but her bare hands. A bit of bad news should be a walk in the park.

"Well, given the state some of the bodies are in, we're not entirely sure yet who's who, and how many VICs we have definitively."

Sandra appeared momentarily appeased.

"But you *can* identify at least some of them, correct?"

"Yes." Harding fought hard against the urge to cap it off with a "ma'am."

"Positively?"

Harding nodded. "Positively."

"Bill."

"Yes."

"Denise?"

Harding nodded.

"Junior?"

"Yes."

Sandra sighed heavily. "And..."

"Aside from Cassie Miller—"

Her eyes opened wide. *A bit too wide,* Harding thought. A false moment. Over the top, like it was a rehearsed gesture. Bad play acting in an otherwise flawless performance.

"Mama is...*here?* I thought she was still living out in Las Vegas."

Harding nodded. "Based on call records and voicemails, it

appears Mrs. Miller became concerned when she didn't make contact with Bill after repeated attempts."

"Her *precious* Billy," Sandra spit out like venom just loud enough for Harding to catch it. "Mama's boy."

"Yeah, so when she didn't hear from the VIC, she came to check on the family and met with foul play."

"I see." Sandra took a long drag and exhaled slowly. "Do you know who—"

Harding cut her off, anticipating where Sandra was headed. Families always wanted to know who was to blame, who did what to whom.

"It's impossible to tell at this juncture, and barring a witness, I don't know if we'll ever be able to explain everything that happened here. We're looking at time of death, primarily. If we can determine in what order things happened, maybe we can paint a clearer picture. Until we have all the data, and that's going to take some time, we're basically playing ping-pong in the dark here, I'm afraid."

"Do you think that's likely? A witness, I mean. Is there anyone left alive?"

Harding shook his head. "Again, we just don't know. The investigation is only three hours old. We've barely scratched the surface of the crime scene, and forgive me for saying, but it is substantial."

Sandra Miller looked disappointed, and it didn't suit her. Harding didn't like seeing her like that. He also guessed Sandra used that look to her advantage every chance she got.

"There are potentially three bodies we've not fully accounted for as of now, so it's not out of the question that at least one of them is alive, either out here or still in there somewhere." *The house of horrors.* "But only time will tell.

Everything will become clearer the more we process the scene and examine the evidence. It's like a ten-thousand-piece puzzle. Right now, we have about two or three pieces locked. But the more we investigate, the more we process, the more pieces will fit together until we have a nice Monet or Van Gogh."

"I'm more of a Rembrandt gal, myself, Detective."

Harding knew nothing about art. They were all just names to him. Meaningless names without context. In truth, he wouldn't have known if Rembrandt was an artist or the genius who invented Play-Doh.

He thought that would be the end of it, the probing for more details, more specifics that just weren't there yet. It usually was with most people. But Sandra Miller was not most people, and he should have known it would take more to satiate her.

"Who's missing?"

Harding hesitated, and Sandra pounced.

"Come on, Detective. You've already told me far more than I suspect you were cleared to. A little more won't hurt."

He laughed. "I bet no one has ever said no to you once in your life."

"Why, Joe Harding, you really are a detective." She smiled, and they shared a laugh. "Now come on, spill the beans."

Harding shuffled his feet and stuffed his sweaty palms into his pockets. They floundered about like a fish on dry land, rattling the contents of Harding's pockets noisily. "Look, if you really want to hear—"

"I do."

"Okay." Harding took a deep breath and sighed. "We have one set of remains we can't visually identify."

Sandra removed the extinguished cigarette from the holder

and lit a fresh one. "Why is that? Do you need a photograph for comparison? I can give you that."

He shook his head solemnly. Sandra inhaled deeply and blew it out forcefully.

"That bad?"

"Worse."

"Decomposed?"

Harding noticed Sandra showed no hesitation. She was unflinching in her determination to hear the grisly details.

"Some, yes. These are...," he trailed off, trying to find the kindest way of telling a relative that their loved one was reduced to chunky human broth.

"Oh, come on, Detective! Don't stop at second base. Go all the way."

"Well, Sandra. One set of remains, and we're assuming they are only one set of remains, is basically...a reduced person."

Harding put it out there, hoping Sandra would bite.

And she did.

"Oh," Sandra said, taking a drag. Then added with an exhale, "I see."

"I'm sorry."

Sandra Miller sighed, but it sounded empty, like she was bored rather than upset.

"These remains," she began, stopping to think. And smoke. The cigarette was already nearly puffed out.

It's a miracle this broad hasn't gotten the big C yet.

"Yes," Harding nudged.

"If you had to guess—"

Harding spoke, but she waved him off as though he were nothing more than an irritating common house fly.

"I know, but *if* you had to guess at this stage, who do you think those remains belong to?"

Harding watched her real close. Sandra Miller appeared to struggle with the word "remains." Other than that, she presented like one of those Italian marble statues. Solid, impenetrable. Impossible to read. Never in all his days on the job had he ever come across a family member at a crime scene who held it together so perfectly—especially a crime scene like this one. *A house of horrors.*

He didn't know Sandra Miller from Arthur Miller, but he got her. Understood her completely. And it pained him to admit that now he was the one squirming on the hook.

"Personally, I won't say. Coroner thinks it's Mary."

That got her. That did...something to ruffle her stoic portrait.

A look of disappointment formed on her face, and it was gone in an instant. But it had been there long enough for Harding to see.

"Well, shit."

Harding was surprised to hear her swear. It felt weird like seeing your teachers outside of school on the weekend just being normal people, doing the stuff normal people do.

"And the other two? The Bobbsey twins?"

Harding had to think on the names, not wanting to offend her by misnaming them. "Alexandra and Toby?"

Sandra nodded, eager to hear Harding's response.

"Toby is unaccounted for at the present time. The remains appear female, so the thought is they belong to either Mary or Alexandra."

"But Toby is definitely not among the deceased, as of now?"

"Correct. Your nephew is not among the confirmed deceased."

"Interesting."

Sandra took a final drag on her cigarette and killed it. She removed the finished butt from the holder and threw it somewhere onto the front lawn. Harding noticed she had a decent arm and excellent aim. Sandra opened her purse—Versace, the genuine article—and tossed the holder into it without looking.

"Show me," she said, more like an order.

Harding was taken aback. "Excuse me?"

Sandra Miller closed her purse and folded her arms across her chest.

"I need to see for myself."

That wasn't a request. Harding took it as the order it sounded like. Under normal circumstances he'd tell Sandra that was out of the question, no can do, off limits to civies. But these weren't normal circumstances, and Sandra Miller was not a normal person. And in that moment, all Detective Joe Harding could do was say—

"Right this way, ma'am. Watch your step." He pointed ahead. "You don't want to step right into... someone and contaminate the whole scene. It'll be *my* ass."

Sandra groaned. *Ma'am.*

"Lead on, Detective. Lead on. I'll follow your ass."

Harding stared at her for an impossibly long minute. There was a glimmer, something. He thought he'd seen something there. Another face for a split second, if that long. Another face on top of hers. Her true face, maybe.

That face scared him to death. Had he been anywhere else, Harding knew he would have shit himself right there on the spot. Somehow, he held it in and held himself together, even as he thought he felt her fingers tapping at his gray matter, searching. Probing.

Now I know why no one ever says no to this broad—
They can't.

Harding smiled at Sandra Miller, politely and professionally, as duty would require. Nothing more laced in between the lines. His interest, curiosity, had gone limp. She smiled back, neither politely nor professionally. It was the kind of Gorgon smile that turns men into stone.

"Yeah," Harding began, stopping to swallow the mouthful of saliva that suddenly filled his mouth. "Right this way."

As Harding crossed the threshold and re-entered the Miller House, *the house of horrors,* only one thought loomed in his head.

This broad is gonna be the death of me.

Home, Sweet Home

The ground beneath Imogen shook like a car hitting a pothole as big as Delaware. It roused her from her sedation. Her eyes, barely more than slits, saw nothing of her surroundings. Wherever she was, it was sealed up tight, and there was not a sliver of light coming in from beyond its walls. And it was cold. Freezing. As cold as Antarctica had been once upon a time. Had there been any light, Imogen was sure she'd have been able to see condensation with every exhalation. The ground beneath her felt solid, metallic. It chilled her fingers to the touch. For a moment Imogen imagined she was a slab of prime beef riding in the back of a refrigerated meat van. *Meat here! Get your frozen meat here! Aged sixteen years!* And maybe she was just that—nothing more than meat. Skin and bone.

In their exploration, her fingers stumbled onto what felt like a clumsily folded cotton blanket. It smelled funky, like a musty basement. There wasn't much weight to it as it was about as thick as skin, but she wrapped it around her head and shoulders. It was the only thing she could do to stave off the bone-chilling cold.

The bit of warmth the blanket offered did little to ease the growing pain in her head, originating where she'd been struck hard by something. She felt around, but there was no blood, only a tender lump about the size of a jawbreaker candy—the kind she used to get as a kid on the Boardwalk in Point Pleasant at the Jersey Shore. What she wouldn't give to be there now. Baking in the sun. Feeling the coarse sand under her back through her beach towel. The smell of sausage and peppers, hot dogs, hamburgers, popcorn, and saltwater wafting through the air as the tide rolled in and out. Shrieks of joy and laughter coming in from all directions. Life was perfect at the beach. A happy place. A happy memory warming her from within.

Imogen recalled the story by Hans Christian Andersen of the Little Match Girl who lit every one of the matches she was supposed to sell on the streets to help support her family just to stay warm on a frozen wintry night. That's how Imogen felt now, like the Little Match Girl—except the only thing she had to stay warm was a flimsy blanket not made for such frigid temps.

She died anyway, didn't she? The Little Match Girl. Died nameless in the street because no one cared to help her. All this time, and nothing's changed. We are who we are. Maybe our time really is up, and this is humanity's last stand.

Imogen shivered in equal parts from the cold and her apocalyptic thinking. Having ventured outside for even just that little she had done, Imogen didn't think the end of the world was far off. Oliver had said things were getting better. The "numbers" were coming down, whatever that meant. *Did he mean the number of dead or the number of infected?* And still every day someone else they knew died. Classmates. *Former classmates.* Neighbors. Relatives. Celebrities. Politicians. Everyone. The virus was taking everyone—rich or poor; Black, White, or other. If you had a pulse, you were fair game.

And it didn't seem like the vaccine was the great white hope everyone thought it was going to be. When all was said and done, Imogen wasn't sure if the vaccine wouldn't have killed as many people as the virus itself. Maybe more? It worked as advertised in some but failed horribly in others...in most. There were videos showing the last minutes of people who had experienced "an adverse reaction" to the vaccine. *I'd say death is one hell of an adverse reaction.* And they were horrific—the vaccine deaths. Beyond horrific. Death by the virus seemed downright peaceful by comparison. Vivid descriptions of the expirations kept Imogen up some nights. They bothered her more than the snippet of the death-cast she'd accidentally watched. *Am I on video now? Is this my death-cast, and I don't even know it?*

She thought it was like everyone was getting a glimpse at their future with those videos. It was like the Grim Reaper himself put them up as if to say, *hey, this is what's in store for you. Don't fight it. You can't avoid the inevitable. You had your chance to change your ways, but you didn't heed the warnings. Now, I've come to collect what's mine. And it's ALL mine.*

Inevitable.

Certain death.

Pre-determined outcome.

Her thoughts had gone full dark. Imogen didn't think they could get any darker than *The Little Match Girl*, but that wonderful Ivy-League brain of hers had said *here, hold my beer.* That kind of thinking wasn't helping in the current situation. But really, what good could it do, given the circumstances they found themselves in, her brain and her? *Perfect together.*

Isn't there some kind of euphoria before the brain freezes to death? Yes. Hypothermia can cause hallucinations and euphoria.

Maybe I'll experience paradoxical undressing. Give my audience a nice show of skin, if anyone is really watching. Show some titty because, Ally, I have titties. I don't have anything to burrow in, except this ratty blanket. Fuck. I guess it will have to do. I wonder if Death will look like that old actor, Brad Pitt, when he comes for me. Old or not, boy can still get it.

Imogen's teeth chattered as her entire body violently shivered and shook.

Could you hurry it along, Mr. Death? I don't know how much more of this I can—

"You have to stop thinking like that," a voice suddenly said in the dark. It sounded like a girl. A young girl. Younger than Imogen, at the very least.

Imogen sat up, but the pain in her head worsened, so she only ended up on her elbows. Her face poked out of the blanket, which was still draped around her head, loosely now that she had moved to a more upright position.

"Who said that? Who's there? Where am I?"

"It's not about where you are, Imogen, but where you are going," the voice said, sounding closer now than it had a moment ago.

Imogen hadn't heard any movement, but somehow whoever was behind this voice had moved closer to her. *Silently moved closer.* She didn't even hear anyone else breathing aside from herself.

"I don't understand. Ahhhh—"

The bump on the back of her head ached. Stars flashed before her eyes. The pain forced Imogen to lower back down to the ground. Her head seemed to hurt less when she was not sitting up.

"He wants you to know he's sorry."

"Who's sorry?" Imogen said, gritting her teeth in pain. "And why?"

"This was not part of the plan. She got to you first."

Imogen winced, but the pain warmed her momentarily. "Who got to me? And hold up a sec. There's a plan?"

The voice laughed. "Of course there is."

"And you think I'm a part of it?"

"You *are.*"

"Girlfriend, I think you have me confused with somebody else. I'm just—"

"You're Imogen Rockwell." The voice sounded even closer now, although it had shifted positions again. It now came from in front of her and to the left. Before, it had been behind her to the right. Not only was it silent, it moved fast, whatever it was. "And you are more important than you know."

Fuck. Maybe this is Death. Bummer, it's not Brad Pitt.

"And I—" The voice moved again. "I am not Death."

Without thinking, Imogen exhaled. Brad Pitt or not, she wasn't in a hurry to cuddle with old Death.

"And neither is Brad Pitt."

Imogen laughed softly as her teeth clattered again.

"Ggg-girl… can yyyou ttturn uppp the heat? Imma fr-fr-freeze to death over here."

"You won't. And I can't."

"Figures." Imogen shivered. "Ss-so what ar-ar-are you? Like… the gh-ghost of Christmas p-past?"

The voice laughed again. It sounded further away.

"I am not. Consider me…a friend of a friend."

"If you were a friend, y-you'd t-turn up the heat."

The voice sighed. "I told you. I can't do that. They want you to be cold."

"Yeah? Wh-why is th-that?"

"So you don't *think*. So you don't," the voice began. When it spoke again, it was practically whispering into Imogen's ear. "Use that Ivy-League brain of yours."

"Pfft. A lot of use my br-brain is. C-can't even k-keep me wa-warm."

"Are you sure of that?" the voice said in Imogen's other ear.

"Wh-what are y-you t-t-talking ab-b-out?"

Now, as the voice spoke, it seemed to come from both everywhere and nowhere at the same time. And yet, Imogen suspected she alone could hear it.

–Has anything strange ever happened in your presence?

"Y-y-es."

–Have you ever been able to move objects simply by thinking about moving them?

"Y-y-es."

–Have you ever made things disappear?

"Y-y-es."

–Have you ever brought them back?

"Y-y-es."

–Have you ever made things happen? Things you wanted to happen.

"Y-y-es."

–Have you ever taken life from a thing?

Imogen hesitated but then said, "Yes."

Impossibly, she felt warmer. *Hypothermia or something else? We'll see if I start stripping next.*

–Intentionally or unintentionally?

"B-b-both."

–Have you ever brought something...back?

Ally.

An image flashed before her mind's eye. Something from the past. Something from when they were younger, much younger. Children. Something she buried deep down in the graveyard of her memories, and now it was digging its way out. Imogen tried to turn away from it—re-bury it deeper if she had to. But the more she looked away, the clearer the image became, until Imogen remembered everything about that awful day. The accident. Ally. And what happened after. *What she had done.*

"Yes," Imogen said sternly, not feeling the cold anymore.

-Thank you for your honesty, Imogen. He was right about you.

Imogen was frustrated but tried not to sound it. "Who? Who is this friend you keep talking about?"

-He wants to welcome you to the Gemeo Project.

Imogen gasped. *Oh, my god. It* is *a cult. I'm never telling Ally.* "Who wants to welcome me?"

There was a moment of absolute stillness. It felt like everything around Imogen had gone away except for her. Nothing made a sound, not even her breath. She wasn't even sure if she could hear or feel her own heartbeat anymore. Everything just faded away.

For a second, Imogen thought the cold had finally killed her. The conversation had been nothing more than a frosty hallucination brought on by hypothermia. But then everything returned. The sounds, the cold, her breath, and the voice. Whatever she was in, a room or a container, shook as though a massive earthquake had hit it. She covered her head, bracing for possible impact from unknown objects in the room—if there were any. It was so completely dark that Imogen could've been in the middle of Area 57 with the U.F.O.s and wouldn't have known it.

But nothing came, except for the voice, and the shaking stopped almost as quickly as it had come on.

"Your Dream Lover, of course."

Imogen shot to her feet, ignoring the pain in her head. *A distraction.* "What did you say?"

"Your Dream Lover wants me to welcome you to the Gemeo Project."

"I knew it," Imogen hollered. "I fucking *knew* it! He *is* real!"

"He is." There was a long pause, which Imogen barely noticed over her celebratory hoots and hollers. But then, finally, the voice added in a cautious tone, "and so is the game."

"Game? What game?"

But the voice said nothing.

"Hello? What game?"

Then, the voice whispered, echoing eerily—

The one you're already playing...

STAYCATION.

The Fourth Interlude: No Way, Jose!

Long before he ever laid eyes on his vampy neighbor in Boston, Jose Garriga knew death was in the cards. He'd been told as much by a friend. Hell, he agreed to it. *Penance for the things I did and for the things I didn't do but should have done.* For Jose Garriga, death was the only way out of it. And maybe the only way to end the game once and for all.

Many winters had come and gone since they'd become unwitting players in the game. Joanne and Jose. Participation by location. If they hadn't lived next door to the damned Millers. If Joanne hadn't been such a damned busybody. If Bob Buchanan had just delivered the mail.

If, if, if...

But they *had* moved next to the Millers, Joanne *had* been busybodying on that damned app, and Bob *had* wanted to be a hero. And he knew all about it—their special friend. So, now here they were, like Judas damned for all time.

He knew everything—this friend—which was amazing since when they'd met, he was little more than a child. *Or so he seemed? He always had old eyes.* Even now, compared to Jose and Joanne, he was still a child. More than a decade later, and Jose could still see the boy in the face that was becoming a man. *Atlas, carrying the weight of an ungrateful world on his shoulders.*

In a way, Jose felt sorry for him. What was happening now and what had happened then had happened *to* him. The boy didn't choose...this. It wasn't fair that he was forced to bear this heavy responsibility. How many years had he been allowed to be a carefree child? Ten? Eleven? Jose couldn't recall. And now, those years were gone, and Jose didn't think getting them back was something his friend could do, even with his extraordinary powers.

But who knows? Maybe Jose was wrong. He'd been wrong about a lot of other things in the last ten years. *Vermont. Joanne.*

After Vermont, his special friend came to him. Even though it'd been over ten years since he'd seen him, Jose recognized Toby Miller right away.

It was the eyes. He's an old soul.

Jose had been wandering the desolate streets—*desolate because everyone else was dead*—trying to process the thing he'd just witnessed. The awful thing Joanne had done. He wanted to run, but how far was far enough to be safe? They'd run from St. Augustine Place and the house of horrors, and it followed them. *No, it never left them. It was always with them, an invisible passenger.* For a moment, Jose considered the unthinkable—ending it all. He hadn't been practicing anything in decades, but he thought given the circumstances, Jesus would understand. How could he not? But Jose couldn't help but wonder what from this hell might follow him into whatever life came next. Purgatory in the house of horrors.

That's when he came—Toby. He explained to Jose that there were forces in motion and, like it or not, Jose and Joanne were a part of it. They'd always been a part of it. A big part of a greater plan, and the time had come for him to play his part.

Jose went to tell Toby about Joanne, about what she had done, but Toby hushed him. Toby already knew everything. *Of course he did.* Toby told Jose that what he saw had been a small sample of what was coming unless he helped Toby finish the game once and for all.

"Game, Señor Toby? I don't understand. What game? We're not playing a game," Jose said, traces of the accent he usually quelled coming through in his confusion.

"Everything you think you know about everything is wrong. What you see is nothing but the dream of a slumbering giantess. All that you are, all that you think you are, is nothing more than pages in a script."

Something burned in Jose's stomach. He knew this. Impossibly, he'd always known this. "All the world's a stage, and all the men and women merely players," Jose said, recalling high school English Lit with his favorite teacher of all time, Pat Lobosco. *I hope she's okay in all this.*

Toby smiled and nodded. "Bill knew a lot more than how to pen a good verse. Poe, too. They had the sight. They saw behind the veil. They were awake while those around them slept."

A part of him didn't want to ask it, but another had to know the answer.

"What did they see, Señor Toby?"

"Do you want me to show you? But be warned, it drove poor Eddie Poe mad."

"Aye!" Jose trembled like a child during a thunderstorm. "I don't know, Señor Toby. I'm scared. This...all of this... frightens me to death."

"You haven't seen anything yet."

Jose paced in a circle, about to lose what little shit he had left.

"Take my hand, Jose. And wake."

Toby held out a hand. Jose stared at it a long time, considering every possibility. In the end, it didn't matter. He knew he was as good as dead anyway. For the first time in years, tears rolled down his cheeks.

"The devil, you know, right?" Jose said.

"The devil is nothing more than a character in a children's picture book compared to what awaits us out there, on the other side of everything."

"You're not really selling it, Señor Toby." Jose laughed. "But I'll take your hand anyway, because I have to believe that we have a chance. This can't be how it ends."

Toby took Jose's hand in his and squeezed gently. "No, indeed it is not."

Something like electricity coursed through Jose's veins, but he felt no pain. Just a slight tingling sensation all over his numbing body, like Novocain kicking in. The hair on his head rose. The metal fillings in his mouth vibrated, pulsing down to the roots. His entire mouth felt like it was on fire. A warm, wet sensation gathered in his groin, spilling slowly down his legs.

"Señor...Tobyyyyy?"

Then, his left leg shook like Elvis feeling the spirit, followed by the right leg. Jose looked a bit like a marionette gone mad. His eyes rolled back in his head as his lids fluttered wildly. Thick, frothy white foam formed in the corners of his open mouth. It flew explosively in every direction when his head started whipping from side to side.

"Ayyyyyy!"

The tingling in his body amped to a feverish pitch. And then, just when Jose thought his heart was going to burst inside his chest, everything stopped at once. His legs wanted to give out beneath him as the rest of him went slack, but Toby kept Jose propped up like a crash test dummy.

Toby pulled Jose's limp body to him, cradling his former neighbor in his arms. Jose's head bobbled about until it rested on one of Toby's shoulders. He felt Jose stiffen, then heave as though he was about to expel his insides.

"Ayyy...Señor Toby. I don't...feel so...good."

"I know." Toby leaned his head close to Jose's ear and whispered, "CROATOAN."

And in an instant, they were gone...*abracadabra*...stepping through the veil...*alakazam!* Pressing through to the other side, the other side of everything. Vermont and home now felt like it was a spot a million miles away, across the universe. Another time, another place. But really, the two places existed side by side. The other side of the veil, standing right beside the world Jose knew all too well.

Jose stood and looked out from the abyss and saw. Yes, he *saw*. Finally. And from there, he saw everything clearly, as though he'd put on the right pair of eyeglasses, and the world came into focus for the first time in his life.

And then he understood.

This is how it ends.

Jose Garriga understood his role in the production, his part to play. And much like Pilate, he accepted his fate. His awakening was complete. The dream of his life was over. And he saw that there were still some things worth dying for.

And today was the day Jose Garriga was going to die.

It's a good day to die, Señor Toby. Good a day as any.

He knew it was coming because he had seen it all those

months ago with Toby when they crossed the veil. Everything else he'd seen passed exactly as he had seen it, including the Irish bitch next door. *The thing that swam underneath her skin. It was a foul, undead thing. An unholy abomination.* And it had to be stopped.

He'd known as soon as he'd seen her—truly seen her—who and what she was. And what she had been once upon a time. But Jose played his role brilliantly, following Toby's direction—right down to the final gasp at the motel door. *Brando would be proud.*

He'd done good. Jose said the lines written for him. Did all the things the role required—right down to fucking the foul thing in a seedy motel three times a week. It made him sick to do it, but it was for the greater good.

Some things are worth dying for, Señor Toby.

The thing had gotten what it wanted from him, and now it was lights out, Jose.

One thing becoming another.

The pain at first had been excruciating, almost exquisite, but now, as he lay there in a pool of his hot blood on the squeaky bed in the motel, Jose Garriga felt nothing but bliss. Death was coming, and it was going to be the sweetest of sweet releases. Better than the first time he shot his wad after jerking off to a popular swimsuit catalog.

The thing—that foul thing—was gone and now it was just Jose and the thing's keeper. Sandra Miller lit a celebratory cigarette.

-Well, this has been fun, Mr. Garriga.

I bet you're the kind of woman that always gets what she wants.

-Every time, Sandra said. Every. Time.

I bet no one's ever gotten the better of you, right? You're always ten steps ahead.

She laughed but agreed. *Twenty steps,* then exhaled a thick cloud of smoke.

–You have to get up real early to surprise me.

I'm an early riser.

–The quick brown fox jumps over the lazy dog. Can you guess who's who in that scenario, Mr. Garriga?

Blood filled his mouth as she reached inside him and moved something else around, but he smiled. A great toothy one, too.

I'm the fox, and you're the lazy—

She squeezed his insides tighter, pulling at them like they were a string of cotton candy.

–Careful how you finish that sentence, Mr. Garriga. I'm not done playing with your insides yet. Still plenty more I can do in there.

Jose laughed, and laughed, and laughed so hard until he cried.

–You think this is funny?

He nodded, thinking but not saying—*I got you, bitch. I. GOT. YOU.*

I've seen how the story ends. And...

Sandra squeezed something inside of him that wasn't meant to be squeezed.

And...you're not going to like how it ends.

Jose grinned like a boy walking into a room of relatives so he can proudly show off his wang for the first time. Then he howled with laughter. It came from some unknown part of Jose, and once it started, he couldn't shut it down. He sounded like a mad scientist, marveling as his creation opened its eyes for the first time, but he didn't care. It would all be over soon.

Sandra Miller—the wolf that wore not sheep's clothing

but the face of an ordinary woman, hiding in plain sight—rearranged the last of Jose's insides. Her fingers moved faster than the blades of a blender. When she finished, she stuck a fresh cigarette in her long black holder, lit it, and then inhaled deeply as she admired her handiwork.

Jose went to speak but choked on a pool of blood that gathered in the back of his throat. The taste of iron was nauseating. He coughed and spat it out, hoping more than a few drops landed on her pristine ensemble—especially that damned fur coat. *What is that? Vicuña?*

-What's that, Jose? I didn't catch that. Not so funny now, huh?

Sandra sat beside Jose on the bed the thing used to fuck him seven ways to Sunday for weeks. She stared into his dull, blood-shot eyes and tisked. The tip of her cigarette glowed as she took a drag, and then she leaned in as though to kiss him on the mouth but blew a lungful of smoke in his face.

He rallied enough to say, "Death...be not proud."

Sandra smiled. "I didn't know you were a learned man, Mr. Garriga. I mistook you for a garden variety laborer." She said "laborer" as though it was a dirty word.

Under other circumstances, this would have infuriated him. *Puta.* But now, he didn't care. She'd get her comeuppance, and she'd get it thanks in part to his sacrifice.

And Joanne.

"I'll see you in hell," Jose said.

Sandra kissed his blood-stained cheek. "Keep it warm for me, dear. I may be a while yet."

Jose heard her gathering up her things, checking her voice-mails, and finally zipping up a coat that Jose knew cost more than he paid for the house on St. Augustine Place.

"Happy trails, Mr. Garriga. I'll pass on your regards to your wife when I see her."

The door to their room opened, and then closed. *Adios.* Jose listened as her footsteps sounded further and further away until they were gone. Then, he heard the roar of a car motor revving to life, followed by a vehicle, presumably hers since the lot had been otherwise empty, pulling out of the motel's parking lot.

All's well that ends well.

He thought about his wife, Joanne, and her part still to be played in the game. It saddened him just the slightest bit that he wouldn't be there to see it unfold, watch her play her part, but he knew when it was all over, they'd be together again. Somewhere nice. Somewhere peaceful. Toby would make it so. He promised he would. *Penance paid.*

"Aye, *Dios mío*," Jose said to the empty room.

But then, Toby was beside him, just as he promised he would be, ready to take him to the place, the happy place, where he would wait for Joanne.

"I did it, Señor Toby." A coughing fit interrupted Jose's speech. "I did it."

Toby took hold of Jose's hand.

"You did. I am so proud of you."

Jose laughed. "She called me a laborer. A garden variety laborer. Ayyeee, *Dios mío.*"

Toby squeezed Jose's hand. "Are you ready?"

Pay no attention to the man behind the curtain. I am Oz, the great and—

"I am, Señor Toby." Jose took a long inhale, and then slowly exhaled. "Tell her...tell Joanne...I'm sorry. And I'll see her soon. I can't feel my legs. Are they still there, Señor Toby?"

"Put out the light, and put out the light," Toby said, closing his eyes. "CROATOAN."

Goodnight, and thank you for your service, Jose Garriga.

To die laughing must be the most glorious of all glorious deaths...

–Eddie Poe, who did not die laughing.

Harding and the She-Wolf

"Watch your step there. It's a little slick at the bottom," Harding said to Sandra Miller as they descended the basement stairs of the Miller House on St. Augustine Place.

West and a pair of junior-looking crime scene techs stepped aside, allowing Harding and Sandra to enter the scene. Harding gave West a small nod of appreciation.

"Thank you, Detective. I think I got it. I'm a Miller. This isn't my first crime scene." Sandra straightened out the material of her flowy top, then the matching form-fitting bottom the moment her heels touched the cement floor, as though there were even the slightest chance a wrinkle might have formed during the short climb down the steps. "So, this is it, huh? The scene of the crime."

She said the last phrase in a mock serious, true crime TV show announcer's voice. Harding thought it was an odd tonal choice under the circumstances. Something else that didn't sit right with him about the broad. But Harding had no clue, yet, what it all added up to. He'd seen his fair share of dysfunctional families react to murder scenes. They'd always been out of the ordinary. Hell, he'd seen one family break out into a fifteen-person brawl literally over the fresh corpse of a recently departed relative. But Sandra's plucky attitude and the bizarre nature of the crime scene itself was one for Harding's personal record book.

"*One* of the crime scenes, yes," Harding said between sucks on a LifeSav-Ahs.

He observed his guest carefully. Her face remained blank, devoid of any reaction to the sights—and smells—around her. Foul. Every crevice reeked of death and decay. The smell was enough to make half the techs that'd come down to the basement dry heave or puke. The aroma was so potently pungent the techs worked in shifts, except for West, who breathed it in like it was five-thousand-dollar Parisian perfume.

But Sandra Miller hadn't so much as winced at any of it or given the slightest indication she'd noticed any of the macabre sights and smells surrounding her. If Harding hadn't known better, he would have thought this was just another day at the office for the glamor girl. But Harding also suspected Sandra Miller wasn't the working girl type.

Harding watched as her eyes buzzed about, scanning the scene like they were recording every gory detail into her memory bank. He half-imagined she'd replay them in her mind's eye later, viewing them as others might home movies. But then, a puzzled look came over Sandra's face, and she turned to Harding.

"Mama?"

Harding cleared his throat. He took a small step to cross around her, then pointed to the back wall. "There."

"Oh, right," Sandra said, stepping toward the area that held the skewered remains of her mother. "Now, there's something you don't see every day, huh, Detective? Even in your line of work, I'd expect that must be somewhat unique?"

"It is, yes. Death by Christmas decoration is a new one for

me.”

Harding sucked so hard at the candy it split in half in his mouth. He swallowed one piece, then rolled the other around with his tongue like it was a wad of gum.

“What’s left of Bill and Denise is in the freezer. Justin is there in the crate. Junior is upstairs. So, where’s my Mary?”

Something again poked at the sleeping bear that was Harding’s gut. Something not right. He just didn’t see it yet.

He indicated with his head the small roped-off section of the floor that contained the pile of stewy-looking goo. That got a reaction out of her. A small one, but it was something.

This broad may not be a pod person after all.

Harding didn’t know, and hoped he’d never find out, how he would react if he stepped into Sandra’s Jimmy Choos and stared down at a molten pile of sludge that had once been a beloved family member. Hell, Harding had cried for seven weeks straight when his childhood dog, Brownie, got flattened by an ice cream truck steps from his house. To this day, he couldn’t stand the taste of Mister Soft-E.

“Detective?”

Harding detected a scrap of emotion in the woman’s voice. He approached her cautiously, not wanting to intrude on her moment with her niece’s remains.

“Yes, Miss Miller?”

“I don’t suppose I can have a quiet moment with my...,” Sandra’s voice broke off. She sniffled, then continued. “My Mary.”

Harding thought that Jenny Aurbach cried more convincingly as “Nancy” in that awful community theatre production of *Oliver* his wife—*ex-wife*—had dragged him to during their brief attempt at reconciliation. Jenny Aurbach was a computer programmer by day and a wanna-be anything else by night. That unlucky afternoon, Jenny Aurbach had tried her hand as a musical theatre actress and failed spectacularly. *Don't give up your day job, hon.* Sandra Miller was no Jenny Aurbach in the tears-on-cue department. It was like the act of crying was beneath her. She couldn't even fake it.

Harding shook his head. "It *is* an active crime sc—"

She turned to him. Her eyes swollen and bloodshot as though she'd just been poked in each of them. But they were dry.

"Please, Detective. I need...I need to say..."

Sandra fanned at her face with her hands like a Southern Belle. *Well, I nevah!*

Harding considered for a moment. The longer he took, the more ridiculous Sandra's fanning looked to him. If they weren't surrounded by dead human beings, Harding might have broken into a raucous fit of laughter. He thought the only things missing to complete the image were white gloves, a parasol, and a great big hoop skirt.

Still, he'd allowed other family members a quiet moment with their deceased loved ones at crime scenes. Harding didn't understand why they'd choose to remember their loved ones as meat sacks and chalk outlines, but he'd never been in their position. Death, especially tragic death, made people lose their marbles. Or at the very least, misplace them for a while.

He peered into her eyes, feeling his resistance wane. *She's doing it again. That thing she does. Charming me. I can't say—*

"I need the room," Harding announced in a commanding voice that wasn't his own.

West shot him an inquisitive look. "Joe?"

"Take five. Grab a smoke. Grab a slice. Food truck is

parked on the corner of Augustine and Camile. Take a piss. Do whatever you gotta do, just don't do it here," Harding said, not meeting West's gaze.

"Joe, she can't be left unsuper—"

"You think I don't know that?" Harding growled. "You were still picking your nose and eating it when I started on the job. Don't tell me..." Harding stopped, composed himself, then went on. "Don't tell me how to do the only thing I'm good at, okay, West?"

West had recoiled at the sudden ferocity, but now inched back towards Harding.

"Sure, Joe. Sure." West looked at Sandra, who no longer looked like a grieving widow but a satisfied trickster from Nordic mythology. His gaze found Harding. He noted there was a glassy faraway look in the senior Detective's eyes that hadn't been there before. "Five minutes. Five."

"Five minutes," Harding repeated, his tone softening as his eyes cleared.

"Okay, smoke 'em if you got 'em," West said to his junior techs, motioning to the stairs. They made their way to the stairs and climbed. West turned back to Harding, who looked like a sad puppy being scolded for shitting in a favorite pair of slippers. "Your five minutes start now, Joe."

Harding said nothing but nodded slowly.

Then, he was alone with Sandra Miller, the she-wolf.

Harding wondered if she was going to tear him to pieces like something had done to her Mary. West probably wouldn't even notice if his goo combined with Mary's to make a gooier pile of stew. West was good, not *that* good, Harding thought.

The basement was deadly quiet. The only thing Harding heard was the sound of his breath. Harding and Sandra eyed each other. *And I'll huff.* The clock was ticking. Five minutes wasn't a lot of time, but it was more than enough to do some damage. Ali could throw a dozen punches in under three seconds, any of which would knock a normal person into next week. *And I'll puff.*

"Detective?"

"Ma'am."

Sandra smiled, and Harding couldn't recall if her teeth had been that white, that *sharp* before. Her eyes bulged and widened. They looked hungry. *So very hungry.*

"My, Miss Miller," Harding said quietly, "what big eyes you have."

And I'll blow your whole fucking house down, Joe Harding.

No Place Like—

When Imogen Rockwell opened her eyes, at first relieved to find she was lying on her bed back in her bedroom, a feeling of relief came over her. The night's misadventure was over and done with, somehow now behind her. *There's no place like home, eh? I should call Ally.*

She looked around her bedroom, taking in the comforts of home. Imogen was so happy to be home that she hadn't stopped to wonder how she'd gotten there. Relief overtook logic, but logic would catch up. And the more she looked around the idyllic bedroom, *her idyllic bedroom*, the more uneasy she became. Imogen's stomach groaned, and she felt like something was about to make a painful return trip up from her belly.

This is off. The whole thing isn't right. This...isn't my room.

No, it wasn't quite her bedroom, but a highly accurate approximation of it. It was close enough to the real thing to an untrained eye, but *her* expert eyes saw the flaws immediately. The bed pretending to be her bed was more comfortable than it ought to have been—more comfortable than it had ever been, even back when it was new. And every one of the sticky stars that made up Orion hugged the ceiling tightly.

This is not my room. But at least it's warm in here, wherever "here" is. This here beats the last here, that's for sure.

She jumped to her feet, surprised to find the ground was solid and not made of quicksand or potato salad or something equally illogical that made sense only in the world of dreams. Because that's what this had to be—a dream. Where else is a room not a room besides a dream?

Imogen wished she could shake herself awake and find herself back in her real house—*there's no place like home*—be sitting on her real bed, staring up at the one peeling sticky star of Orion, listening to Ally drone on about boys or janitors or "custodial engineers" or, really, anything. What she wouldn't give just to hear her friend's voice now.

I told you, girl. It's a cult. And I'm the "dumb one."

Or maybe talking to Ally could wait.

She walked the length of her doppelgänger bedroom. Even the dimensions of the replica room were off in just the slightest way. Imogen knew it was eleven steps from her bed to the desk in the corner. Fifteen steps from the bed to the closet. Six steps from the bed to the window. In every instance, the distance was off by a step or two. Barely noticeable. But she noticed.

And the smell. Or more precisely, the lack of an ambient smell. Where were the comfy smells that made her room *hers*? That unique combination of aromas that said Imogen Rockwell lives here. A sprinkling of baby powder with a touch of TK-1 and a dab of lavender.

But there was no perfumy after-smell, no baby powder, and no lavender, either. There was...nothing. The room smelled almost industrial, like a hospital before they hose it down with bleach.

Even more unsettling, outside her bedroom window was... nothing. A virtual wasteland. It was pitch black. Not a single streetlamp blinked in the dark, and no stars twinkled in the night sky. *Assuming it* is *night.* Everything that should be outside of her window was not there.

Imogen remembered that winter back when she'd been in the third grade where she had hamsters. *Roger, Mark, Mimi, and Lola.* Sometimes she'd cover the hamsters' habitat with a small blanket so they'd be tricked into thinking it was night. Then she realized the poor things weren't getting any sleep, since they were nocturnal animals, so she stopped. But it was already too late for poor Lola. Drove the gal mad. The poor thing ran herself to death on the exercise wheel after running for three days straight without a wink of rest. *Run, Lola. Run. R.I.P.*

That's how she felt now—like a rat in a cage without an exercise wheel in sight. But maybe that was a good thing. Without anything else to do, Imogen could see herself running non-stop until she dropped just like little Lola.

Then Imogen noticed something on the bed. Something that had not been there a minute ago. She approached the false bed cautiously, weary that there could be more surprises lurking in the seven steps it took to walk from the window to the bed.

"What the fuck?"

There on the bed lay a garish Halloween mask with a hand-written note. Written in all capital, blocky lettering were the words: *PUT ME ON. NOW.*

Imogen picked up the note and examined the writing, hoping she might recognize it. But she did not. The writing was plain, neither neat nor messy, perfect nor imperfect. It was just ordinary.

That thing is not touching my head.

The mask stared back at her. Its strange, lifeless eyes

taunted her, almost daring her to put it on. At first, she couldn't recognize the cartoonish face etched on the mask, but then it came to her.

"Jinkies," Imogen exclaimed in her best Velma Dinkley voice.

Velma, from the old *Scooby-Doo* cartoons. That was the face crudely depicted on the mask. Velma fucking Dinkley.

It wasn't even that Velma's face was crudely rendered on the latex mask. It was more that it looked like the nerdy gal's face appeared to be melting off its skull. The skin sliding right off the bone as though it'd been boiled for hours until tender. One eye sat higher than the other, and the droopy eye was offset. The right cheek sagged as though it was caught mid-drip. Velma's signature black spectacles sat crookedly on what was left of a button nose. One lens was popped out, gone completely. The hair on top of the mask's head was partially singed, while the other bits of hair poked up wildly, as though Velma had just woken after a long night of partying in the back of the Mystery Machine. And perhaps worst of all was Velma's mouth. It was locked in a horrific-looking scream. One thing becoming another.

It's like Velma meets "The Thing."

Imogen picked up the mask, considered tossing it out the window, but stopped dead in her tracks when she noticed what had been tucked under the mask—a second note. The handwriting appeared to be the same or similar enough that only an expert could spot the inconsistencies.

She set the grotesque mask aside so she could get a closer look at the second note. Her blood chilled as she read the words:

Staycation.

The Rules—

Dead Speak

"Oh, you stupid, stupid, girl," Sandra Miller said as she stood over the pile of gelatinous human goo with a generous helping of disgust paired with a pinch of pity. "Look at you now. Just look at you."

In all her days, she had never seen a person end up in such a liquidus state. And for this to have happened to Mary, *her Mary*, was unacceptable, if that mushy pile even turned out to be Mary in the end. It would not do one bit.

To be frank, she thought she was handling the situation quite well. A few short years ago, Sandra would have arrived, metaphorical guns blazing, and leveled what remained of the place. Sent them all straight to hell. But that wasn't smart. Brashness drew attention, and she did not want attention. The Millers had thrived precisely because they avoided drawing attention to themselves. When you live in the shadows, what's the sense of shining a light into the dark? Mama Cassie used to say that.

And look at you now, Mama. Just look at you. Not so haughty now, are you? And your precious Billy. The pathetic loser. I should have finished him off in the womb. And just look at you both now. I beat you. I. FUCKING. BEAT. YOU.

Sandra smiled. The thought of parts of Billy resting in the

meat freezer beside parts of his Missus, as their own kids had eaten them, warmed her insides. She didn't give two shits how it looked to the Keystone Cop hovering behind, looking over her shoulder. What really mattered was how it felt, and it felt good. Goddamned devilishly good.

Still, Sandra knew she probably shouldn't underestimate Joe Harding. He seemed rather adroit for an average gumshoe. It was probably best not to dismiss him so readily. Plus, in time, he may serve a purpose. The more the merrier. And it didn't hurt to have a bona fide New York City Homicide Detective in your back pocket. He wasn't unattractive either. There had been *something* there for a moment or two up on Billy's front porch. Harding wanted to fuck her. Sandra was sure of it. She didn't have to read his mind to know. *Men are all the same.* It was written all over his face, and in the way he fawned over her. He was awkward, like a fifth grader with a boner handing out Valentines.

And for just a moment there, Sandra wanted him, too. She wondered how his rough fingers would feel slipping inside of her, and then withdrawing slowly, only to be rammed back in. The Detective was solid in stature, although clearly not a gym rat. Sandra pictured him naked, on top of her, devouring every square inch of her real estate. The thought of his thick nightstick pounding her into next week practically sent her into a howling fit. *It's been a while.* Had she allowed it, she might have turned into a puddle there on the porch. *Business first, playtime later.*

Back to business.

Mary. Or what was left of her.

Sandra bent down to get a closer look at the goo. It really was nothing but a pile of mush. Gore. Sinew. A bone or two. Some hair. *Fuck.* For all she knew, Harding and Co. had stumbled onto the remains of Jimmy Hoffa. There was no way to identify them as belonging to Mary without testing them, and testing took time. At least, conventional testing did.

But Sandra Miller had a better way.

"Detective?"

"Ma'am?"

"I don't suppose you could fetch me a cold bottle of water, could you? This is a bit much for me." Sandra stifled a laugh. "I'm feeling a little...faint."

Harding stepped closer to her.

"Ma'am, I really shouldn't—"

Like she'd done earlier, Sandra Miller charmed Joe Harding.

"Water, please. Now. Thank you."

For a second, Harding only stood there, dumbly, as though some of his brains had just been sucked through his nose.

Resistance. I like that in a man. Your will is strong. It will be so much fun breaking you into a million pieces, Joe Harding.

But then Harding's legs moved to the stairs. They sluggishly carried him up each step as though he had three hundred pounds of Idaho's freshest potatoes strapped to his back.

"Detective?"

Harding stopped.

"Would you be a doll, dear, and get the door?"

A second later, Harding said, "Yes, ma'am." And then he closed the door on his way out like a good little soldier.

Oh yes, Joe Harding. Sandra Miller was definitely wet now. *We're going to have so much fun together. Just you wait.*

She licked at her lips.

Business first.

Sandra reached down into the sludge pile and grabbed a

clump of bloody hair.

"Now, let's see who you belong to. Belonged to." She considered the clump. "Mary, or Alex."

Then Sandra tilted her head back and opened her mouth impossibly wide. Her muscles and bones stretched beyond what was normal for a human jaw. Opening wider and wider, until it looked more like the entrance to a deep, dark cave than a mouth. Just a big, round black hole encircled by two sets of glistening white, razor-sharp teeth. A long, slick tongue slithered out of the cavernous mouth and wagged about, waiting to be fed.

Sandra Miller dropped the bits of hair and gore down the shaft and swallowed it whole in one big throaty gulp. The serpent tongue withdrew, satisfied with the offering. Sandra's mouth closed in on itself, morphing back to human.

When Sandra's jaw finally snapped back into its normal position—well, everyday position—her eyes began to pulse and glow. Every dark corner of the basement was draped in their eerie green flickering light. Slowly, Sandra rose out of her Jimmy Choos, levitating a good four feet over the over-priced clogs. Her arms shot straight out, so her body made a perfect "T." She wriggled as though caught in a trap, then settled. Her head twisted from side to side, as if Sandra's whole face was being slapped by a powerful but invisible, hand. Then, her body went still and limp. Still suspended in mid-air, a slow, raspy moan escaped her open mouth.

"Who goes there?" the voice inside Sandra Miller bellowed.

A sound like static poured out of her mouth as Sandra's head jerked about. An antenna scanning for a signal.

"Is that...youuuuuuuuu?"

The sound of a thousand screams filled the Miller basement.

It was a wonder no one upstairs heard them. Nor did they feel the house tremble down to its bones. *Keep them distracted.*

"Is that you, Auntie?" a familiar voice came through.

Sandra Miller laughed maniacally. "It is, my dear, dear Mary."

"Oh, Auntie. Look at what's become of meeeeeeeeeee—"

Suddenly, the mini family reunion was cut short by Andy West, the coroner. From the bottom of the stairs, he shrieked in abject horror. The sweaty plastic bottle of ice-cold water he'd brought down for the grieving Miller woman fell to the ground and exploded.

Not terribly long after, Andy West followed the water bottle and exploded, too.

Part of him, anyway.

Staycation 2.0

The rules:

1. *You must wear your assigned mask at all times. No exceptions.*

If you remove your mask at any time, for any reason, you're out.

1. *When the bell rings, you must draw a card. Cards can be found on the kitchen table.* **If you fail to draw a card, you're out.**
2. *The timer begins when the last player has drawn a card. Each player must complete the action indicated on their selected card before the timer goes off.*

If you fail to complete your action in the allotted time, you're out.

1. *Players can use any found objects. Nothing is off-limits.*
2. *The game is completed when only* **one** *player remains.*
3. *Failure to participate in the game, will result in expulsion.*

Imogen sank onto the bed that was not really her bed.

Staycation. The game.

She'd heard of it, of course she had. Everyone heard the stories. The salacious rumors. The whispers. Occasionally, a short video made it online, supposedly recorded by someone either playing the game or who had beaten it. Imogen thought these videos, not that she'd seen more than a couple of them, looked staged. Deep fakes, maybe. They were rare and never stayed online for long before the internet police took them down for violating community standards—which only made Imogen believe more firmly that they were bogus. Film students reviving a forgotten urban legend.

And until a moment ago, Imogen would have bet her life that's all they were—stories, fakes, the stuff of urban legend. But here she was, locked inside a room that wasn't hers but made to look like it, with a creepy Velma mask, and an even creepier set of instructions.

She'd woken up here—came to, more like it—in this place, wherever it was. Before that, the last things Imogen clearly remembered were the walk to the Coffee Cavern, the empty streets, the quiet, the boarded-up house, the writing, *CROA-TOAN*, and being knocked out. How she'd gotten here and by whom was still muddy in her brain. All she knew for certain was the lady—yes, it *had* been a female—that turned her lights out, had the smallest trace of an accent in her voice. Almost like it wasn't supposed to be there but came through anyway. None of it made sense. Yet. As Velma Dinkley would say—*looks like we got another mystery on our hands.*

Imogen recalled Ally mentioning something about the game around the time the first lockdowns began. That felt like a lifetime ago. She'd almost missed the mention of it since

Ally sandwiched it between talking about Bobby, again, and something about a rumor the virus was manufactured by a twelve-year-old would-be influencer in Norway trying to go viral—

"There's a joke in there somewhere," Imogen had said.

"What? Are you dissing my Bobby again? Let it go, Imo. Just let it goooooo."

Imogen laughed. "MENSA called. They want their membership card back."

"Ooohhh. A they/them. I like it. Sexually liberated. Probably open to butt stuff. Are they hot? You can tell me. They're hot, aren't they? I mean, with a name like Men Sa, they'd have to be, right? A damned waste if they weren't. Don't tell me if they're not, but they are, right?"

"Yes, so hot. They're so hot, your eyes'll blister just looking at them."

"I fucking knew it. Didn't I say it?"

"That you did. That you did."

"I mean, can you believe they're just taking girls off the street and forcing them to play this stupid game? It's sick. Fucking perverts."

"Slow down, partner. What game?"

Ally sighed, then whined. "I, like, literally just said. Don't you listen to me, Imo?"

"Honestly? No, not always. I don't miss much, usually."

"Imma let that one slide 'cause I love you, bitch."

"Aww, love you, slutbag."

"Anyway! As I was saying...yeah, Pedro's cousin, Gabriella, you know Pedro, right? The hot soccer player from Long Acre. My god. If I could just play with his ball—"

"Moving on..."

"Yeah, so Pedro's cousin Gabriella said she saw a girl get snatched right out in broad daylight. They put her in the back of a big ass truck or something. It was like some Mexican lady, I think. The grabber."

"Wait, where was this?"

"Um, let me think."

"Don't hurt yourself."

"Fun-nnnyyyy. It was in Black Oak. The Super Center parking lot."

"Shit!"

"I know, right? It's like crazy."

"So, people saw this girl get grabbed and no one tried to stop it?"

"I don't know, Imo. I guess not. I mean, she ended up missing for like...I don't know... a few months."

"Jesus."

"Right? Had her face on the milk cartons. Bet that's a collector's item now."

"I'll get you one off Z-Bay for your birthday."

"You're too good to me, Imo."

"I know. But hold up, Al. What's this have to do with the game?"

"O-M-G." Ally smacked her forehead on the other end of the phone. "The game! When she finally made it home, I heard she looked like something the cat dragged in, but whatever. Had crazy eyes. Like, PTVD eyes. I think she offed some people."

"P-T-S-D, Al."

"Right. Well, she didn't say anything for like three months. Well, almost anything. She just kept saying 'I won...I won the game' over and over again. So yeah, they forced her to play the game somewhere. I don't know. Gabby said she thought it was like in the back of one of those lonnnnnggg trucks. You remember? When this lockdown shit began, the roads were, like, empty. Like…tumbleweeds and shit."

"Yeah, empty except for—"

"Cargo trucks," they said in unison.

"Essential workers," Imogen said. "No one would think to look in the back of the trucks, because everyone was too busy clapping for them as they drove through our neighborhoods. Essential-fucking-workers."

"B-B-BINGO!"

"But Al. What's this game?"

"Oh, come on, Imo. You know. *The* game. The one no one likes to talk about, like ever. The one our parents get all weird-like if you ask them about it."

A light began to burn in Imogen's brain.

"Oh, *that* game."

"Yeah, duh! Stay-fucking-cation."

God, I fucking miss Ally.

Then, something caught her eye in the far-right corner of the bedroom, just above the door. It was a digital sign. On it, the words "pre-game set" flashed. Imogen didn't remember seeing that there before, but she supposed it might have been there this whole time. It was possible she might have missed seeing it in the general confusion of things.

Come on, girl. You know it wasn't there, right? Why you lyin' to yourself?

Imogen wondered what "pre-game set" meant. There'd been nothing in the rules about it. Unless she missed something? She grabbed the paper with the rules printed on it and looked it over. Then, she flipped the page over and saw written in the same hand as the rules and the mask directive—

Turns of Play:

Pre-game set. Twenty minutes. Players ready themselves for gameplay.

Gameplay begins with the first round of card drawing.

A round ends when the timer counts down to zero. The first round is one hundred and eighty minutes in length. Each subsequent round shall decrease by fifteen minutes.

After a three-minute pause in play, during which time players who did not complete their actions are removed from play, the drawing of cards will commence, and a new round starts at the buzzer.

Gameplay is repeated until only one player remains, and the game is won.

All she kept saying is I won. I won the game.

FUCK.

"Players ready themselves for gameplay? What am I supposed to do? Pray, pee, or what," Imogen wondered out loud, setting aside the instructions. "Fuck, this sucks."

She lay on the ground and knocked gently.

Doesn't sound like a cargo truck. But I think that's how they got me here. I must have passed out from the cold, and then they moved me here? Maybe?

Imogen sat up and pressed her back to the bed. She glanced up at the digital display and noted that sometime recently, while she'd been reminiscing, it had begun counting down.

16:27:03.

"Sixteen minutes until I die," Imogen said.

The twisted Velma mask looked even less appealing than it

had when Imogen first laid eyes on it. The thought of putting it over her head so it touched her skin, her face, made Imogen want to hurl.

It probably smells like a used jockstrap in there. There's no way Imma put that—

"You're going to have to put it on if you want to win the game. And if you want to get out of here, and see your friend again, you're going to have to win the game," the voice Imogen recognized from earlier, the child's voice, had returned.

"You're back. Thought you were gone. I don't suppose you can get me outta here?"

"There's only one way out, I'm afraid, and that's—"

"To win the game. Yeah, I got it."

"I'm sorry, Imogen. This wasn't supposed to happen."

Imogen laughed. "Yeah, well. The story of my life."

"You don't really know the story of your life, though, do you? That's why you reached out to us in the first place...to find out who you are, where you come from."

"I suppose you're right. But in fourteen minutes, none of it will matter. I've never been very good at games. I don't see how Imma walk away from this. I mean I can't—I won't—just kill someone."

"You've done it before."

"That was an accident!" Imogen was on her feet, ready to go ten rounds with the disembodied voice. "And besides, that one doesn't count. I...I brought her back."

"Do you trust me, Imogen Rockwell?"

Imogen laughed. "Trust you? Hell, I don't even know you! Maybe you did this to me. You and the whole damned Gemeo Project."

12:34:22.

"Well, what would you like to know?"

Imogen sighed. "I don't know. Let's start with a name. You got one?"

"I do. It's Alex."

"Alex. That's a nice name. Short for?"

"Alexandra."

"Alexandra. Very nice. Sounds very regal. You got a last name to go with the first?"

"I do. Miller. I'm Alexandra Miller, but you can just call me Alex."

10:08:57.

"Well, Alex, are you gonna let me see you?"

"I can't. Not yet, anyway."

"Mysterious. So why can't I see you? Doesn't seem fair seeing as how you can see me."

09:10:37...

"You can't see me, Imogen, because...I'm dead."

Go West, Young Man!

"Where the fuck is West? Has anyone seen Andy West, the coroner? Little guy. Squirrely. Dressed like he stepped out of a runway show in Milan," Harding said to everyone within earshot, standing in the front room of the Miller house. "Anyone? Anyone? Bueller?"

He received nothing but blank stares and shoulder shrugs in reply. Even the *Ferris Bueller* reference failed to crack a smile. *Pre-pubescent punks. It's a classic.*

Harding popped a LifeSav-Ahs, but it did nothing to relieve the ache at the center of his brain, which was worsening by the second. Harding had never experienced a migraine headache in his life, but wondered now if his number was up. *There's a first time for everything.* He rummaged through his pockets, finding only what he expected to be there—a few loose coins, car and house keys, and two rolls of LifeSav-Ahs. Wint-Oh-Green and Pepp-Ah-Mint. But nothing for his head.

"Fan-fucking-tastic. A house full of the NYPD's best and brightest investigators, and the coroner goes missing. You can't make this shit up. I bet Dennis Franz never had to deal with this bullshit."

Harding knew the pop-culture reference was dated, soaring right over the heads of the mostly youngish officers in his company, most of whom had probably never heard of either Dennis Franz or *NYPD Blue*, or knew why Franz's flabby rump made TV history back in the day.

"Sorry, Joe," a junior officer said. She appeared as confused as he was.

"Yeah, sorry, Joe," someone else said from the next room.

Harding rubbed at his temples.

Everything around him felt like it was slipping away from him, like it was in the future, and he was in the past, and the two timelines were growing further apart with every passing second. The corners of his vision blurred and darkened. His legs felt unsteady, as though he just stepped off the stool at O'Malley's Pub on 9th and 45th for the first time after hours of drinking.

This...isn't right. I...don't feel...good. She did something to me. That...Miller bitch. She got inside my head.

A sharp pain stabbed at his head. It almost knocked Harding right off his feet.

Fuck. She's still...in there...Goddamnit. Get. Out. Of. My. Head.

"Joe? You alright?" someone Harding couldn't see asked.

"Joe?"

Harding waved an unsteady hand and took a small step, stumbling as he took another step and then another, moving to the basement door.

"I'm fine! Fine," Harding shouted back. He knew he sounded intoxicated. The haphazard way he stumbled about the scene cemented the image of a drunk in the mind's eye of everyone there who witnessed it. *Fuck. Fuck.*

Harding stuck out his arms and held onto the wall like it was a life preserver. Before him, the basement stairs appeared steeper than they had been the last time he'd climbed them.

And, if Harding was correct, it seemed like the number of steps had doubled, maybe even tripled. Even more impossibly, they were moving. Not like an escalator in a predetermined, orderly manner. But moving in a wild, unpredictable way like steps in a video game.

He stood frozen at the top of the landing. A thin coat of sweat covered every inch of his body, and his legs felt as though they had been fitted with a custom pair of cement shoes by Capone & Co. out of Chicago. He wanted to take a step forward; he tried to do so, but his feet and legs wouldn't budge. *Stay put, fool. You know what's down there. Do you want to end up like—*

"Is that you up there, Detective?" Sandra Miller called to him. The song of the siren. Her voice sounded far closer in his ear that it should have given that he was upstairs, and she was tucked away somewhere in the basement. "Come on in. The water feels wonderful."

Harding told himself, come hell or high water, he was making it down those steps. She could do her worst, but he would do it just to spite her. She was a mere guest at his crime scene. Yes, he would make the descent—even if it killed him.

He reached out his right hand and grappled the banister. Then, repeated the action with his left hand. Harding guessed to the outsider he might look more like a guy who's terrified of heights trying to step onto a roller coaster platform than a seasoned NYPD Detective about to come face to face with an unspeakable evil.

One foot came off the ground. Harding's entire leg shook as he planted his foot on the first step. He laughed, feeling feverish all over, as sweat further blurred his vision. The salty perspiration stung his eyes, but he dared not wipe at them. Harding knew if he removed even one hand from the banister, he would go tumbling down those steps faster than Jason Miller in *The Exorcist.* He gritted his teeth and set his other foot on the first step.

With every step forward, five new steps appeared ahead of him. It took a few minutes, but soon Harding found himself in a steady rhythm, climbing down the never-ending staircase. But then, just when it felt like he was making progress and the ground was in sight, a dozen more steps would materialize, and Harding found himself back at the top all over again.

And then there was the shooting pain in his head. The closer he came to the bottom, the more intense the pain in his head grew. Harding was seeing stars behind his eyes. The botched root canal he'd endured a few years ago felt like a skinned knee in comparison. He didn't know anything could hurt like this.

Harding stopped, closed his eyes, and took a breath. Every nerve in his body crackled with electricity. This was killing him. He knew it, and yet he also knew he had to get to Sandra Miller. His gut told him to press on.

"Come now, Detective. You're so close." Sandra Miller stopped to cackle, then continued in the sultriest voice Harding had ever heard. "I'm so close, Detective. Don't stop now."

Harding pressed on. He kept his eyes tightly shut and just kept his feet moving, one after the other, climbing step after step after step.

There are only so many steps. There can only be so many steps. Eventually, I'll land on rock bottom.

And then, sure enough, after descending what must have been fifty thousand steps, Harding's feet finally landed on something solid. His heart raced in his chest, beating out a rhythm that'd give the fastest dance tracks a run for their money. He was drenched from head to toe in perspiration, and still sweating profusely, looking as though he'd taken a shower fully dressed in his work clothes.

But he'd made it to the bottom, to the basement, and he was still alive. For now, at least, he was still alive.

Harding reached into his pocket and fished out a fresh LifeSav-Ahs. It stuck to his clammy hand, staining his fingers white as he shoved it into his willing mouth. He opened his eyes just as the peppermint flavor flooded his mouth, hitting his system like a drug, and then Harding nearly choked on the small white candy as the gruesome sight of Andy West's severed head came into focus. He saw himself reflected in West's lifeless brown eyes, mouth twisted open in a silent scream, resembling the inspiration for Munch's famous painting.

Then, as if the nightmarish vision could not get any worse, West's mouth dropped open and moved as the bodyless head spoke. Harding stumbled back onto the steps. He landed hard, wincing as the small of his back instantly ached.

"Hello, Detective! Look what you made me do!"

The voice did not belong to the late Andy West, but to Sandra Miller, who had a hand shoved up into West's decapitated head and was operating it like a puppet. West's mouth opened and closed. His eyes darted to the left, and to the right, then up and then down. At one point, West's blood-stained tongue popped out, waggled, and then retreated into the dead man's open mouth.

"Hey! Joe! Know why my ex left me?" West's mouth froze, and his eyes appeared to bulge. "Because he said I had no HEAD game!"

"Jesus Christ," Harding shrieked, pressing himself tighter to the stairs, ignoring the soreness in his back.

West's tongue flicked like the tongue of a snake. "Whaddaya say, Detective? Want some good, sloppy, wet, jaw-dropping... head?"

Sandra Miller's head fell back against her shoulders, and, once again, her jaw stretched wider than humanly possible. A series of gurgles, snaps, crackles, and the occasional pop spilled out of Sandra's set of super-sized chompers.

Harding's hands clawed at the steps, digging in vain, until two of his fingernails cracked and broke off. Instinctively, they kept clawing as blood oozed out of the tips of his fingers.

Sandra's monstrous jaws flapped as a cackle that would have made the Wicked Witch of the West shit green filled the basement. Harding screamed, then his own mouth sealed up tighter than the financial books at the Vatican. His teeth dug into the soft, tender flesh of his tongue. Blood filled his mouth, the iron flavor not mixing well with the aftertaste left by the LifeSav-Ahs. Harding's feet thrashed and kicked at the air. In another instant, his head whipped to the side as a steady stream of puke decorated the steps, then slowly oozed down them, moving like the titular creature from *The Blob*.

Harding's sudden vomit-fest made Sandra laugh harder.

He wondered how no one upstairs had heard any of this. But then he remembered the absolute chaos of the scene, both inside and outside of the Miller House. When he'd arrived at the house, Harding thought the noise level had to be at least ten decibels above a KISS concert. And his ears still rang from time to time after he'd seen the Kabuki-clad foursome at The Garden. *The originals, before the two imposters stepped into those impossible to fill platform boots.*

This broad is gonna be the death of me.

In one movement, Sandra Miller made the distance that

lay between Harding and herself. She towered over him, straddling his body and the steps as though she were ready to fuck them both. In one hand, Sandra held Andy West's noggin by its matted hair. And she ran the other hand down the length of Harding's torso, making a beeline downtown.

"No, don't," Harding implored weakly. "Don't k-k-kill me."

Her serpentine tongue slithered out of her mouth and licked at the sides of Harding's sweaty, vomit-crusted face.

"Why on earth would I want to kill you, dear? This is only the beginning. I want to leave you with a little souvenir. Something to remember your good friend Sandra by."

Harding's frenzied eyes darted to West's head.

"Something else, I mean."

"Oh, god," Harding whispered. *There are no atheists in the foxhole.*

"I think it would be best if you closed your eyes for this part, Detective. It might get a little...messy."

Harding's eyes closed, and for a moment, he never wanted to open them again; never wanted to see the horrors that lay on the other side of the darkness.

West. Poor, poor Andy West. What the fuck am I going to tell his boyfriend? Steve? Or is it Brian?

"Don't worry about that now, Detective. I'll take care of everything. That's what friends are for, right?"

Get out of my head. Get out of my head. Get out of—

The pain felt exquisite as Sandra tore into his soft flesh, but Harding found he had no voice with which to scream. The house of horrors had taken it all from him. It had taken nearly everything Joseph P. Harding had to give, but not quite everything. Yet. There was still time for the house to take everything but the sweaty shirt off his back.

Harding's part would be recalled later, much later. Some sixteen years after the events at the Miller House on St. Augustine Place. Right around the time the plague virus— *SARS2-460N1*—hits. It will be ten times more contagious than COVID-19 and fifty-seven percent more deadly. And despite some promising early results, there will be no vaccine. Mankind's last stand against its greatest unseen, unknown enemy. And Joe Harding would be in the thick of it, fighting the good fight. Fighting again for his very life.

But today, back where it all began for Harding, the Miller House, the house of unspeakable horrors, he'd lose his pound of flesh. He'd squeak by with what remained of his life. Andy West wouldn't be so lucky. But, as promised, Sandra Miller saw to the late Andy West. The evidence would say that West blew his head off using his own firearm. Another casualty of the Miller House. Harding wouldn't have to face West's boyfriend, *ex-boyfriend,* or lie to the man's grief-stricken face.

The evidence tells the story.

But Harding would know differently. Detective Joseph P. Harding would always know the truth, and it would haunt him even more than the horrors of the Miller house itself. The truth would slowly eat away at his insides until no amount of Tums would take away the ache in his gut. The truth never stays buried for long. The best you can do is tuck it away some place in the back of your mind and forget about it for a while, until the day its undead hand comes a-knocking at your door, demanding its pound of flesh.

Harding would wait for it then. Wait patiently for his number to once again be called.

As he came in and out of consciousness, Harding watched as

Sandra expertly set the scene. She placed West's head and body in the perfect position to be consistent with a "self-inflicted gunshot wound to the head." Then, she tidied up after herself, careful to remove all trace evidence of Sandra Miller from the scene.

"It'll be like I was never here, Detective."

Harding groaned.

And later, no one, save for Joseph P. Harding, would ever recall Sandra Miller visiting the house of horrors.

"But you'll know. Detective. You'll always know, won't you?"

"Just...just..."

"Yes, Detective? Spit, don't swallow."

"Tell me one thing. Just tell me one thing."

Sandra straddled Harding's prone body at the bottom of the stairs. After she'd finished with him, Harding slithered down the steps like a Slinky until finally crashing to the floor, unable to move.

"If I can, certainly, Detective."

"How...how did you know?"

"How did I know what?"

"How did you know what was going on here?"

"Ahh. That."

"Cassie Miller came to physically check on Bill—"

Under her breath, Sandra whined, "Fucking mama's boy."

"—and the family when she got no response from repeated calls, texts, and emails. But you?"

"Yes?"

"But you never called. You never checked in. There's no record of you ever—"

"The game was my idea. A suggestion to my impressionable

niece. A test, really. As for the rest? What is it your lot always says? The simplest answer is usually the correct one."

She bent to his ear and kissed it gently.

"Happy trails, Detective Joseph Paul Harding. I'll be seeing you."

Sandra rose and turned to the steps, readying herself for the climb. But she froze dead in her tracks. The color in her face drained instantly. And Harding thought she trembled ever so slightly, and for a moment, her cockiness was gone, replaced with dread.

"You?"

Her voice sounded shrill. Shaky. *Afraid.*

Harding turned his head a couple of inches until he could just barely make out the shadowy figure standing at the top of the Miller's basement steps. It was a child. But the more Harding stared, the clearer the picture became, despite the figures on the landing wearing the darkness. There was not just one child up there, but two—one carrying the other.

A voice came from the top of the landing. A single worded response, sounding more sure, more determined than Harding expected. He trembled as the child roared—

"YOU."

As Sandra Miller raced up the steps as fast as her Jimmy Choos would allow, the figures disappeared. For once, it seemed someone was five steps ahead of her. He thought he heard something else, too. Harding thought he'd heard the child say "CROATOAN" just before Sandra tore ass up the stairs. But surely he'd misheard that.

"No, no, no!"

Those were the last exasperated words Harding heard from the Miller broad before she left his field of vision.

And as he lost sight of the back of Sandra's exotic vicuña coat and her ass, which Harding thought should have been shapelier given the woman's obsession with appearance, Harding saw something he'd missed before. Hiding right there in plain sight.

A camera mounted to the ceiling. No, *cameras*.

The simplest answer is the correct one.

She knew because she was watching them play the game.

Harding laughed despite the intense pain it caused him.

"I'll be seeing YOU, bitch."

Real soon.

Out, Damned Spock!

"Jesus Christ, did you just see that? Did everyone just fucking see that?" Imogen Rockwell screamed through her demented Velma Dinkley mask as she flicked pieces of brain matter off her shirt. Just then, she didn't care if talking or screaming was technically permitted or not. The rules didn't say.

Imogen went to cover the mask's twisted mouth when she realized the voice that spilled out of it was not her own. It didn't sound like anyone's voice, but rather it sounded like a flat, emotionless AI-produced voice—the kind that greeted everyone at checkout stands before the virus came; before most people started using expendable "shoppers" to brave the outside world while they stayed tucked safely inside their homes, safe from the poisonous air.

Imogen realized she might as well have been saying "paper or plastic, cash or credit" rather than screaming at the sight of the guy in the Mr. Spock mask's head being blown into more little pieces than a ten-thousand-piece jigsaw puzzle. It all came out of the mouth's mask sounding the same.

There's a voice changer in the mouth. Has to be. And some sort of localized detonator. Fuck. And why is...this mask...on so tight? It feels like it's constricting like a boa around my neck the longer I wear it. If the game doesn't kill me, the mask will...one way or another.

Imogen tugged at the mask, but it didn't give one bit. Instead, it seemed to cling even tighter to the whole of her head, like one of those "face hugger" critters from that old sci-fi flick, *Alien.* Oliver loved that movie. They'd watched it together a few times, even though it wasn't Imogen's cup of tea. She loved that Oliver jumped out of his skin every time that damned little space slug burst out of that dude's chest right in the middle of supper, blood soaking through the guy's pristine white tee shirt. *Because in space, no one wears dingy whites.*

Six of them were playing the game when it began.

Now that Mr. Spock was...out, only five players remained.

Imogen, aka "Velma Dinkley"; a pudgy blonde-haired Cabbage Patch baby doll, who looked as though it had been dumpster diving for most of its miserable life; a sunglasses and bandana-wearing Jimi Hendrix, whose face looked as though it had contracted pox and a side of some strain of flesh-eating bacteria; a mangy, fat orange cat Imogen assumed was Garfield, its beady eyes a dead giveaway. She noticed the fat cat was the only one wearing a full-body costume, complete with a scraggly tail, and not simply an acid-trip inspired pull-over mask on top of their head with over-sized navy-blue mechanic-style coveralls on the bottom. Imogen practically swam in hers, but she had to admit, they were pretty comfy.

And finally, last, but by no means least—

No...no fucking way is that supposed to be...nah, it can't be, but...is that—

Josh. Fucking. Groban.

I hate that fucking guy.

Josh Groban. Crooner extraordinaire, who despite a plague

celebrated his eighth consecutive year in residency at Vegas's former red-hot spot that was now barely lukewarm, The Swallows—whom everyone now just calls "She Swallows." It came to be known as the place has-beens go to take their dimming stars for one last hurrah; a place where geriatric fans are all too happy to fork over obscene truckloads of cheddar to gaze upon their former stars just one more time—even if said celebs were all way past their sell-by date and wrinkled beyond recognition. Just one last time...like the good old days...before their lights burned out.

There's no getting away from that guy. He's gonna follow my ass into the next life, warbling until my ears bleed.

Groban's droopy, dorky face was sculpted in all his constipated—*I really have to take a shit boys and girls, but let me just try and hit this one note first*—glory. It was really the only look the guy had in his toolbox. The only other semblance of a look was a dim, lights out and nobody's home kind of expression, which was probably close to true most of the time.

It didn't matter if it was a low note or a "high" note—he never really hit those ringing highs, just pretended the low ones were high ones—Joshy Baby always, *always,* appeared on the verge of pinching out a loaf in his Depends. And his one-foot-in-the-grave fans ate that shit right up, like a kid gorging on Halloween candy.

But like all the other nightmarish masks in the game, Josh's face had seen sunnier days. The terror etched in the crooner's bugged eyes told a different story, like whatever he was going to pass through his puckered-up bunghole was going to tear the little man apart. *Keep that hole puckered, Joshy, baby. Keep it puckered.*

"How did they know?" Imogen stammered, picking the last

little bits of Mr. Spock off her clothes. "How did they know he wasn't gonna do it?"

The others glanced at each other, shrugging in silence.

"But we shouldn't, like, lose our heads over this," Garfield purred. The voice came out squeaky and high-pitched, like the fat cat had just huffed on a helium balloon in a back alley in the dodgy part of town.

The small crowd booed.

"But, in earnest, I guess we know what 'out' means," Jimi Hendrix said, pointing out what had once been Mr. Spock's head but now looked more like Kibbles 'N Bits. His voice was low in tone and had a thick Asian-flavored accent. "Should we, I don't know, say a few words or cover him up?"

"Or her," Imogen corrected.

"Excuse me?" Jimi said.

"How do we know Spock—our Spock—was actually a 'he'? Could well be that our Mr. Spock was a Ms. Spock under the hood. We all sound...well, different. Altered. And these coveralls leave a lot to the imagination."

"Wow, you're like, so smart," Garfield said dreamily while pantomiming cleaning one of its bloody paws. Their Spock may not have traveled the galaxy, but his brain matter made it from one end of the kitchen to the other—and beyond—with ease.

"Don't be ridiculous. You're over-thinking it. As usual." The Cabbage Patch Kid squealed in a deep velvety baritone that could have easily once belonged to the long-departed soul singer, Barry White, who was now little more than soul food for carrion eaters. "Oh, my god. That's just sick. His head...oh my god. This whole thing is just...sick. Who's doing this to us?"

Behind their mask, someone coughed. Imogen thought it was little miss Cabbage Patch.

"I think you're asking the wrong question," Imogen said.

She stared at the timer mounted above the front windows in the living room that, like her twin bedroom windows, looked out at nothing. Nothing but the dark. There were only forty-five minutes remaining in this round of play. *The first round.*

Jesus Christ, this is only the first round.

So far, no one had completed the action dictated by their chosen card. Each player's chosen actions were kept secret from the other players. The cards had been arranged in six neat stacks on the kitchen table. One pile for each of them, indicated by a small neatly typed place card—the kind they used at fancy-ass soirees and dinner parties in the movies. Spock. Jimi. Cabbage. Garfield. Velma. Josh.

We'll only need five piles now.

When they first gathered in the replica Rockwell kitchen just over two hours ago, they'd shuffled about like a motley crew of middle-schoolers who otherwise didn't know each other from Adam but were forced to coalesce into a team and play a game of kickball by a wanna-be drill sergeant sporting a baseball cap, military-style dark sunglasses, matching track suit, and wearing a whistle around their neck like a solid-gold crucifix.

Another electronic sign hung on the opposite side of the kitchen. This one resembled a generic yellow "walk/don't walk" box. But instead of "walk/don't walk," this custom box had "talk/don't talk" imprinted on its square face. It had been asleep when they first gathered, but when the last of them—Josh, because...of course Josh—entered the kitchen, it woke instantly, flashing "don't talk" in red. And for over two hours, no one had spoken a word until Spock's head went boom.

At first, no one wanted to draw a card from their pile, but a sudden jolt under Jimi's mask got the party started. Their cards in hand, they could do little more than stare at each other dumbly from behind their masks, offer a weak wave, or a shrug, or both.

Imogen had done none of the above. She'd switched on that Ivy-League brain of hers and was taking apart the room in her head, looking for the seams, the inconsistencies. *The room's weaknesses...*because there had to be weaknesses.

And that's how she'd get out of the funhouse. It was a copy, and not even an exact copy. Worse, it was probably a lot like that Swedish So-Easy-To-Assemble-By-Yourself shit furniture that had been all the rage for a time—you know, in theory, Part A was supposed to line up perfectly with Part B, but it rarely did; not without a lot of extra blood, swearing, and tears—

Am I supposed to have this many screws left over?

—said moments before a set of bookcases came tumbling down.

But Imogen knew that somewhere in this fun house, some-where, they'd made a mistake in their calculations, and she was determined to find it. She had her Ivy-League brain on her side, not to mention her new ghost-friend, Alex Miller.

But she couldn't think about that, Alex Miller, not when the game still needed playing.

Imogen continued, "I think we should be asking ourselves, why *us*? This can't be random, us being here. Together."

"Oh, it's just like one big, bad dream," the grotesque baby doll said.

Garfield stopped cleaning itself long enough to add, "Or like a bad trip. It's like, I don't know, maybe we're all like just hallucinating. None of this is really happening."

"Doctors can have hallucinations, too," Joshy Baby said, more to himself than to the group.

I know that. I've heard it before. Somewhere—

Then it hit Imogen, where the line came from.

Invasion of the Body Snatchers.

The original. The black and white one. The version with Kevin McCarthy.

The one she'd seen a hundred times with her dad, Oliver.

Imogen was about to say *Dad?* when the yellow traffic box switched on and rudely flashed "don't talk."

"Well, shit," Garfield said. Then quickly added, "Sorry. It slipped out. Like, I'll stop talking now. I swear. Right now. Please don't like zap me or anything. For real."

The cat was referring to an instance earlier at the start of the game when the "don't talk" had been flashing and the Chatty Kathy in the baby doll mask could not zip her mouth shut. She'd got out two whole sentences before something in the mask appeared to jolt her quiet, like a shock collar for a yappy canine.

Now they all knew their masks could do a hell of a lot more than just zap.

They could also go BOOM. SPLAT.

As the clock ticked on, Imogen was sure of only two things:

Even without *seeing them,* Imogen positively knew the face behind the mask of three of the four remaining players, and she had to find a way for all of them to get out with their heads still intact.

But there were still forty-plus minutes of play left. *Just the first round.* And, unless she wanted to end up like Spock, she'd have to complete the action on her card—

Kill a player of your choice using only the frying pan from the kitchen.

Imogen hoped something would happen in the next forty-odd minutes to end the game. Even though the rules were very specific about how each turn was to play out, maybe the first round would be considered a draw on account of Mr. Spock's exploding head.

Not likely, but a girl can dream.

The stranger seemed the likeliest of victims, but Imogen couldn't see herself doing it. Just taking out a stranger who later might turn out to have been Chelsea Fucking Clinton. If she knew for certain that the real Josh Groban hid under one of these masks, it might make the choosing easier. But her gut told her Joshy Baby was on a bender preparing for his early evening show at She Swallows.

That left the fat cat, the baby doll, and the imposter Groban.

With only these options, the choice was obvious.

The fat orange cat. Garfield.

Yes, Garfield would have to go if it came to it.

There was no way she could take out Oliver and Janet.

But Ally…

After all, she'd killed Ally before, twice, and she'd brought her back.

Maybe, just maybe, *god forgive me*, she could do it again.

And if not, maybe it would buy them enough time for Imogen to find the way to get Oliver, Janet, and the potential Ms. Clinton out of the funhouse.

Smile for the Camera, Joe!

"What's up, Joe?" Vallance said as he slid up behind Harding.

In front of them, the house of horrors tempted, the *true* house of horrors in The Willows. The others were just a distraction. Harding knew it in his bleeding gut.

"This is it. This is the one," Harding muttered as parts of him went numb.

Yes, *this* was the house where the real game had been played, where someone had been *tested*. The fine, unshaven hairs on the back of his neck stood at attention as soon as he'd sidled up to the house's front walk. *One of these is not like the others. This is the one. This is* the *house.*

Beneath the sturdy veneer Harding constructed, his insides trembled. The other officers didn't know, but he did. He had no doubt what they'd find inside—cadaverous carnage, perversion, and inhuman cruelty.

And that was the point of it. Ostensibly, it looked like a game to the layman. A sick game devised by a mad genius. But underneath, it was a test. Harding knew it was because the Miller bitch had told him as much. *The game was my idea. A suggestion to my impressionable niece. A test, really.* The game at the Miller house had been a test for Mary Miller, and she had failed it spectacularly, reduced to a pile of spilled chunky soup.

That Mary Miller had lost the game and young Toby Miller had emerged from the home as the apparent victor came as something of a shock and delivered a Mike Tyson-sized blow to Sandra Miller's ego. She had slipped up. Misjudged, underestimated, and made a critical error. That the omniscient Miller bitch had been blindsided by a child, her nephew no less, was something Harding knew kept Sandra Miller up some nights. It kept him up too, but not for the same reasons.

Back when the Miller investigation still had a fresh coat of paint on it, Harding was sure he'd seen Toby Miller, clutching the presumed lifeless body of Alex Miller, at the top of the basement stairs. Somehow, Toby Miller slipped out of the house of horrors and evaded detection by the over hundred NYPD officers that had been on the scene—all the while cradling his dead sister's body. The whole thing felt like a dream, even now, all these years later. One moment Toby Miller had been there, and the next...holy David Copperfield, he'd up and vanished like a fart in the wind. And much like Sandra Miller, leaving zero trace evidence that he'd ever been there.

For some time, Harding thought he'd imagined it all. Or most of it. Members of the Miller family, Cassie Miller, and USPS worker Bob Buchanan had been massacred in some fashion and the Millers had by all accounts been playing a game that expedited their deaths. But Sandra Miller's serpentine tongue, West's head talking like a ventriloquist dummy, and Toby Miller's vanishing act...*Croatoan.* They all felt like a false memory, and the more time went by, the more jumbled the memories became.

But there were always the scars to remind Harding it had

been real. *She* had been real. The nosey neighbor, that Garriga woman, had written about it in her supposed tell-all book, *The Evil Next Door.* But she knew even less than Harding and Co. He felt she should have titled it *Well, Maybe* because it was two hundred and fifty pages of mainly just observations she'd made while stalking the family from behind her curtains, a few basic facts like—the Millers were dead—and then a lot of wild speculating. Harding thought the book wasn't fit to wipe his ass with.

The book came and went faster than most fads once the shock wore off, and she'd disappeared less than a year later. Went completely off the grid along with her husband after she'd lost her shit at a book signing. In the end, more people talked about the videos captured at the signing than they ever did about her book. That was the last Harding knew of her. He hadn't even thought about her until—

"Jesus, Joe. Looks like I picked the wrong week to quit sniffing glue," Vallance said quietly, almost with reverence, as they crossed the threshold of the house. The house that did not belong there.

Harding cracked a smile. It was a good tension breaker. "Ah, you finally watched it, huh?"

"Yeah. Pretty funny for an old movie."

Harding wanted to throttle Vallance's face for calling *Airplane!* an "old movie," even if it was just that. Christ, Harding had grown up watching that movie in the Asofsky's basement. *Gone With the* Fucking *Wind* was an old movie.

Instead, Harding just nodded. "Yeah, they'd never get away with half of those gags now."

"What a time to be alive, huh, Joe?"

"Indeed, it is." *Indeed, it is, but for how much longer?*

Harding stopped abruptly, Vallance nearly falling over him, as something tickled at his nostrils. His senses woke up, startled by something from the past. A fragrance. Something that screamed—

Sandra Miller.

Harding would recognize her unique scent anywhere. Even after all these years, the sense memory came flooding back to him. The ritzy perfume that she likely had made custom. The sweet and sour smell of her cigarette smoke. Even the aroma of that damned vicuña fur lingered in the air.

She's been here. The Miller bitch.

It had taken over a decade, but the past finally caught up to him. *She* had finally caught up to him. This time Harding knew he'd not let her get away. This time it would be game over for Sandra Miller if it was the last thing he ever did.

This broad is gonna be the death of me.

"You okay, Joe? What's up? You got something," Vallance whispered into Harding's ear.

"Yeah, maybe."

"What?"

"A ghost."

Vallance shook his head. "A what—"

"Has CSU been through at all yet?"

Harding listened as Vallance thumbed through several pages in his detective's notepad. "Um, yeah. Looks like they did a preliminary sweep. Cyber is still performing their initial sweep, as you requested. Sy's around here some place. Arrived about twenty, twenty-five minutes ago."

Harding approached what appeared to be a cat—an impossibly big, fat, shaggy orange cat—tucked behind the sofa and pressed against the wall. Only the closer he came to it, Harding knew it wasn't a cat. *I guess he was supposed to be the family dog, Joe.* It was what remained of an average-sized person wearing a cat costume. The head was gone. The mess on the wall, floor, and sofa told Harding a localized detonation device of some kind had blown it off.

Maybe Sy can find bits of the bomb in all that. Reverse engineer it. He's good, real good but...maybe no one is that good.

"How many?" Harding struggled to get out. "How many VICs?"

"Um," Vallance stopped to check his notes. "CSU says four so far. This one here, one in the kitchen, one in the powder room, and one upstairs in a bedroom."

"Four," Harding repeated, speaking the word out loud but saying it for himself to hear.

Harding knelt to inspect the remains of the costumed kitty. He gently pulled one of the VICs hands out of the jumper, freeing it from the material that made up a paw. The skin was smooth, tight, and wrinkle free. *Shit.*

"She's young. A juvie, most likely."

He tucked the hand back into the costume and set it down with care.

"Text Sy. Ask him about the cameras."

"Now, Joe? Shouldn't we let him do a pre—"

"Now, Vince. Do it now."

The grave tone of Harding's voice spoke loud and clear to Vallance.

"Yeah, sure. On it, Joe. Gimme a sec."

Vallance stepped away, clacking at his phone's small, glowing screen.

Harding inspected the room. A typical Vegas suburban living room. Nothing too out of place, except maybe the vinyl record player, which looked too new to be vintage or neo-vintage. After a brief resurgence in popularity about fifteen years ago, vinyl once again went the way of the dinosaur. They were about as rare now as tin ashtrays and realistic-looking cap guns.

But then something caught his eye. A flicker of light, almost like it came off a candle in the wind. It had been there for less than an instant, Harding was sure of it, and then it was gone. But he waited, sure it would be back. And a few seconds later, it was.

The light streamed from under a door tucked in the corner of the room. A coat closet, Harding assumed. He approached with caution, hand floating in the neighborhood of his service weapon.

"Hey, has anyone checked the—"

Suddenly, a fit of deep, chesty coughs came from the other side of the closet door. At first, Harding was rooted in place. A mix of adrenaline and fear. But then, he sprang into action and was at the door faster than a jackrabbit. He unclipped the revolver, taking it into one of his trembling hands. On the other side of the door, the coughing fit raged on.

"Hey! Hey," Harding shouted over his shoulder. His commanding voice momentarily stilled all other activity. "Get me a paramedic. ASAP. Vince! VINCE!"

Vallance ran to Harding's side. "What do you got, Joe?"

"A live one."

A wave of energy pulsed through the room. Hushed tones and muffled chatter on the radios followed. *A live one!* Someone in the next room shouted out an open window to send over the paramedics. *Priority one.*

"Vince?"

"Yeah, Joe?"

Harding's heart raced in his chest. His breathing was excited. Accelerated. "Cover me."

Vallance unsheathed his weapon. "Got you, Joe."

Harding nodded. "On three?"

"On three, Joe."

Harding swallowed, then licked at his lips. He gripped the knob in his clammy hand. The metal felt cool on his burning hot skin. "One..."

But you'll know. Detective. You'll always know.

"...two..."

This is only the beginning.

The pounding in Harding's ear was deafening. A trickle of sweat dripped down his forehead as the coughing fit worsened.

I'll be seeing you, Detective.

"...THREE! Go!"

"Go, Joe!"

Harding turned the knob and nearly tore the door off its hinges.

"Do not fucking move! Hands where I can see them!"

Coughing, followed by a muffled, "Don't shoot! Don't shoot!"

Harding's gaze lowered to the closet floor. "Show me your hands!"

"Jesus, fuck," Vallance cried. "Is that a fucking Cabbage Patch Kid, Joe?"

The baby doll coughed. "Joe? Detective Joseph P. Harding?"

The voice was female. Strained, from the coughing most likely, but an adult female. One with which Harding was not formerly acquainted. *But she knows me.*

Harding turned his head to Vallance. "Medics now."

Vallance eyed Harding curiously

Harding mouthed the words *she's got the virus.*

"Shit. Right," Vallance said before returning his weapon to his side and hauling ass out of the living room, and right out the front door.

Harding studied the Picasso-inspired baby doll mask. The woman's hands shook faster than a Ferrari. They were covered in a thin layer of perspiration. *Fever.* And there, between her legs on the floor, the source of the flickering light—a portable self-powered broadcast cam. A red light pulsed on its top, indicating it was both on and sending video out to a feed.

Not seeing a weapon, Harding housed his revolver as he leaned to the costumed woman on the floor of the closet.

"I'm Detective Joe Harding. And you are?"

Under the mask, the woman breathed heavily. "Janet. Janet Rockwell."

"Well, I'm glad to meet you, Ms. Rockwell. What—"

"She...she...," Janet began before she was seized by a violent coughing fit.

Damn, virus or vax?

Harding reached to Janet's head, to the grotesque mask covering her face.

"No, Detective! Leave it! Leave it on. I beg you."

Harding's hands rose up in surrender.

"It's...the virus. I have it," Janet said solemnly. "I think. I also got...the shot. So, it could be that."

"Okay, but either way, help is coming."

Beneath the mask, Janet laughed without a stitch of humor. "No one can help me now, Detective Harding. I was a goner before any of you got here."

Harding didn't know what to say. He knew Janet was right;

the reaper was coming for her any second now, but he didn't want to sound rude or insensitive.

"It's alright, Detective. Just...just...get my daughter back, okay?"

"Your daughter?"

Harding leaned in closer, hoping the novelty mask would protect him from her rotten air.

"Imo...Imogen. Imogen Rockwell. She's...she's not..."

Janet coughed. Something wet splashed against the mouth of the mask.

Blood.

"She's not what, Janet? Who took her?"

Janet coughed up her lungs a few more times until the fit eased up enough for her to talk again. "She wasn't mine. I didn't birth her. We...we...adopted. Oliver and I. I...I couldn't conceive. She was...was...my own little...Cabbage Patch Kid."

She laughed before another round of wet coughs silenced her.

Harding waited for it to pass, looking over his shoulder for the paramedics, who were still nowhere in his sight.

"Imogen. That's a real nice name, Janet."

"There's...there's someone else here, Detective Harding... someone else...in the house," Janet murmured. "Not...not playing...the game."

Harding moved in closer to the abstract nightmare mask. "Who's here, Janet?"

She wheezed and coughed. Harding winced, hoping he was in that ninety-seven percent effective rate for the shot, but remained rooted in place.

"I think it's a...a...ghost. I know how that must sound, Detective Harding. But...but I'm not crazy."

Something shivered up Harding's spine. Anticipation. He knew what was coming next.

"Imo...Imo...Imogen called her Alex."

Fuck me. She's talking about Alex fucking Miller.

The woman attempted to speak but gurgled and heaved instead.

Blood. And a lot of it by the sound.

"Who took her, Janet? Who took Imogen?"

Janet's voice was lost under a series of coughs, cries, and chokes. She tapped a sweaty finger on the surface of the camera. Harding picked up the camera and turned it to his face, seeing himself reflected in its shiny lens.

Behind the mask, there came a low laugh that began more like a growl. Slowly, the growl turned to a laugh, which became a cackle. A blood-curdling, pulse-pounding, nerve-racking cackle. Harding knew it at once—

It was the kind of a cackle that would have made the Wicked Witch of the West shit green. Sandra Miller.

Harding dropped the camera as he stumbled backwards.

"Sandra?"

"I thought you'd be happier to see me, Detective," Sandra Miller's voice came through the locked lips of the mask.

Harding's hand went to his weapon. He fumbled, not able to get a solid grip on its handle. Finally, after what felt to Harding an eternity, he had the barrel of the gun pointed squarely at the Cabbage Patch Kid's head.

"Smile, Detective Harding. You're on Candid Camera."

"Sandra Miller, freeze!"

The mask's eyes pulsed red as something beeped, slowly and steadily, under the hood of the mask. Soon, the beeping accelerated until it was just one long, uninterrupted tone. But the mask's red eyes kept on flashing frantically as though they were screaming.

"I'll be seeing you, Detective."

Harding, who by now realized what was coming, dodged to the ground, and rolled out of the way—

"Tell Imogen I love her. I've always loved her."

Janet's own voice, and not Sandra Miller's

—a split second before Janet Rockwell's head went BOOM and exploded all over the closet. Harding thought he saw an eyeball roll down the hallway, while something that might have been a stiff upper lip landed at his feet.

Paramedics rushed in, finally. Vallance trailed close on their heels.

"Joe!" Vallance hollered as he crept to Harding's prone body.

"There's a girl. A daughter," Harding began, stopping to dust bits and pieces of Janet off his jacket. "We have to find her. Imogen Rockwell. That's how we end this."

Twenty steps ahead.

"Once and for all."

Harding took a breath and made his way through the scrambling emergency personnel, who were already too late to the party, and walked out onto the front porch where the scene felt less chaotic at the very least. And, if he wasn't mistaken, there may have even been a slight, *very* slight, breeze in the air tonight. He'd take it, no matter how weak it was blowing.

He was sweating like a pig, and he knew it. His face felt like it had been dipped in a baptismal basin. And Harding didn't give a fuck about trying to conceal it. To his way of thinking, at least he hadn't lost his breakfast, lunch, and dinner on the front lawn. He still had that going for him.

Harding dabbed at his face with a napkin that reeked of takeout deliciousness that he'd found folded and tucked in his back pocket. It was a futile task for something so flimsy, and paper-thin, but Harding kept at it until the little napkin was nothing more than a ball of soggy nothingness. He squeezed it in his palm, surprised how much liquid spilled out onto his shoe. Then, he tossed it somewhere ahead of him, toward the street, but where it landed exactly, Harding couldn't say. Something else had caught his eye.

Son of a bitch.

The thing he saw, the impossible thing, stood at the end of the drive. It smiled and gave a small wave of recognition. Harding looked around, convinced he had lost whatever sanity he still had left in his hard head, but no one else seemed frazzled by the sight of Andy West, the very dead Andy West, standing calmly at the end of the drive, holding his own severed head in one hand, and waving with the other. It was the smile on West's face that really got under Harding's skin.

She defiled that head. Used his head like it was a puppet. The Miller bitch. And now, here it is once again, smiling at me.

Just then, someone rushed out of the house and pushed past Harding. It nearly scared the literal shit out of him.

"Jesus Christ. It blew her whole fucking head off," the EMT said before finding a spot on the front lawn that had not been vomited upon and proceeding to let her rip.

Harding raised his eyebrows to the EMT, who looked back between chunky bursts, as if Harding's bushy brows could say *hey pal, you should see the fucked-up shit I've seen.*

"Hey! Hey, Joe," West called, waving his free arm frantically in the air. "Joe!"

Harding resisted as long as he could, but then made eye

contact with the deceased coroner.

"Joe! Does this head made me look fat?"

Same old West.

Harding responded with a literal eye roll and then walked to join the grinning apparition at the end of the walk.

"What...," Harding began, then looked around. He definitely did not want to be seen talking to himself on the job. That's the first step in a long series that ended up in one place—the funny farm, which wasn't so funny. When Harding was sure the coast was clear, he continued. "What are *you* doing here, West?"

West tisked. "I knew you'd forget."

"Forget what?"

Then, West said, in a put-on and over-the-top ghostly voice. "I've come, Joseph P. Harding...to...take you shopping."

Harding nearly pissed himself in relief.

"Really? I thought you'd like this." Harding indicated his soiled shirt. "It's Armani."

"Hmm. Let me...just..." West's arm brought his head closer to Harding to inspect the shirt. "Yeah...it's a knock-off, Joe. Sorry. Nice try, though."

"Thanks, I think." Harding laughed, and then steered back to business. "What're you doing here, West? Not that I'm not happy to...see you."

"It's awkward, isn't it? I told him it would be awkward."

Harding nodded. "It's a little awkward, yeah."

"We've been—"

"We?" Harding interrupted, but the ghostly visitor ignored him and continued on as though Harding hadn't just asked a question.

"—watching you, Joe. A long time. And now that you

remember everything, he thinks you might be ready to know the rest. So, if you think you're up for it, if you think you can handle it, there's something he wants to show you."

Harding swallowed hard. *Who?* He retrieved a Tums and popped it into his mouth, missing the minty flavor of the LifeSav-Ahs candies. *Show me what?* His teeth chomped at the chalky calcium carbonate fake candy and swallowed the broken bits whole.

"Yeah? Who wants to show me something, West? And what is it they want to show me?"

"You know who, Joe," West said, sounding gravely serious for the first time. "Go see for yourself. It will blow your mind."

Harding noshed at the last bits of the stomach soother still lingering in the corners of his mouth. "Ok, I'll bite. Thrill me."

"You know where to go," West said as he pointed a finger toward The Willows' main entrance gates. "Time to go home, Harding."

And there—beyond the gates, beyond the sirens and the emergency responders, beyond the looky-loos and the press—its ghostly visage beckoned in the dark of the desert night. Rising out of the sand, standing where no other homes stood. The Miller House. The House of Horrors.

Harding approached. He didn't have enough Tums in his pocket for this, so whatever he had on hand would have to do. The closer he got to the Miller House, the further away everything else felt. He looked over his shoulder and The Willows was nothing but a pinpoint of light miles away. And yet, he'd only been walking a minute or two—at most.

He walked up the drive, headed for the porch, and stopped as the front door opened. Harding didn't know who he expected to see on the other side—the thing that was Sandra Miller, Grandma Miller hanging from a bloody set of antlers, or the pile of sludge that once was Mary Miller?

His mouth went dry, and his heart skipped about a dozen beats as the shadowy figure in the doorway slowly came into view. He recognized the eyes at once, from years of staring at old Miller family photos. *Old eyes. An old soul.*

It was none other than Toby Miller, grown up.

"Hello, Detective."

Make It Stop!

Imogen Rockwell thought about getting the frying pan out of the kitchen pantry and smashing in someone's face with it. If she thought it would end the stupid game outright, she'd do it—gladly. But she knew it wouldn't end anything. The alarm would only sound when the round ended, whoever was left would have to draw another card, and they'd sail into round two. Then round three, then...for however long it took until one person was left alive. Or maybe by the end, they'd all just refuse to play and watch as each of their heads popped like water balloons.

Tick tock, tick tock...

Everyone felt it. The passing minutes felt heavy. Somebody would have to make a move soon. Someone would have to do something, or they were all going to die in less than thirty minutes.

Tick tock, tick tock...

For twenty minutes, they all stood around, gawking at each other wordlessly in a communal state of shock. Someone, maybe Joshy Baby, had put a sheet over Spock, but the image was still there; a sheet couldn't erase it from their stored memory banks. No one said anything as Spock's headless torso was covered up by a cheap store-brand bed sheet. What was there to say? *Sorry, you should have just played the game. At least the sheet is clean. Live long and prosper. Happy trails, Mr. Spock.*

Imogen wasn't positive, but every time she got closer to Jimi, she thought she heard muffled sobs underneath the mask. She was surprised Jimi's mask hadn't zapped its wearer for a show of emotion, no matter how muted. Although shows of emotion were not specifically forbidden in the rules, Imogen thought they were not encouraged either. The zaps came on like cattle prods, to keep the meat in line. Since Spock's head went BOOM, the cattle had behaved good as gold, better even. The house was so quiet the gentle hum of the HVAC came out more like the roar of an electric guitar.

Everyone was quiet except for Jimi.

Imogen wondered if, though they seemed strangers to her, Mr. Spock and Jimi Hendrix weren't *acquainted* with each other. Something had to give them away to each other, in the same way Imogen thought she had positively identified Ally, Janet, and Oliver. Their little tics and speech patterns revealed who they were, despite the technological interference.

Maybe it was the same for Jimi and Spock.

She thought again about her action card—

Kill a player of your choice using only the frying pan from the kitchen.

Fuck that. No.

Imogen decided she wasn't playing this stupid game anymore. Even though there were plenty of times she'd wanted to bash Ally's head over the years, she couldn't see herself actually going through with it—even under these fucked up circumstances. Ally was a pain in the ass of the highest order, but she was Imogen's pain in the ass. They had a shared history. *I killed her twice.* A long history. *And I brought her back. Twice.*

And there was no way she could just bang some unknown rando's head into tomorrow, either. Janet and Oliver's heads were both similarly off the table for banging. The only head banging Imogen would be doing in the foreseeable future was some banging of her own noggin to some righteous death metal. The next time she ventured into the living room, Imogen would have to check the vinyl to see if her favorite record had been copied—Dakotah Dark's *Midnight Offerings.*

"That's it," Imogen said. "I'm not playing this stupid game."

She reached into the top pocket of her coveralls and rummaged until her fingers found the action card she had tucked there at the start of the round. *This is just the first fucking round.* She drew it out and tore into it until it was in almost as many pieces as Spock's head.

"I'm not killing anyone. You hear me? I'm *not* killing *anyone*," Imogen yelled as she threw the torn pieces of her action card high into the air. It came down like an early snowfall as Imogen stormed out of the kitchen.

Jimi, Joshy Baby, Garfield, and the ugly Kid followed, hot on her heels.

"But you have to. *We* have to play," the Cabbage Patch Kid stammered, stopping only to cough once. Then twice. "The rules are clear. Do you want to end up 'out' like that, that, that—"

"I don't know. I think like he's called Mr. Spock or something. Maybe Dr. Spock," Garfield said, sounding almost as uninterested as you'd expect the fat orange cat to be in the proceedings.

"Mister. It's Mister. Everyone knows that," Imogen said. Her temper bubbled to the surface. "Doctor Spock was some whack job flower child who wrote a bunch of highly inaccurate books about raising children. Fucked up an entire generation."

"I don't know about that," the Cabbage Patch Kid grumbled. "My mother read Dr. Spock, and I think I—"

"I rest my case," Imogen said before the ugly Kid could finish. "Look, I'm not playing along with this sadistic shit. I'm not a murderer."

"Is that… is that what your card told you to do? Kill one of us?" Joshy Baby piped up from the back of the room.

The ugly Kid coughed again.

"Yep." Imogen emphasized the "p" for dramatic effect.

"Who?" Jimi asked.

"That's the best part. Dealer's choice." Imogen pointed to herself, then turned her hands into finger guns and fired blindly at the crowd.

"I bet it was me. I mean, like, *if* you were gonna do it. I bet you were gonna pick me," the fat cat said from the couch, where it had begun lazily lounging as cats do.

Imogen made a zipping motion over her mouth, then threw away the invisible key.

"Haha. Bitch, I knew it was me," Garfield said. "I still love you, though. I'd have killed me, too. Just so you know. I'm dispendible."

Imogen laughed. "Not a word!"

"No, it was *me*," Jimi said. "I'm guessing you all know each other. Yes?"

Imogen, Joshy Baby, Garfield, and the Cabbage Patch Kid looked at each other, but no one spoke right away.

"I think I know who all of *you* are," Imogen said, indicating

Joshy Baby, Garfield, and the Kid. She turned to Jimi. "But I don't know *you*. I don't think—"

"Don't you, though?" Jimi said.

"Ha, I knew it. You reek of TK-1, Imo. I can smell you like a mile away," Garfield aka Ally giggled.

"No, I don't know you," Imogen said.

"What about Agnes...Mr. Spock? Did you know her?" Jimi said as he moved closer to Imogen. "Think."

"Ding! Ding! Ding! Give the girl a prize. Imo, you called it. Mr. Spock *was* a Ms. Spock. Maybe a Mrs. Spock. Holy shit." Garfield laughed as she cuddled a throw pillow.

"Agnes? That was her name?"

"Yes. Did you know her, Imogen?" Jimi pressed. "Think. Think real, real hard now."

Beneath her Velma mask, Imogen closed her eyes. "Agnes... Agnes...Agnes?"

Think real hard now.

"Stop this. Now," the Kid growled. She might have said more, but she was silenced by a cough.

Agnes...Agnes...Agnes...

Think real hard now.

Tick tock, tick tock...

"Pumpkin?" Joshy Baby sounded worried.

"Earth to Imo. Come in, Imo," Garfield shouted from the sofa. "This fucking mask is so itchy. Is anyone else itchy? I need to take this off. Like now. This itch...is gonna..."

She tugged at the mask. It didn't budge. So, she tugged harder. Then, harder and harder, until finally it gave just the slightest bit. Ally felt a rush of cool air as she made a fresh gap between her skin and the mask.

"This itch is gonna fucking KILL ME!"

It all happened so fast.

First, the cat's bulging eyes went red. The LED lights embedded in the eye slits turned on and flashed in rapid succession. From inside the mask, Ally did not see the flashing eyes. But she heard the warning alarm ringing inside the mask. Everyone in the room did, too. No, not a warning alarm, but a....

"Ally! No! Don't," Imogen screamed. She went to run to the couch but was tackled by Joshy Baby. They fell hard onto the living room carpet. Joshy Baby grunted through the mask as his knee slammed right into a corner of the coffee table.

... a countdown.

After five piercing warning sounds, the fat cat's eyes burned so bright they hurt to look at. Jimi turned away, and the Kid instinctively covered her head as she dropped and crawled to Joshy Baby and Velma just as—

Ally's head went BOOM!

Splat.

Her body rolled off the couch and fell into the compact cavern between the wall and the sofa, wedging itself there perfectly.

"Ally! Fuck! No. No. No. Ally," Imogen screamed into Joshy Baby's chest as he pulled her closer to him. "ALLY!"

Joshy Baby groaned as he tried to bring them both to a standing position. The pain in his knee stabbed him worse than he'd expected. He turned to the Kid, motioning.

"Take her."

The Kid drew Imogen into her arms, trapping her there, and then moved her away from Joshy Baby and the blood-soaked scene. Bits of Ally dripped down the wall as the sofa swallowed up her blood like a sucking baby.

"Come, Imo. Come," the Kid said softly, fighting back the need to cough. She looked back over a shoulder to Joshy Baby. "You alright, dear?"

He laughed. "All things considered, yes. I'm fine. The coffee table doesn't belong there. It's too close to the couch."

"It's bigger than ours," Imogen said between sobs.

"What?"

"That table. It's bigger than ours. That's why you hit into it. Everything is just a little off."

Joshy Baby turned back to examine the table. "Well, I'll be."

"Oh, Ally," Imogen said. "My stupid fucking Ally Cat."

Ally Cat.

It just came out. Imogen hadn't called her "Ally Cat" since they were eight or nine years old. It was a nickname she grew out of, to be replaced with more age-appropriate monikers like "slut-face," "ho-bag," and "mouth4hire."

Jimi stepped into the tight circle that was Joshy Baby, the Kid, and Velma—aka Oliver, Janet, and Imogen. The Rockwells.

"I know this isn't the best time for this, but the clock *is* ticking. We have ten more minutes until the first round is over. And then? Who knows," Jimi said, his tone sounding nice and easy, like a John Denver tune. *Country roads...*

Imogen checked the electronic screen. Jimi was right. They were running out of time.

Tick tock, tick tock...

"What was your action?" Imogen asked Jimi.

"Excuse me?"

"On your card. What was your action?" Imogen clarified.

Jimi laughed. "I had none. My card was blank."

"Wait, yours too?" Joshy Baby asked.

"Mine was blank too," the Kid said.

"I don't understand. This is just...just...so fucked up. So, basically, you all were supposed to just, like, let me kill one of you? Do nothing to stop me? Do nothing, period?"

Jimi nodded. "That's the game, Imogen. It's not about me, or Oliver or Janet. It's all about—"

"Me," Imogen finished. "This has all been about me, hasn't it? Right from the beginning."

Jimi nodded again. "Agnes. Tell me about Agnes, Imogen."

Think real hard now.

Tick tock, tick tock...

"I don't...I just don't know an Agnes."

Think harder. Now.

"Agnes...it rings no bells. I'm sorry." Imogen sighed, frustrated with herself and with the game. "Who is...I'm so sorry. Who *was* she?"

The Kid tugged at Imogen's arm. "Don't do this. Not now. Don't do this."

"Janet," Joshy Baby implored.

"No, Oliver. No. I won't let this happen here. Not *here.*"

The Kid tugged more forcefully at Imogen's arm as though she could drag Imogen somewhere else, somewhere safe, somewhere far away from this house—

—*of horrors.*

"Janet. Baby?"

By now, the Kid sobbed uncontrollably underneath her latex mask.

Tick tock, tick tock...

"It's time. She needs to know. It's okay. We knew this day would come."

Joshy Baby looked at Jimi and gave a slight nod. The Kid let go of Imogen's arm and ran out of the living room. Her heavy footsteps resounded up the stairs. Then, a door slammed shut.

Joshy Baby leaned down to Imogen's head, and with their masks separating skin from skin, he kissed her forehead.

"I'll be right back. Let me go check on your...on Janet."

And then it was just Jimi and Imogen. They stared each other down like two gunslingers at high noon. The electronic screen began a loud tick with each passing second.

Tick tock, tick tock...

There were now less than ten minutes left in the first round.

Jesus Christ. The first fucking round.

"Agnes? Who was she?" Imogen finally asked, ending the silent standoff.

"She was your mother. Your *real* mother."

Do you ever feel like you don't belong? Do you feel alone even when surrounded by friends and family? Do you ever think that you were meant to be somebody else? That you are, in fact, someone else. Do you have questions, the kind that keep you up all night staring at the stars? This is the Gemeo Project. Are you ready to begin your journey?

"Agnes Miller."

The Final Interlude: The Miller Family Curse

Agnes Miller was stunned. The news wasn't what she had expected, or what she had prepared herself to receive. At first, she thought it was a mistake. It had to be. What they were saying just wasn't possible. All the doctors since she was twelve had said the same thing—

Her soil was bad.

Inhospitable for life.

Barren.

And there wasn't a thing anyone could do about it.

That's how these things go.

Wasn't meant to be, I guess.

A damned shame. You're a fine-looking woman. Smart, too. Your kids would've been something.

No reason you can't adopt.

Plenty of men out there don't want kids. Get yourself one of those.

You're an auntie, correct? Your brother and his wife have a bit of a brood, don't they? Denise used to be a patient of mine. But then her employer had to switch providers. Ah, what can you do? Focus on being the best auntie you can be. You'll forget all about wanting one for yourself. And I think you'll find they're a lot less messy that way, too.

Yes, Agnes Miller's "woman doctors" shared a lot of opinions over the years concerning her barrenness. But none could ever explain it. The *why* of it—why was her body born incompatible with motherhood?

Some things just...are the way they are. It's god's plan, my dear.

Agnes Miller had wanted to slap the smirk right off that arrogant OB-GYN's face and shout at the top of her lungs—*fuck god's plan!* But she did no such thing.

Instead, she turned down the flame of her rage, from boil to slow simmer, and made an anonymous call to the board saying that old Doc Greene had touched her inappropriately during her last four exams.

It wasn't *entirely* a lie. The old Doc's fingers had lingered longer in parts they shouldn't have lingered once during her last four visits, but did it really matter at that point? Once, twice? Who can be sure? Behind the mask, who could say for certain that the old Doc wasn't salivating like a starving man every time he gazed upon a patient's cooter. No, *her* cooter, because hers was surely the prettiest of them all.

It had been old Doc Greene's successor, Dr. Simms, who delivered the miraculous news, after a fumbled explanation about Doc Greene's sudden "retirement." Agnes Miller couldn't help but smile while Dr. Simms fell over his own feet trying to account for Doc Greene's sudden disappearance and his name being unceremoniously removed from the sign.

She could have thrown Simms a life preserver, but it was more fun watching the sweaty man do the doggy paddle in the middle of a tsunami.

"But that doesn't change the fact that all of us are here for you every step of the way in your miraculous journey." *Click the sparkling tree graphic to begin your journey.* "And I know I speak for everyone in the office, past and present, including old Doc Greene himself, when I say congratulations. You're going to be a mother, Agnes Miller."

"A what now?" was all Agnes Miller could manage as the shock stunned her dumber than Eric Trump.

Simms laughed one of those loud, fake laughs that Agnes detested. It turned up the flame of her rage just a notch.

Maybe another anonymous phone call to the board...

"A mother, Mom! Whip out the cigars and champagne because Agnes Miller, come on down, you're pregnant! About seven weeks, give or take. So, no cigars or champagne for you."

Yes. Another phone call was definitely in order.

"But...that's impossible."

Seven weeks.

Simms did that tedious fake laugh again. Agnes's temper turned up two notches for that insult.

"I don't know about that, Agnes, because your baby is saying 'I'M POSSIBLE'."

Damn it all. I'm just going to choke the cocksucker right here.

Agnes Miller did not strangle her obstetrician, nor did she report him to the medical board for his insultingly fake laughter. But she did flip off Little Mz. Perky Sugartits, the office's current grossly under-qualified eye-candy, on the way out after she made the mistake of saying *have a nice day, MOM!*

The drive home had been a long one, longer than usual. Agnes drove past her exit on the Cross County Parkway and kept driving until she realized her gaffe in Hartford. She might have kept trucking all the way to Maine, but that pesky little gas light came on and roused her from her somnambulist driving.

Good god. Hartford? Do they pump gas for you in Connecticut? I'm liable to get shot if I get out of the car to "fill 'er up." Ick, what a god-forsaken spot. Hartford. At least it's not Staten Island.

Agnes found a nice man to fill up her tank while she waited comfortably in the car—with the engine still running, just in case. He'd refused the tip when she offered it to him, saying something about it being a pleasure to help out a damsel in distress.

A damsel? In distress? Who does he think I am? Lois Fucking Lane?

She wanted to flip him off as she sped away, leaving the shit stain that was Hartford, Connecticut in her rearview, but Agnes just smiled and said *my hero* in the driest of voices. She didn't know why she was the way she was. Quick to anger. Her rage was always simmering just below a boil. It didn't take more than a piece of lint on her favorite skirt or a hair out of place in her professionally sculpted do to turn up the flame, and simmer quickly became boil over.

Anger. Resentment. Bitterness.

Those were Agnes Miller's three favorite flavors, mixed to make the perfect shit sundae with her barrenness the cherry on top. She'd have to remove the cherry now, on account of her current "condition." Who knows, in five years, maybe ten, she'd replace that cherry with "motherhood" because wasn't that what most women did—complain first about not having kids, then complain about them after they'd arrived?

But why am I like this? Tens of thousands of dollars later, and the best any shrink could come up with was that Agnes Miller had "mommy issues." *Pfft. Billy's got the mommy issues.* She used to call him "Norman," after cinema's favorite mama's boy, Norman Bates. They'd all teased him mercilessly about the way Cast-Iron Cassie doted on brother Billy. *Maybe it's because he's the only boy? Maybe it's because he's really adopted? Maybe it's because he's secretly an alien that looks human?*

The Miller girls had a lot of theories, fewer answers, and a growing resentment towards Mama Miller and her darling Billy Boy. Little by little, Agnes Miller distanced herself from the family, starting with a truckload of extra-curricular activities in high school that kept her dance card full seven days a week. She'd gone away to college, because of course she did. And went as far away from home as she could—the University of Alaska Anchorage.

Ha, let's see you ask me to come home on the weekends and holidays now.

She loved the experience of being away from the rest of the Miller clan and thrived in Anchorage. For the first time in her life, she did not feel strangled by Cast-Iron Cassie's fierce gaze. Agnes had a large circle of friends, was considered popular, and was even well-liked among her peers and neighbors. The simmering rage, like everything else in Anchorage, seemed to cool. For a brief time, Agnes Miller thought she'd live out the rest of her days in Anchorage. Far from the rest of the Millers. Far from Mama Miller.

But the family business called her home.

Billy had delivered the bad news. Car accident. Julie Anne had died instantly.

Oh, that's terrible. How's Franklin—her husband, now widowed-husband—*holding up?*

It was a stupid question. Everyone knows it's a stupid question, but still we go on asking it as if the answer is ever going to be anything less than *oh, they're broken up about this, I'll tell you what.*

"About as you'd expect, Aggie," Billy had said.

The silence between them told Agnes there was more to it. "Billy?"

He exhaled on the other end. "I'm still here, Aggie."

"What is it you're not telling me? There's something else. I can feel it. What is it?"

After a long, drawn-out pause, Billy finally said, "Sandra."

As if that one word, that single name, was enough of an explanation. But Anchorage Agnes had been out of the game for a long time. It would take more than that to fill in the blanks.

"Sandra...was killed too? She was driving the car when it happened? What? I'm confused here. Give me something more, Billy."

For a moment, it sounded like the line went dead, a regular occurrence in Anchorage. But Agnes thought she still heard Billy's quiet inhalations and exhalations on the other end.

"Billy?"

He held his breath, then slowly let it out with a whispered, "Sandra...was in the car, Aggie. She walked away without a fucking scratch. Jules' car was totaled. But Sandra...not a fucking wrinkle in that damned vicuña coat of hers."

"Oh, Billy."

"Remind you of anything?"

Dad.

They simultaneously had the thought, but neither said the word out loud, like uttering it might summon Old Scratch himself. All the whispers they shared with Jules behind closed doors about Sandra and the accident that killed their father came flooding back to her.

"There's more, but..."

"But?"

"Not on the phone, Aggie." He sounded positively paranoid. "She could be listening."

She?

Sandra.

"Alright, Billy. I'm coming home."

He released a huge sigh of relief.

"Good. Good. Aggie?"

"Yes, Billy?"

"Don't tell anyone you're coming."

"Can I at least tell Charlie?"

"Who's Charlie?"

"My husband, Billy. Charlie is my husband."

Had been for going on ten years now.

"You're married?" Billy laughed into the phone, but it was not a humorous one. "Well, congratulations, Aggie. Does Ma know?"

Agnes hesitated to answer, unsure why. Finally, she said, "Yes, I...think so. I didn't tell her, but she sent a gift."

"I look forward to meeting him. Bring him. I don't care how. Remember, don't tell anyone in the family you're coming. It's not safe. Just come straight to my house after you land. You still have the address?"

He knew she did. Agnes sent holiday greetings and birthday presents to the kids every year. It was more his passive-aggressive way of saying *you should have visited sooner.*

"Yes, I have it. See you soon, Billy."

That was seven and a half weeks ago.

Now, she was miraculously with child, and Billy was dead.

And Denise was dead. Junior, that little shit, was dead. Mama was dead. Mary was dead, they believed. And Toby and Alex were...gone. "Unaccounted for at this present time" was what the flatfoot said. Harding was his name. *Detective Joseph P. Harding.* And there had been something else, a look, when he'd said that last part. *Unaccounted for at this present time.* The gumshoe looked as though he'd seen a ghost. Maybe even two.

Toby and Alex. The Bobbsey Twins. They differed from the rest of Billy's litter. They always seemed to be talking to each other, reacting to each other, laughing, smiling—without ever saying a word aloud. And even though they were the youngest of the group, they seemed to be the eldest. *Old souls.*

The Miller Family Business, Billy called it. She corrected him, calling it *the Miller Family Curse,* just like those old Brooklyn biddies used to do. But they both knew what it was and what it meant, no matter what they called it. But Agnes preferred to pretend it was all just make-believe, like Santa for adults.

The siblings shared a huge laugh when Agnes went to leave and couldn't find her car keys. It appeared to make Billy madder than Agnes thought it ought to have, and several times she heard him demanding they "put them back." They turned up, the keys, forty-five minutes later, buried at the bottom of her over-sized and over-stuffed purse. Agnes and Billy both swore they had turned the purse inside-out several times, but there had been no keys.

It was during this brief interlude, while Billy and Denise were busy tearing the house apart trying to solve the case of the disappearing keys, that it happened.

Agnes found herself alone with the Bobbsey twins, Alex and Toby. They each had a crazed sort of smile painted on their small, round, angelic faces. If Agnes didn't know any better, she might have thought she was about to be Village of the Damned-ed. But Alex and Toby weren't like those evil kids in the movie. They were kind, compassionate, overly empathetic. Although Agnes had only spent any real time with them twice during their short lives, this visit being one of the two, she felt as though they carried the weight of the world on their shoulders.

They cornered her in the kitchen. Instinctively, Agnes backed away until there was nowhere left. But she just *knew* she was in no real danger. Toby stood on her left, and Alex on her right. They looked at each other for confirmation, then giggled mischievously.

Toby placed both of his small hands on her belly, followed by Alex, who did the same. And then something happened to Agnes Miller, something she could never explain. Something ran through her body, energy maybe, and made a home somewhere in her lower regions. Now, she knew it had homed in on her womb.

The kids laughed again and then ran out of the kitchen, leaving Agnes on the verge of tears with her ample ass pressed up against the fridge. Something that felt like a magnet poked at her left cheek, but she dared not move. No, Agnes Miller *could not* move. She had just been part of a miracle, and she didn't know what to do with that.

Seven weeks.

Later, alone in her rental car, a shitty Chevy that smelled like a frat house, Agnes Miller cried and cried until she was, as they say, all cried out. She was as dry as the Nile, which dried up six years ago. The Eerie evaporated five years ago. More would follow.

But she couldn't get Billy's words out of her head.

"You're talking about the end of the world here, Billy," Agnes had said to her brother.

"I am."

Agnes made a face, a face that said *yeah, okay, tell me another one, Billy.*

"Think about it. Really think about it. You've been up in Alaska what, fifteen, twenty years now?"

"Something like that," she said, sipping at her piping hot cup of Earl Grey. It was about the only thing Agnes thought Denise knew how to prepare properly.

"How cold did it get up there last winter?"

Agnes knew where this was going. "Cold enough to turn your balls blue."

"But not as cold as the year before, or the year before that, or—"

"I get your point, Billy. We've pissed off Mama Earth, and she's coming for us. It's out of our hands. We've had our time, and soon we'll all be dust in the wind."

"What if what's happening out there isn't natural but…man-made."

Agnes nearly spit out her tea. "Man-made? What are you going on about now, Billy?"

"What if we could stop it, Agnes? What if all that we see and seem is but a dream within a dream?"

"Get your head out of the books, Billy. You'll be quoting the Bard next. I traveled over four thousand miles for this? This is crazy talk, Billy. C-r-a-z-y. I could have you locked up for talking like this. Thank you for the visit and the tea."

Agnes gathered her coat and rummaged through her bag for her keys.

"It's Sandra, Aggie. It's fucking Sandra. You know it is," Billy whispered. His face had gone white, and he looked on the verge of puking. "You know I'm right."

"No, this is crazy talk. Good day to you, sir. Good day!"

Agnes felt her temperature rising, but she would keep her cool.

No telling what this nut-job is capable of.

That was then.

And now he was gone, and Agnes couldn't tell Billy that he'd been right—about everything. At the funeral—*funerals*—Sandra was the only dry eye in the house. Agnes felt her sister's eyes on her the entire time, watching her every move. There were a few times she felt like Sandra was poking at her insides as though *looking for something.* It terrified her. And then Sandra had cornered her in the ladies' room, asking about hers and Charlie's love life.

Was she—getting any? Did she get over her "woman problems"? Any Millers baking in her oven?

Agnes told Sandra to mind her own business, but even then, she felt her sister trying to get deeper inside of her. *To the womb.*

Agnes flew straight back to Anchorage after the last Miller was put in the ground. She'd even attended the mailman's funeral, Bob Buchanan, because she felt responsible, some- how. That nosey neighbor, the Mexican woman, had made a spectacle of herself—again—at Bob's send-off. She tried to speak with Agnes after the Buchanan funeral, mumbling about ghosts and voices.

Agnes thought the Garriga woman sounded as loco as her late brother Billy.

But now she knew better.

Agnes had gotten pregnant even though Charlie hadn't so much as leered at her in months. *Seven weeks.* And even if he had, and they had, her soil was bad. She couldn't have kids of her own. All the doctors agreed on that point at least.

The kids had done it to her, somehow. Billy's kids. With the touch of their hands, they created life inside her barren belly. *Created fucking life.*

So, maybe the rest of it was true. The Miller Curse, and the Miller Family Business, and all the other far-out things she'd discussed with Billy the day her body had been impregnated. *Sandra...*

Agnes and Charlie Miller moved twice during her pregnancy. Each time moving deeper and deeper into the Alaskan wilderness, hoping she could hide from Sandra's all-seeing eye. They drove two hours one-way for her check-ups, then found a Yupik midwife to home deliver and then take care of the babies when they were born.

Agnes knew she couldn't keep them. It wasn't safe for any of them. The only chance they had was to be flown to the mainland and surrendered for adoption.

Do you ever feel like you don't belong? Do you ever think that you were meant to be somebody else? That you are, in fact, someone else. We're Gemeo Labs. And this is the Gemeo Project. Click the sparkling tree graphic to begin your journey.

Keep them separated. That was the only way to keep them alive.

Agnes laid her eyes on her babies for just a moment before they were out the door, and hopefully on their way to safety. She buried thoughts of her kids deep down, just in case Sandra's tentacles came calling. But now and then, when the nights were cold and dark, Agnes Miller wondered how her twins were getting on in the world.

And that's how it went for sixteen years.

Until she'd gone for a walk and woke up with Charlie in a strange house where she was told to put on a costume and play *the game*. Billy and his family were playing a game, too. That's what the detective had said. *House gone wrong.*

He didn't last long, that detective. He packed up his shit first chance he got and high-tailed it as far from the Miller house as he could without looking at the rearview.

But then, just then, Agnes knew he hadn't gone far enough. There was no place far enough. Sandra had found them. She had found them all. And no matter where they went, how far, she would find them again.

They'd all been wearing masks, but Agnes knew the moment she saw Velma Dinkley that she was *hers*. She didn't need to see the face or hear the voice to know. Agnes felt the same energy inside of her as she had when Alex and Toby pressed their hands to her belly. And for a moment, she swore she saw Alex at the end of the hall out of the corner of her eye. There for less than a moment, and then gone again.

Agnes would not play the game.

Sandra's game.

She would rather die than give her the satisfaction. So, she did. And just before her head went BOOM, Agnes had two thoughts simultaneously—

I'm glad I got to see at least one of my babies again before the end, and I wonder how the other is—

BOOM!

Spppplatttt.

The Dead Girl, Part Two

"It's okay. You do what you got to do," Jimi said, handing Imogen the over-sized frying pan. It was new. Still had the tags on it. "Do it now while Janet and Oliver are upstairs. That'll buy you all some time, at the very least. End the round. Properly."

"I can't. I just...no...I won't do it."

He indicated the electronic ticker visible from where they stood in the powder room just off the kitchen. "You don't have a choice. Either I go, or we all go. 'Sides, there's nothing left for me now that she's gone. Do it."

Four minutes.

"Just close your eyes and swing. I won't fight you. I can't. Drew a blank card, remember? My head will likely be separated from my body if I so much as look atchu funny."

This is all about you.

Imogen held the weighty cookware in her hand, wishing now she'd signed up for softball back in the day. She wasn't much of a jock, but she assumed she could pull off a basic swing. It shouldn't take much force with that thing to deliver a death blow. It had to weigh near ten pounds, maybe twelve. And, thanks to the mask, she wouldn't have to see the result of her handy work.

She hesitated. Resisted. "What if I miss? What if—"

Jimi laughed. The nostrils of his mask inflated, then quickly deflated. "You won't miss. I got a pretty big head. At least, that's what Aggie used to say."

Three minutes.

"I don't want to do this."

"I know. Me neither. It's not like I got up this morning and said oh hey, it might be nice to get my head knocked in by a skillet."

Imogen laughed. The frying pan shook in her trembling hands.

"No, I definitely did not have that on my bingo card." Jimi stopped to clear his throat. "How much time we got left?"

"Three minutes. Less, now."

"Alright. Listen to me, this must be done. You hear me? So don't you spend whatever time you got ahead of you feeling bad about me. Kill me, so you can live. That's the game. That's what Aggie would have wanted. For you to live. And maybe Oliver and Janet too. Do it for them. Maybe you can figure a way out of this."

Tears streamed down Imogen's cheeks. Her face had gone numb.

"Do it. Kill me."

Imogen did a few practice swings, stopping the pan just short of Jimi's melon-sized head. Then she wound her arm back and held it there. Every muscle in her arm locked and loaded, shaking from the tension.

Two minutes.

"Do it."

"Hey, what's your name?" Imogen said between sobs.

Jimi laughed so hard his shoulders shook. "Charles, but you

can call me Charlie, if you like. Everybody does. Aggie only called me Charles when she was…"

His voice trailed off, but Imogen got the picture.

Her muscles ached. They felt like jelly. Her biceps twitched underneath the sleeve of the coveralls. *Tick tock, tick tock…*

Sooner rather than later, before her arms gave out, she'd have to bring down the pan if it was going to do any real damage. And the clock was ticking. *Tick tock, tick tock…*

"Sorry, Charlie."

One minute.

Jimi, aka Charlie, chuckled. Imogen cocked her head.

"It's like that commercial. The old tuna commercial. The tag was always 'sorry, Charlie'. Probably before your time. Look it up…when this is over. Think of me. Maybe laugh. Okay?"

"Okay," Imogen said softly. "I will."

"On three?"

Imogen nodded but then verbalized her agreement in case Charlie had closed his eyes in preparation for the coming darkness. "On three."

The ticker flashed and beeped obnoxiously. Upstairs, Imogen heard the shuffling of feet.

Thirty seconds. Twenty-nine…

"One," Charlie said, his voice dry and scratchy.

"One."

Twenty-six. Twenty-five…

"Two."

"Two," Imogen parroted back.

Twenty. Nineteen…

"Imogen?"

"Yeah, Charlie?"

"Get that bitch for me. And for Aggie."

Imogen's eyes let loose a bucketful of tears. "Done."

"Do it now, Imogen," Alex's voice suddenly echoed in her head.

Fifteen.

"Thr—"

Imogen brought the frying pan down, slamming it into the side of Charlie's head before he could get out the whole word—*three.*

His body jerked and flew against the wall of the pocket-sized powder room. He was pinned between the wall and the commode. Trapped like a bear in a trap.

"Sorry, Charlie," Imogen cried as she smashed the pan into his head again, and again, and again, her rage growing exponentially with every swing. One side of his head had caved in completely, but she kept swinging and swinging as his legs kicked and his hands jerked about wildly.

Five.

BANG!

Four.

BANG!

Three.

BANG!

Two.

BANG!

One.

A buzzer resounded throughout the house.

BANG! BANG! BANG! BANG!

A mechanized voice came over a hidden intercom system—

Round one...complete. R-R-RESET. Twenty-minutes to round t-t-two.

BANG! BANG! BANG! BANG! BANG! SORRY, CHARLIE! BANG!

BANG! BANG! BANG! BANG! BANG! BANG! SORRY! BANG! BANG! BANG! BANG! CHARLIE!

As Imogen wound her arm to bring the pan down again, Oliver, aka Joshy Baby, seized hold of her arm and held it in place. Blood coated her fingers and made a spectacular splattering trail of crimson up the length of the coveralls.

She didn't have to look to know there was nothing left of Charlie's head on top of his shoulders. Beneath the deformed and deflated Jimi Hendrix mask, what had once been Charlie's head, now looked more like a plate of corned beef hash.

"He's gone, pumpkin. You can stop now."

The pan slipped out of Imogen's hand. No one heard the bang or the clatter as it hit the floor over the combined sounds of Imogen's wailing and Janet's incessant cough. Oliver folded Imogen into his arms and directed her into the dining room—the only room on the main floor that was not painted red with blood. *Yet.* He tapped the wall switch and the dozens of small lights on the overhead chandelier buzzed to life, illuminating the sleek, ultra-modern black dining table.

He untucked a chair, motioning for her to sit. Imogen fell into the chair and sobbed into her hands despite the mask blocking contact between her hands and face. Slowly, her head leaned forward until she had it pressed into the table, where it remained in place as she continued to wail and sob.

"We can talk about...the family stuff another time, obviously," Oliver, aka Joshy Baby, said as he began absentmindedly stroking the scraggly hair on top of the demented Velma mask's head, which was now spray-painted red.

"Obviously," Janet added between coughs.

"Dammit, Janet. Make yourself useful. Get some water or something. I'm sure you found the wine bottles by now. Why don't you have a glass or ten?"

Janet, aka the Cabbage Patch Kid, drew both her hands to her waist in a defiant stance. "And how are we supposed to drink anything, Einstein? We have no mouths!"

He glared at her through the mask, only easing up when she coughed again. Imogen stirred, poking up her head just slightly as though she were testing the waters.

"It's okay. I'm okay. I don't need anything. Really."

Imogen hoped she sounded convincing because even she had her doubts.

"See? She's fine, Oliver."

Oliver knew Janet was sticking out her tongue underneath that ugly Kid mask like the petulant child she turned into whenever the going got rough. And this qualified as "rough," so he let his anger cool.

"I have to pee," Janet announced suddenly, and then disappeared up the stairs again. The sound of the door closing shut in the master bedroom soon followed, and Oliver and Imogen breathed a little easier. The tension in the room dropped instantly now that hurricane Janet had relocated.

"She's coughing, Dad."

"I know."

"Like, a lot."

"I know," Oliver snapped. "Sorry. This is all a bit much. Sorry. The coughing started a couple of days after we discovered you were missing. Ally told us about your half-baked plan to break into the Coffee Cavern. We'll talk about *that* another time as well. So we went out looking for—"

"A couple of days?"

"Yeah."

"Wait, how long was I missing? I mean, how long before we

all got...here?"

Oliver, aka Joshy Baby, cocked his head. "Don't you remember?"

Imogen shook her head. "It's...I don't know. Fuzzy. I was someplace...cold? Indoors, but like ice cold. Felt like we were moving, like driving. Highway driving. Bumpy. An ice truck? Do they still have ice trucks? That's all I really remember. It was just cold. It's not much."

He took one of her hands in his. "Pumpkin, it's been over two weeks since you went missing."

"What? Two weeks?"

He nodded. "Nearing three, I think."

"Do you think Mom has it? The virus? She sounds bad."

Oliver, aka Joshy Baby, squeezed her hand.

"Dad? What aren't you telling me? Does Mom have the virus? Do you have it too?"

"Listen to me. Do not react. Do not let her know that you know. Agreed?"

Imogen nodded.

"So, you were missing a few days, then a week, then two."

"Yeahhh, and..."

"We were going out a lot, like a lot a lot, to look for you. Police recommended we get the shot..."

"Shit! No! I'm sorry. I didn't mean for this—"

The grisly reports she'd read about the numerous deaths by vaccine filled her head all at once. Imogen tried to get out of the chair, but Oliver held her in place, seizing both her arms with more power than Imogen thought he had in him.

"Shhh. Sit. Down. Don't. React."

Imogen complied, lowering herself slowly.

"It's not the virus that's killing her, is it? It's the vax."

"Indeed."

"Fuck."

"Indeed."

"Dad, I'm sorry. I'm—"

"It's not your fault, pumpkin."

A heaviness filled the air and hung over them like a storm cloud. Then, her head jerked up and Imogen looked at Oliver, trying to see the face underneath the grotesque caricature of Josh Groban.

"Dad...are you...okay?"

She suspected he smiled under the mask, which was his tell.

"I'm fine, pumpkin. Just fine."

Imogen knew he was lying. She bit her lip and cried as quietly as she could, hoping he wouldn't see or suspect.

Twelve minutes to play.

Imogen nodded to the ticker in the hallway.

"What do we do?"

Oliver, aka Joshy Baby, eased his grip on her arms until he'd released her.

"I guess," he began, rubbing his eyes through the mask. "I guess we play the game."

Eleven minutes to play.

"Look, I really don't want to get into this now," he said, but she cut him off.

"Then, don't. It can wait. It'll have to wait."

But Imogen knew even beyond the game, there wasn't any time left.

Oliver and Janet were as good as dead already. Another set of clocks began ticking, these hidden inside of her parents. The vaccine was now a ticking time bomb waiting to go off inside of both Janet and Oliver; although it seemed like Janet had a head-start, if the cough was any indication.

Soon, they'd bleed. First from their ears, then from their eyes, then from everywhere. Then the coughing would worsen. They'd lose control of their bowels. Their skin would itch, and then feel like it was roasting. Blood and puss-filled blisters would form all over their bodies as endless streams of vomit and excrement expelled from their orifices until they were empty. Finally, the fever would take them to a happy place called Delirium, where they'd die in a steaming pile of all that they once were.

And that was just based on the few reported instances of vax deaths Imogen had scanned several weeks ago. For all she knew, for all they knew, it was so much worse than what had been reported...what was still being reported. Imogen guessed she'd have the answer before the end of the game.

Together, they sat, looking at each other across opposite sides of the modern table Oliver was sure Janet would hate, but instead had loved as much as he had. As a family, they shared many happy times gathered at that table, Ally included, even if the one they were currently sitting at was only a replica of the real thing back home. *There's no place like—*

For now, they could pretend. And that's just what they did until—

"OLIVER!" Janet screamed from the upstairs bathroom.

"Janet—"

"Mom—"

Oliver and Imogen spoke at the exact same time.

"Go," Imogen said. "GO!"

Oliver was out of his chair so fast it flipped over onto the floor. A second later, Imogen heard his feet take the steps two at a time. She didn't know he could move that fast. From downstairs, she could just make out the faint knock followed by an even fainter—

Janet?

The bathroom door clicked open, and then all Imogen could hear was the gentle hush of crying before the door clicked closed again.

Ten minutes to play.

Imogen felt restless. She had to do something. She *needed* to do...something.

The adrenaline was pumping through her system. Her heart raced as though she'd just sucked down three XXL Iced Americanos with a side of Angry Bull energy drinks. She wandered into the fake living room, pretending not to notice what remained of her best friend wedged between the couch and the wall. But Imogen knew she was there, of course she did, and her heart sank a bit more knowing it.

It was too quiet. That's what was bugging her. Not a creature was stirring, not even her Ally cat. The thought made her smile for a second, but then reality came crashing down and Imogen teared up behind her demented Dinkley mask.

She thumbed through the vinyl records, and recognized most, if not all, as ones that resided in the genuine Rockwell abode. The one she wanted, Dakotah Dark's *Midnight Offerings,* was tucked all the way in the back—just like in real life. Hidden like a dirty secret.

Janet tried to ban "the devil's music" from the Rockwell home, but Oliver had intervened on Imogen's behalf and a compromise had been reached. Imogen could have the Dark albums in the house, but she was not to play them when Janet was home. An easy deal, since Imogen loved nothing more than cranking the volume up to ten, running through the house, room to room, up the stairs, down the stairs; all the while making "devil's horns" with her fingers and singing along to the one and only Dakotah Dark.

Nine minutes to play.

She placed the record on the turntable and clicked the player on. She watched as the record's gravestone label spun around and around and around. As she lowered the needle to the grooves, Imogen hoped the universe would grant her this one thing. This one small thing. *Just let me hear Dakotah Dark one more time. Just one more time. That's all I ask.*

Imogen closed her eyes as the record hissed and popped, then skipped. But then, the most glorious thing she'd ever heard came through the speakers.

Dakotah. Fucking. Dark.

Now, she could really pretend she was home. Everything almost felt all right, normal even, despite the pile of corpses decorating the fake Rockwell house Imogen was trying her damnedest to forget.

The lead guitar screamed and wailed, an intro worthy of Old Scratch himself. A series of impossible notes and chords that no human being had any business playing. Then the drums kicked in. Just a steady, low bass drum. *Bum. Bum. Bum.* Beating like a heart. Imogen banged her head to the rhythm. And then, finally, came the seductively smooth voice of the devil's child himself—

Dakotah. Fucking. Dark.

Seven minutes to play.

Imogen howled along with Dakotah, note for impossible note. It felt tribal, like she was exorcising herself. Purging her soul. Shaking off the figurative and literal ghosts and demons that held her down, kept her back. She was a murderer. Again.

What kind of person kills another? *Cain and Abel. Macbeth. Julius Caesar. O.J. Okay, so it was a long list.*

Before Charlie, she'd killed her best friend twice. It didn't matter that somehow she'd been able to bring the air-headed Ally back from whatever lay beyond the abyss. She had still killed her. And Charlie. It didn't matter that he asked for it. Murder was murder. It didn't amount to a hill of beans if killing Charlie bought them all twenty more minutes of life, or twenty more years. She still had to kill to get them.

Dakotah Dark understood death. He'd understand the conflicting emotions at war within her psyche. If only she could commune with the macabre maestro, but he was worm food. Had been for years before Imogen was even born. The closest she could get was this. A musical séance to raise the spirits.

Back in his day, at the height of the satanic panic, they used to say that if you played his records backwards, you could hear Dakotah read from his personal grimoire. Imogen never tried it. Before, she had been too afraid she might conjure something from the pits of Hell, especially after the Ally incidents.

But now?

Now there was nothing to lose. They were all probably going to die in that fake house. Would a pack of hellhounds really make things so much worse than they already were?

Imogen stood before the record player, watching the record spin in endless circles. She could do it. Just click the power off, move the needle to the end of the record, and manually spin it backwards.

As she debated conjuring the Devil, something more foul, more profane entered the room. But Imogen couldn't hear its approach over the deafening decibels of Dakotah Dark. It made no attempt to hide itself or quiet itself as it slid up to her. The foulness of its essence soiled the very air. It snarled and grinned, baring its black teeth. Imogen had wanted to commune with death, and so the dead thing came to her, answering her black prayer.

Imogen clicked off the turntable. The house again fell quiet. She reached for the needle. *Do or die time.* But no. Imogen froze in place. All was not quite quiet. There was something. Something new in the room with her. Right behind her.

Imogen heard it wheezing. The rancid smell of its breath penetrating the latex nose of her mask. The stink made her want to throw up, but she swallowed it back down.

Then, a sudden and loud BOOM from the upstairs bathroom, followed by a mournful cry—OLIVER! NO!

She wanted to turn around. Turn around and run up the stairs to see what the hell had just happened, but that would mean turning and seeing the creature that stood behind her. The thing that brought death. The thing that *was* death.

"Ohhh," the thing hissed. "I think Daddy lost his head."

The undead thing howled with laughter. Imogen spun around on her heels until she was face to face with the wicked thing that smiled at her with its fetid mouth and decayed teeth. The foul thing that stared at her with its black, cold, dead eyes. The thing that had once been Mary Miller.

Imogen went to scream, and then it was gone.

But in its place stood a sturdy-looking Mexican woman, who raised a block of wood over her head, and then struck Imogen with it.

"Gotcha," Joanne Garriga said in a voice that wasn't entirely hers but was hers mixed with the essence of Mary Miller.

Imogen recognized it at once as the same voice she heard when she'd first been grabbed on her way to the Coffee Cavern. And somehow, she knew, as sleep overtook her, that the game had just ended.

Dream Lover, Part Two

It was dark. So very dark. *Black.*

Olivia Christine Lovejoy couldn't see a foot in front of her, let alone the hand she thought she was waving in front of her face. *Full dark.* She felt a strange rush of emotions, from hope to astonishment, but fear had no place among them. Olivia felt fearless. Insanely brave. Invincible.

Mostly, she was excited; excited because she wasn't alone. He was there beside her in the dark, her Dream Lover. She knew it, even if she couldn't see him. He was there. She felt his presence. It was everywhere around her, enveloping her. And it took away any doubts or fears she might have been feeling.

"Where...are we?" she asked.

"On the other side," he said.

His voice came from both everywhere and nowhere, but Olivia heard him loud and clear all the same.

"The other side of what?"

"The other side of everything."

Olivia went to say that she didn't understand, but she suddenly felt something tugging at her, pulling her along gently. She thought it must be his arm, but it was so dark Olivia couldn't really say for certain. Instead, she offered no resistance and allowed herself to be led. She knew he would never hurt her, her Dream Lover. Toby Miller. He'd had plenty of opportunities to do her harm, and never once had he so much as ruffled the hairs on top of her head. Wherever he meant to lead her, Olivia would follow, even if he meant to walk them up to the gates of Hell and ring the bell.

"Look," Toby began, his voice trailing off into a million ghostly echoes. "There."

At first there was nothing, but then the very dark itself rippled as though someone had thrown a pebble into a pond of murky water. Smoke and light rose out of the ripples. Olivia now could see her person in the dark, her hand waving in front of her face. She did not see Toby, but knew he was there. Close by.

In the motion of the thousands of ripples, an image formed, swirling and bubbling until it came clear and in focus—

A room. Dimly lit. A heavy snowfall outside of a window. Two women. And one of them was screaming. The other, covered in blood, shouting over the painful screams of childbirth—

"Push, Agnes! You have to PUSH!"

The woman in labor, Agnes, closed her eyes as she pushed and pushed and pushed until she screamed with the thunderous voice of a thousand women. The room appeared to quake just before it went still. The midwife disappeared between Agnes's open legs, and soon after, the sound of not one, but two, infants introducing themselves to the world rang out.

"Twins, Agnes. You have twin girls."

He was beside her then in the dark, pointing a long finger at one of the screaming newborns. The image froze. Olivia couldn't look at him. She was transfixed by the frozen tableau in front of her.

"That's you," Toby said.

Olivia didn't have to see his finger to know which of the infants Toby was pointing to. Somehow, she just knew. It felt like she had always known. This moment locked away somewhere in her memory banks. And now, it was free. Everything was coming back to her. Broken pieces becoming whole once again. Her brain rewiring itself. Forgotten memories filling the empty jars of her mind.

"And that's your mother. Agnes Miller."

Olivia's eyes welled with tears she did not know she needed to cry.

"My mother?"

"Yes."

Her cheeks felt wet as Olivia said in a child-like voice, "Mom?"

She stepped closer, until she was standing face to face with the frozen image of her mother's exhausted, sweaty face. But there was something else there, too. A smile. A small one, but it was there. And Olivia saw it.

"Hi, Mom," Olivia said, reaching out a hand to touch her mother's cheek.

Toby crept up beside her. "And that one there is your sister."

Olivia laughed through her tears, sniffling as her eyes traveled to the infant cradled beside her in the midwife's arms.

"My sister?"

"Yes. Your twin sister."

Olivia couldn't stop the smile that came across her face. It had a power all its own. A great, harnessable power that had ignited somewhere deep inside of her. Oh, it had always been there, and from time to time Olivia had made use of it—

Mahalo—but it was turning on now. *Really turning on. She* was turning on now. She felt it everywhere in her at once. An energy. An impossible energy. It warmed her insides and lit every corner of the darkness until there was only light. Her light. And now, there would be no going back. There would be no putting out the light. It was time to shine.

She said aloud, every word taking on a new meaning, "Do you ever feel like you don't belong? Do you feel alone even when surrounded by friends and family? Do you ever think that you were meant to be somebody else? That you are, in fact, someone else."

"Her name is Imogen."

Olivia turned her head to Toby, who likely never looked more pleased in the entirety of his life.

"You have the answers. You've always had the answers, haven't you?"

There was a glint in his eyes. "So have you."

Olivia laughed and cried at the same time. "You're...my... our—"

"Yes."

The image was gone in a storm of clouds, thunder, and crackles of pink and yellow lightning. As the smoke swirled and swirled, a new image formed—

Two children giggling as they placed their hands on Agnes Miller's once dormant womb.

Olivia lost her breath for a moment, but before she could say anything, the clouds rumbled, and the image changed again—

A woman Olivia did not recognize—

"My mother," Toby said softly, reading her thoughts. "Denise Miller."

In her arms, Denise rocked baby Alex. The child's tiny hands reached out, grabbing hold of a lock of Denise's hair. She laughed as she lowered her nose to Alex's cherubic face.

"You like pulling your mama's hair, don't you, Alexandra?"

Denise gently pried the baby's fingers from her lock, but Alex had quite the grip. Impossibly strong for one so small, so new. So young.

"That's one helluva tight grip you have there, Alexandra. Come on now, Mama needs her hair back."

Alex giggled and kicked her feet. Denise laughed back, rubbing her nose to Alex's nose. The baby eased her viselike grip on Denise's locks, and Denise sat upright, momentarily marveling at her child. Her *special* child. Yes, most mothers think their children are special, but this one, Alexandra Miller of the Bronx, *was* special. And Denise knew it. Somehow, she knew even then that this child, her child, had a purpose. A larger purpose than she could ever understand. All this, and more, was written plainly on Denise Miller's face and clearly seen in her loving eyes.

Then, baby Alex fussed and fidgeted until she had finagled Denise into holding her up on her knees—inches away from Denise's mama belly. Alex laughed and smiled and then placed both of her hands on Denise's belly in the same manner she'd done years later with Toby on Agnes' barren belly. Denise gasped as the hands made contact and something happened to her. Something indescribably wonderful.

Her body twitched and without thought her hands slipped from Alex, but the infant neither teetered nor tottered, instead found her own legs, and stood of her own accord. Denise's eyes rolled back in her head. Saliva formed at her mouth, foaming up like a rabid dog. Then, inch by inch, her body floated off the bed until it hovered about four feet above the messed-up sheets and blankets below. All the while, Alex kept her hands in place, standing on her own two feet.

Olivia looked at Toby, who did not react to the scene as it changed.

Nine months later—

Denise howling in the delivery room. Billy holding her hand. *Push, push, pussshhhh!*

And then, the doctor holding up Toby for the world to see.

"That's me, in case you were wondering."

Olivia laughed. "Yeah, I got that."

Toby smirked. *She's fun. I like her.*

He raised a hand to the image and made like he was erasing it with an invisible eraser. The image faded into itself as a rush of new pictures came to the surface of the dark clouds—

Toby and Alex as kids.

Disappearing toys. Disappearing plates of food. An entire car vanishing from sight.

Then, one dark and stormy night, the entire Miller house up and disappeared.

In a flash, everything was gone. The images. Toby. Everything had gone black.

Then, out of the dark, a new voice—

"Staycation. The rules," Junior said, reading from the folded paper.

Alex and Toby giggled in the background, but then the image bled into another—

Cast-Iron Cassie's death by Christmas antlers. And then, another—

Bob Buchanan's thirty lashes from Mary Miller. And another—

Justin Miller. A dog crate. *Poor, poor Justin.* Another—

Alex Miller. Blue-faced. Another—

Punishment is good. Bones cracking in Junior Miller's legs.

Punishment is severe. More bones cracking.

Punishment is absolute. The lifeless, broken body of Junior Miller lying in a growing pool of his own blood at the bottom of the Millers' stairs. Then another image—

Denise and Billy Miller, stuffed into a meat freezer. Another—

Alex, Justin, and Toby at a dream-like tea party. Then—

A snarling hell hound. Then—

The undead Millers—Denise, Cast-Iron Cassie, and Billy—rounding the stairs, dragging Mary Miller to her end, tearing her body in half like it had been made of papier mâché. Mary's screams resounded as everything went to black.

Then—

The beast that was Sandra Miller charming her way into the Miller house. Beguiling that detective. Then—

Sandra Miller tearing the head off the coroner, Andy West, with her bare hands that looked more like claws. Then—

Sandra Miller's mouth opening to cavernous proportions and swallowing a bit of the sludge that had been Mary Miller. Then—

Sandra Miller pointing a clawed finger at Toby as he held Alex in his arms at the top of the stairs. *Youuuuuuuu!* Then—

Toby walking out of the Miller house, cradling Alex in his arms, and disappearing into the night. Then—

Sandra Miller giving chase. Bursting through the open front door of the Millers' house of horrors like a machete-wielding psycho in the movies. Only to find no Toby Miller. No Alex Miller. The creature raged. But then, its eyes fell on something. Someone that might be useful, or at the very least fun to play with for a while.

A sturdy-looking Mexican woman talking to reporters, enjoying every bit of the morbid attention. Talking like she knew...like she knew anything.

The creature grinned and stalked its prey. Distracted by the cameras and the flash bulbs, Joanne Garriga never felt Sandra Miller's claws touch her shoulder. Never felt the foul thing that she had slipped inside of Joanne's meat sack. The evil virus. Never felt Mary Miller move in. Then—

Toby standing on a neighboring roof, watching Sandra Miller drive off. Watching as Joanne Garriga returned home with her husband, Jose, and closed their front door, bringing into their home, into their lives, a most unwelcome guest. Then—

Imogen Rockwell at four, five, six, ten, twelve, thirteen, sixteen years old. The Rockwells. Ally. Then—

Imogen and the Gemeo test. Then—

Jose Garriga, laughing as he died. *To die laughing...*Then—

Joanne Garriga under the control of Mary Miller, knocking Imogen unconscious. Picking her body up with ease and tossing it into the back of an unbranded eighteen-wheeler as though it was a softball. Then—

Imogen Rockwell shivering in the back of the truck with only Alex's voice for company. Then—

Joanne Garriga taking Ally, taking Oliver, taking Janet, taking Agnes, taking Charlie to—

The replica house. The Willows. The macabre masks. The game. Staycation 2.0. Then—

A house of horrors. Ally, dead. Charlie, dead. Oliver, dead. Agnes, dead. And Janet, dead.

And Imogen Rockwell...in the clutches of Mary and Sandra

Miller, being moved yet again, but this time in the trunk of Joanne Garriga's car. Then—

Olivia. Recently. At home. Watching TV. A news report interrupts some inane Christmas-themed rom-com she'd been watching with two of her friends, who were now safely part of the Lovejoys' "plague bubble." *Local teen goes missing.* An image flashes on the screen.

"O-M-G...she looks like you," Lana squealed, pointing to the image of Imogen Rockwell.

"For reals. She looks *just* like you. Like...you could be sisters," Penny, the other bubbled friend, agreed.

"Wow, Olivia. You look just like the dead girl!" Then—

Olivia sneaking out of the house. Getting into her yellow eco-friendly car and pointing it west—to where Imogen Rockwell had gone missing. Then—

You look just like the dead girl!

An email. A hit. *Click the sparkling tree graphic—*

Then—

Driving past The Greasy Spoon. Hungry. Closed sign. The diner in the rearview. Then—

You look just like the dead girl!

Driving past The Greasy Spoon. Again. Lights on. Somebody's home. Then—

You look just like the dead girl!

Flo. The Village People. The jukebox. The sexed-up tweens. Herbie. *That's Officer Hunt.*

Then—

Sitting opposite Toby in the booth. Then—

It all went away. Gone in an instant. But something came through the dark, traveling to Olivia as though she were a lighthouse calling the ships home.

Darkness. Cries. Apologies.

Imogen.

Then—

Echoes. Disembodied, ghostly echoes of all that Olivia had seen and heard.

Toby took Olivia's hand in his. "Come, it's time."

She was crying and hadn't even known it. "Time for what?"

"Time for you to wake up."

The dark grew cold. A storm was coming. A big one. It rumbled and boomed somewhere in the distance. The air hummed with electricity. Brief flashes of light sliced the dark, lasting a fraction of an instant.

Olivia squeezed Toby's hand tighter.

"There's something I need you to see," Toby said, leaning to her ear. Olivia had no space to respond because Toby quickly went on. "CROATOAN."

And the storm came. A hellish storm. In it, the end of the world.

He led her to the top of the abyss, and like a carnival barker with a cane and top hat, Toby showed her the world beyond the veil. A world invisible to the dreamers but just as real as the waking dream they call reality. *Is all that we see and seem—*

"It's coming," he said, pointing to a thundering cloud many, many miles ahead of them. "The end of all things."

And then Olivia saw it. She couldn't stop the shriek from escaping her lips.

There, in the center of the cloud, the monstrous thing that called itself Sandra Miller.

Family Reunion

Olivia Christine Lovejoy was on her knees, sobbing into the dust of The Greasy Spoon's parking lot. Toby Miller leaned himself against the flat hood of her little yellow car, giving Olivia both some physical space and a bit of time. When the crying-fest pushed past the ten-minute mark, he approached Olivia with marked concern.

"It's...a lot, I know," he said, creeping down beside her, dust and sand blowing into his eyes.

Olivia howled with laughter, but there were still some tears thrown in. "A lot? A lot? I think that just might be the understatement of the fucking year, Toby! We're talking about the end of the world here!"

He nodded. "We are."

"And like, right now, that..." Olivia didn't know where exactly to point, so she just picked a spot and hoped it was in the correct vicinity. "That world is just right there."

"It is."

"Fuck." She laughed again, trying to swallow it all down. Process the wonders she'd been shown. "And...we're here. But here isn't here? It's really...there. But we don't know it because we're all mostly just like...asleep."

Toby sighed. "Something like that, yes. I knew you were a

smart girl. You're just like Alex. Miss Ivy League."

"Oh, don't be placating me. This is fucking incredible. I feel like my head is going to explode. Ahh."

Olivia rubbed at her temples as her forehead wrinkled in pain. Another headache was coming. A good one, too.

"Need some c-c-coffee, d-d-dear," Toby mouthed, but it was old Flo's voice that came out. He held up a fresh Greasy Spoon cup of Joe.

Olivia fell on her side, laughing. "Oh my god. Oh my god. That was all you, wasn't it? I should have known. I don't know why it just hit me now. Flo, Herbie, the fucking Village People. That was all you."

Toby winked. "Some of it was *you*." *The Village People.*

Weird or not, Olivia took the cup of coffee and pounded it back. Her head needed that java jolt. "Oh wait, you have to tell me. What was up with that British guy in the bathroom?"

"What British guy in the bathroom?"

He sounded genuinely confused.

"Stop it. You know. The proper guy in the little bow tie. He was all like 'I say, do you mind?' I thought he was gonna hand me some expensive mustard or something. For real."

But it rang no bells for Toby, who just shrugged and said, "Are you sure you saw what you saw?"

"Oh, I know there was a little British man with a bow tie and a monocle back where the bathrooms were supposed to be."

She stared at him for a long minute before Toby couldn't hold back the laughter anymore and it came spilling out of him, loudly and joyously.

"Dammmnnn, you almost had me, Toby. Almost."

Toby wiped at his eyes. It felt so good to laugh with another person, like he used to do with Alex. Being with Olivia felt just like that to him, and he hadn't realized until that moment how much he missed it. How easy it was to let the weight of the world go for just a minute and be young and carefree again.

"I don't know. I saw him in a commercial once. Alex and I used to drive our father crazy, walking around talking in British accents all day. Justin had gotten us plastic monocles from the Toy Shoppe at the mall. I think that was the last straw for Dad." *Poor, poor Justin.*

The mood shifted for Olivia. She felt like a wet blanket had been tossed at her.

"I'm sorry, Toby. About your family, I mean. Justin. Alex. Your—"

"You have a sister," Toby said, barreling right over Olivia.

"Seems like I do. Imogen Rockwell. Kinda sounds like a mystery novelist, right? The new thriller by IMOGEN ROCKWELL."

Olivia laughed so loud she almost missed what Toby said next.

"Want to meet her?"

But she'd caught it, and suddenly Olivia was on high alert.

"What did you say?"

"Do you want to meet your sister?"

Olivia's eyes bugged, and she rolled her head around her shoulders as if saying, *well, duh.*

"Fuck yeah."

Toby got to his feet, dusting himself off. "Now?"

Olivia repeated the bulging eyes and head roll. "Now's good."

She rose to her feet, not as easily as Toby had done, but stood and dusted her pants off, which had been covered in a yellow-orange dust.

"Let's go then," Olivia said, heading for her solar sedan. "It's probably open. I have no idea where the keys are. Or my purse. Or anything. That Flo got me all discombobulated. For real, I thought she was going to kill me a couple of times."

She glanced over her shoulder. Toby remained rooted in place. The boarded-up diner looming in front of him. He eyed it, eyes locking in like a radar.

"Toby?"

He did not look back at her, just went on to say, "She's not out there. She's *in* there."

Olivia, who had made it to her sedan by now and had the door open, slammed the car door shut and hustled herself over to Toby.

"What do you mean...she's in there? Nothing's been in there for quite some time. I mean, I don't think we were really in there, were we? Wait. Were we? I'm confused."

Are you sure you saw what you saw?

Toby said nothing, but closed his eyes and threw his head back. Something in his neck cracked. Then his arms went out to the sides as his legs slid apart in the sand. Olivia gasped as Toby Miller's body rose off the ground, higher and higher until he hung there, perfectly still, about seven feet in the air.

"Toby!"

Suddenly, his eyes flew open. And then, slowly, his head moved back to center as he brought his right arm out in front of him. His long, slender fingers stretched out from his hand as though they were searching for something, trying to touch something impossibly beyond his reach. But then the ground beneath Olivia rumbled and shook. It felt like an earthquake. She was thrown off her feet. Her little yellow car's alarm beeped uselessly.

"Toby, what's happening?" Olivia called, but either he didn't hear her over the sound of the earth groaning, or he couldn't hear in the trance-like state he'd slipped into. "TOBY!"

Olivia slid back, heading to her car. She just wanted something solid to hold onto. The angrier the earth sounded, the harder it rumbled and shook, the more she just wanted to hop into the vehicle and drive off into the sunset and forget all about—

The Greasy Spoon slowly imploded in on itself. It looked as though it were eating itself from the inside out. First, the windows blew out, sending bits of glass in all directions. Olivia was far enough away that none hit her but came close enough. Then the roof rattled until it collapsed in a cloud of dust and debris.

Olivia couldn't help herself. She jumped into the driver's seat and pulled the door shut, locking it as though that could keep the outside from getting in. She didn't want to watch but had to. She just had to keep looking at the death of The Greasy Spoon. The window fogged as Olivia pressed her face right up to the glass and stared out in both wonder and trepidation.

The welcome sign, which had eventually become a farewell sign—

CLOSED. Thanks for 57 fabulous food-filled years!

—lit up. The letters swirling and pulsing as bright as they likely had on day one.

Then they all shattered, and the sign exploded in a fury of smoke and orangey-red sparks.

Happy trails, Greasy Spoon. You had the best coffee.

From the ground beneath the diner came a horrible yell, as though a gigantic cave troll had opened its mouth and was now trying to swallow the box-car diner up into its jaws in one greedy gulp.

Toby's fingers tensed and reached for the rubble of the box-car diner.

Again, the ground cried and yelled, shaking itself furiously before there were no pieces of The Greasy Spoon left standing. Toby's body went rigid. His legs came together, fitting so snugly they appeared to be glued to each other. Then, his left arm joined the right, and he aimed both hands, both sets of extended fingers at the demolished diner.

"Oh my god," was all Olivia said as the broken bits of the diner started to vibrate and depart of their own accord, clearing the demolition site completely as something unearthed itself. Something that had been *under* the diner all this time. Something big. Really big.

"Ahhhhhhhhh!" Toby screamed as he excavated the buried shipping container.

Sweat flew off his fingertips and dripped down his face as the container rose higher and higher out of the ground. His arms shook as though he was a weightlifter trying to bench too much weight. But he held on, and the container continued to unearth itself until the whole of it was visible.

By now, Toby was panting, his focus on the container laser sharp. He gritted his teeth, and with one final enormous pull and push, an ear-piercing cry came out of his depths as his mouth fell open and—

The glass in Olivia's windshield and windows shattered, she took cover as—

The container rose just a little higher, hovered in place for a moment, and then fell to the earth, landing on solid ground with a tremendous *THUD!* The entire parking lot was lost in the backsplash of dust and rubble that followed. When it had finally cleared, Olivia ran from the car and found Toby, who, like the container, had crashed to the hard ground below.

She took his head into her hands and tapped his cheek. "Toby? Toby? Can you hear me? Say something."

There was a second where Olivia thought he was dead, as his body was entirely slack, and Toby was unresponsive. Then he cracked a small, but exhausted, smile. He pointed to the container and said, "Go on. Go say hi to your sister. I'll be alright. I just need…a second or two to catch my breath."

Olivia didn't know if she believed him about only needing a few seconds, but she placed his head back down with the greatest of care and then made her way to standing. Without thinking, she dusted herself off, only to walk deeper into the dust cloud that surrounded the newly unearthed container.

She approached it cautiously, not because she was afraid, but because she was nervous. *What will she be like? Imogen. Will she like me? Will I like her? What if—*

"Go on," Toby groaned, getting to his feet. He didn't bother to dust himself off, seeming to enjoy his ragged look. "She's going to love you. And you're going to love her."

Olivia looked back at him and nodded. He returned it in kind. "Go."

Olivia inched towards the container's door. As she did so, it shook and seemed to breathe; the metal going concave and then releasing. Olivia realized this was not because they, she and Toby, wanted to get in, but because something wanted to get *out*.

Without warning, the door flew wide open, banging into the side of the container. The clanging rang through the dark container. A fresh dust cloud rose over the doorway, but behind the dust Olivia could just make out the outline of a person. She stood with an arm out, her right arm, and her hand pointed at where the door had only a moment ago been closed and locked.

And just for a moment, the small outline of another was visible. The outline of a child. Olivia could barely discern it before it was gone. At first, she thought it was a trick of the light or an optical illusion, but the new reality of her world knocked that thought away.

The figure, still shrouded in the dark, had Olivia's same build.

The figure moved towards the open door.

Olivia could only wait with bated breath.

The figure seemed to have the same hair as her.

Olivia's heart raced as the figure inched towards the light. She didn't think she'd even been this nervous in her life. As the figure inside took one step, and then another, and then emerged from the container, Olivia gasped—

They had the same face. Not just the same, but *exactly* the same.

You look just like that dead girl!

Imogen and Olivia gasped simultaneously. But the shock of seeing their own faces staring back at them quickly gave way to an overwhelming need to embrace. They ran to each other with such intensity that they nearly knocked each other over as their arms encircled, drawing their bodies as close to one another as they could.

Olivia held onto Imogen for dear life.

And Imogen held onto Olivia with such ferocity, as though this was all a dream, and she could wake at any second. Now that she had Olivia, Imogen never wanted to give her back.

"Imogen, meet Olivia. Olivia, meet Imogen," Toby said as he entered their space.

The sisters reluctantly released each other. Imogen howled as her eyes landed on Toby.

"Holy shit, it *is* you! Dream Lover!"

She didn't allow Toby to speak. Instead, Imogen threw her arms around him and pulled him to her. If she had squeezed him any tighter, Toby might have popped like a pimple.

"Thank you," Imogen whispered into his ear.

"I'm sorry. I tried to—"

"It's okay. I had Alex to keep me company and teach me a few tricks," Imogen said, nodding at the blown-out door.

"She's an excellent teacher," Toby said, closing his eyes. He allowed himself to take the feeling in, the warm embrace of another person. A loving embrace. It felt nice.

A second later, Olivia joined the group hug, and Toby Miller felt happy.

So very happy.

But he knew, somewhere out there, off in the distance, the storm was gathering. It wouldn't be long before it blew in and took everything, everywhere with it. No, it wouldn't be long before everything ended.

Unless—

The Gemeo Project

"Welcome to the Gemeo Project. Olivia. Imogen," Toby said, withdrawing, reluctantly, from their group embrace.

"What is it, Toby? What does it mean?" Olivia asked.

Imogen agreed. "Yeah. It's been driving me crazy. My friend…"

"Ally cat," Toby said quietly.

"Yeah. Ally said it was a cult."

"It's not a cult." Olivia laughed. "It's definitely not a cult. But I think matching attire would be a hard no from me."

"Agreed," Imogen said to Olivia, then turned to Toby. "Come on. Spill it, Dream Lover. What is Gemeo?"

Toby grinned. He liked them. Both. And he'd turn the world over to keep them alive. "It's an old word. A very old word."

"You like old words," Olivia chided, then pushed impatiently. "But what's it mean?

"Yeah, Toby. What does it mean?"

Olivia quickly turned to Imogen. "Oh, right. That's the correct way to say it. *What does it mean?*"

Imogen cackled.

"Miss Ivy League!"

They said this at the same time, followed by a simultaneous squeak and squeal.

"In case anyone still cares," Toby began, smiling ear to ear, "Gemeo is an old word."

"Yeah, yeah," Olivia said, motioning for him to get on with it.

"A very old word," Imogen said with equal impatience.

"A word that means—"

Imogen and Olivia said it at the same time, without thinking—

TWIN!

"Indeed," Toby said.

"Ha," Imogen cackled.

Olivia smacked her forehead. "Why didn't we just Peegle that? It had to be out there somewhere, right?"

"That word pre-dates Peegle, I'm sure," Toby said, as he turned to walk away. "Come."

"Where are we going?" Imogen called to him.

"Yeah, where are we going, Toby? And can we maybe, you know, stop and eat first?"

Imogen nodded. "I could eat."

Toby did not look back. Just kept walking.

"Okay, well maybe just a coffee, then? To go? Hey!" Olivia kicked at the sand. "I wish you could've met Flo. She made great coffee."

In an instant, a fresh to-go cup of coffee found its way into both Imogen's and Olivia's hands. Olivia raised it to her mouth and savored every drop as it warmed her belly.

"Thank you, Flo," she called out, raising a cup to the air in salute. "Thank you for not killing me.

Imogen took a sip. "Oh, that's good. Almost as good as the coffee at the Coffee Cavern."

"Coffee Cavern?"

"Yeah, I work there. Or I did. Before all…this, you know?"

Olivia stopped and stared at Imogen. "Wait, you work at a coffee bar?"

Imogen nodded. "Yep." She smacked the "P," for dramatic effect. "Coffee helps my headaches."

Olivia was practically salivating. "Do you get a discount? Could you get *me* a discount?"

"Nah," Imogen said, shaking her head solemnly as though she'd just lost a dear friend. *She had, but she wouldn't think about Ally now.* "Yours is free."

Olivia threw her arms around Imogen, spilling a few drops of Joe onto Imogen's shirt. "I think I love you. And not just for the coffee."

Imogen hugged Olivia back tighter.

At last, they each felt complete. Like the part they had been missing had finally been found. Their two pieces of the puzzle sliding into the other perfectly.

"Come on!"

Toby had gotten far ahead of them. He almost looked like nothing more than a tumbleweed in a sandstorm. The sisters ended their embrace and chased after him.

"I need your help with something," he called back to them.

When they finally caught up to him, the pair realized they had wandered roughly five hundred yards into the Nevada desert. The Greasy Spoon now lost in the blowing dust somewhere behind them. They found Toby, down on his knees, kneeling reverently before a make-shift marker that read: *A. Miller.* They came up and quietly sat beside him.

"I don't need to tell you the evil we're facing," he said. "And there's a long, difficult road ahead of us. Nothing is written in stone. Nothing is for sure. You're going to have to dig deeper than you ever thought you could. You're going to have to fight harder than you've ever fought for anything in your life. It's an impossible task, but we have to try. Because that's what we do. That's what we are. Who we are. We have one chance to end this game. To end it forever. To change the world. One chance. If we fail, everything, everywhere ends. And she wins. They win."

"We can do this. I'm with you, Toby," Olivia said, placing a hand on his shoulder.

"Let's do it," Imogen agreed, placing her hand on his other shoulder.

"We can't do it alone. There's someone we need if we're going to win this. And I need you to help me," Toby said, suddenly overcome with emotion.

"What? What do you need us to do?" Olivia asked, squeezing his shoulder.

Toby closed his eyes and sighed.

"We need to bring Alex back."

Lazarus

They sat for a time, communing in silence. Their energies combined, traveling through each of their bodies, swimming back and forth between Olivia, Toby, and Imogen, completing the circuit. Toby felt himself restored, his battery recharging after unearthing the container and piercing the veil with Olivia. Imogen and Olivia felt themselves awakening. Their power activated and coming to the surface, breaking through the years of trying to keep it buried. Forgotten. Hidden.

At that moment, the three were one. Their light blazed through the dark. The desert night looked as though it were on fire. The wrath of the gods came down to judge man for his sins. Anyone within a hundred miles felt the surge, the energy. The *power*. Electricity soared through the air. It rose from the earth like black gold. And for an instant, there was something new, something the dreamers hadn't felt in a long, long hard year.

Hope...

For a fraction of a second, if that, the veil had been pierced. Their combined energy punched a hole right through it. Toby guided it, led its tendrils to the depths of the other side, and took what was his; took back what should never have been taken. And if there was a price to pay for it, Toby would pay it later, gladly. But for now, his hand took from death his sister Alex Miller and brought her back to the other side, to life.

And he spoke—

Lazarus, come forth!

And she that was dead came forth, bound hand and foot with grave clothes.

The Las Vegas sky was ablaze with lightning. Thunder boomed and a heavy rain fell, coming from nowhere. But the rain loosened the ground just enough so Alexandra "Alex" Miller could reach a hand out of the cold ground that had been her grave, the remote spot in the Nevada desert where her brother had picked to stash her remains over a decade ago.

Toby grabbed her hand, squeezed, and then pulled.

Lazarus.

Come forth.

Heroes

"It's time to go. You ready?" Harding asked Toby.

"A minute?"

Harding nodded. "Okay. We'll be in the car."

Toby listened as Harding's heavy steps receded until he was gone.

The rain had stopped, but Toby's hair was still dripping water into his eyes. Alex brushed the hair away from Toby's eyes. They stared at each other for a long while, in silence. Then they pressed their foreheads together.

"I missed you," Toby said quietly.

"I know," Alex said back. "I missed you, too. You got big. You weren't supposed to get big."

"Do you think she knows?"

Alex's eyes searched for the newly minted Miller twins, Imogen and Olivia. They too appeared to be having a moment.

"Something stirs, but," Alex began, studying the twins a moment longer. "But it remains buried. For now."

Toby placed his hands on Alex's shoulders, and then she placed hers on his. They pulled each other closer. And it felt like no time had passed at all. They could've still been two playful kids in their parents' home in the Bronx. Their pieces still fit perfectly together, and Toby knew, no matter what, they always would.

Olivia and Imogen pressed their backs into Harding's SUV, neither saying anything but neither uncomfortable in the silence. Speech was unnecessary. Words, even old words, could not convey what passed between them in the quiet.

Olivia's right hand tapped out a rhythm on her thigh. *Tap. Tap. Tap.* She repeated it several times, then her hand would hover just above her thigh for a moment, and then it would tap out the rhythm all over again from the top.

"What IS that?" Imogen finally asked, breaking the silence. "I know that. How do I know that?"

"I don't know," Olivia said, still tapping away. "It's right.... there. It's like... RIGHT THERE but I can't see it. I know I know this. I know I do."

Imogen began tapping away at her thigh in time with Olivia. "Yeah, me too. What is that?"

Olivia groaned. "It's like an earworm from hell. It's been in my head since..."

She stopped tapping and eyed Toby and Alex.

"Since? Don't leave me hanging," Imogen said, ceasing her own tapping.

Silence returned. The well-greased wheels of Olivia's mind spun around and around.

"Since I saw Toby tap it out in the diner," Olivia finally said just above a whisper.

At these words, Alex and Toby seemed to tilt their heads the tiniest bit, just enough to give them a better view of Olivia and Imogen.

"Huh," was all Imogen managed to get out at first. But the longer she looked over at Toby and Alex locked in an embrace, the more unsettled she felt. "Verrry interesting, indeed."

A short time later, Alex and Toby joined Harding, Imogen, and Olivia at the SUV. Harding opened the back door, motioned with a hand like a well-trained chauffeur, and invited everyone to embark.

Alex hopped in first, giving Harding a wink and a nod. As Toby prepared to climb in, Harding used his arm to block the way.

"Hey, tell me one thing?"

"Yes, Detective?"

"Am I crazy?"

Toby laughed. "Maybe we're all a little crazy, Detective. Or maybe this is nothing more than a dream."

"Within a dream," Harding added quietly.

Toby nodded. "So maybe you're not crazy yet, but as Master Yoda once said to a young Luke Skywalker—"

Harding dropped his arm, freeing the way for Toby to climb into the vehicle. "Another one with this D&D shit. Can't a guy get a simple yes or no answer anymore? Get in."

"No, and as Master Yoda warned—you will be! You will be," Toby said, doing a fine imitation of Frank Oz as Yoda, capping it with a laugh that would have made even Yoda smile.

Harding shut the door and then slid himself into the driver's seat. He looked back over his shoulder, taking in the motley assembly of faces that stared wide-eyed back at him—

Imogen Rockwell.

Olivia Christine Lovejoy.

Toby Miller.

And, most unbelievable of all, Alexandra "Alex" Miller.

"Alright," Harding said as the engine roared to life. "Let's go get this bitch."

Everyone enthusiastically voiced their agreement as the

SUV turned onto the long winding road ahead of them. The remnants of The Greasy Spoon were now little more than a speck in the rearview mirror, a distant memory.

Harding, eyeing Toby in the mirror, asked, "Where to?"

Toby turned to the window and gazed out at the vast acres of flat, nearly barren desert. Then he turned to the road. The road ahead of them was dark. There seemed to be nothing ahead and nothing behind. No lights to lead the way. But their path was sure, and their way was true. They were heroes. Just for today. And this was their day. This was their time. And, come what may, they'd fight until the last of them was standing, if that's what was asked.

"To destiny, Detective. To the edge of the world." Toby started, paused a moment, then finished the thought. "Til Valhalla."

"Til Valhalla," Imogen agreed, taking Olivia's hand in hers.

"Til Valhalla," Olivia said, taking Imogen's hand and Toby's hand in her own.

"Til Valhalla," Alex Miller said last, resting her head on Toby's shoulder. "You have bigger shoulders now."

Up ahead, the storm clouds ignited from the inside. Their lightning could be seen for miles over the flatlands and illuminating the far-off mountain peaks. The earth seemed to tremble as the SUV pressed on through the darkness. On through the endless night. On through the merciless desert. On and on—

Til Valhalla.

Epilogue - ¡Vaya Con Dios, Bitch!

Joanne Garriga hummed as she steered her shit box of a car through the dark. Her headlights did little to pierce the endless black on the road ahead of her. But she wasn't worried.

Jesus loves me, this I know...

There wouldn't be many cars where she was going.

... for the Bible tells me so.

Just the one.

Little ones to him belong...

An over-sized SUV full of dreamers that were already as good as dead.

... they are weak, but he is strong.

From inside her darkest depths, the rotten place where Sandra had injected Mary Miller, a voice sounded. *Soon, little brother. I'll be seeing you. Soon.*

But then, another voice, from an even deeper place, from the place Joanne Garriga kept her secrets hidden from the Miller bitches, just like Señor Toby had taught her to do. This voice...Joanne's true voice...her own voice said—

Vaya con dios, bitches.

Vaya. Con. Dios.

Til Valhalla.

Bonus Content

Want to see the jukebox playlist, Flo's secret pie recipe and more bonus material?!

Download a copy of the playlist to add to your listening queue (no Josh Groban, please!).

And what is the secret behind Flo's killer pie? Do you have all the ingredients?

Also enjoy a bonus chapter plus more content!

Just tell us where to send it!

https://dl.bookfunnel.com/yoklltlccp

Acknowledgements

No Josh Grobans Were Hurt Writing This Book

Welcome back, Staycationers!

It feels like only yesterday we got on this wild ride together. And now, here we are again, one year later for more! C–R–A–Z–Y!

If this is your first-time riding, welcome. We have plenty of room, so make yourself at home.

Yo, ho, ho and a bottle of gum!

There be **spoilers** ahead, so if you've jumped back here to see if your name is in the credits without first reading *Lockdown*… **turn back now!!!** And come back when you're all caught up. We'll wait. I promise you.

Seriously. **Go**. We'll be waiting…

Now that that's out of the way, let's get on with the show…

Sometime before *Staycation* went to press in 2023, Andre, Natasha, and I spoke about the possible future of *Staycation*—did I have any ideas about continuing the story, any interest in developing a sequel… and so on.

Basically, it was the kind of conversation a writer dreams of having with their publisher. Except, for me, *Staycation*, was a one-off. A single nightmarish story contained in a compact binding. But the idea of finding a way to go on excited me. And, if I'm honest, scared me just a little.

I sat with it for a few weeks as we put the finishing touches on the cover for *Staycation* and I made a few last-minute tweaks to the first book's already wild ending. And I gotta be honest here—I wasn't loving the initial ideas I was coming up with. They felt forced. It was like *how can I retread what I've already done, and get the same reaction without turning into a parody or a cliché of myself.* (*cough, cough... M. Night, looking at you,)

I mapped out a large story arc that would cover two more *Staycation* books, largely separate stories with a unifying thread, but the more I toiled with it, the more I hated the idea of going back into it just to re-do what I've already done.

I realized that I had no interest in telling those stories. It just felt like a *Saw* movie to me, and I didn't want to go there, as much as I enjoy a good Jigsaw flick.

So, I'm sorry if that disappoints you. Truly, I am.

For me, there was only one path forward. And that was the one that got me REALLY excited.

I always—*always*—intended to revisit Toby and Alex Miller, maybe some ten years down the road. That's ten years OUR time, not their time. I felt, as Harding might say, in my gut that there was more story there. But I wanted to put some miles between the Millers and me before checking back in on my favorite twins. Tell some other stories first. It seems that fate had other plans for the three of us.

I spent a long, long weekend re-reading *Staycation* about four times and everything I needed was there in the original novel. The threads just needed a little pulling, and that's what I did for the next few months—did a lot of pulling. And then, little by little, Toby and Alex showed me the story they wanted to tell. And it just felt right. It clicked pretty quickly, and little has changed from my initial notes to this finished novel on my end.

For me, the only logical way forward with *Staycation* was to continue to be unexpected. To go right, when you thought I'd go left. Stick to the uneasiness, dread, horror, and wild twists that made *Staycation* a wicked treat.

The real game, dear reader, is between you and I. Can I surprise you? Do you think you know where I'm going? Can I trick you into believing the impossible?

Hopefully, yes.

It wouldn't be a *Staycation* story without some mind-fucks, so I hope I was able to, erm, fuck your brain good. In the end, much like our first outing together, everything had to serve the story, or it was cut. I am a firm believer in story first. Action without story is like playing Pac-Man. There's no explanation for anything, it just is what it is. No depth. And while I still love me some Pac-Man—truly, I am a hardcore retro gamer—the stories I want to tell are about people, sometimes fucked up people, and that takes time to develop. Be patient, and let the story suck you in. In our age of instant gratification, it makes me a little sad to see so many reader comments on-line about books I loved and still love asking when it gets good... does anything happen? Oy. I've been led astray on occasion by writers who let's just say led us out into the wilderness and left us there to die. There was no pay-off. If you give me your time, and several hundred pages, I will make it pay-off. But you have to trust me, and know that every single line in *Lockdown* has a purpose.

All that said, I hope you LOLed at some of the familiar *Staycation* tropes I tried to weave in; some not even remotely subtly, and others hidden a little deeper. Did you get all of the Stephen King references? The Broadway and theatre nods? **All** of the Easter eggs? Are you sure? You might want to go back and check again...

And sorry not sorry, I'll never stop ruffling Josh Groban's feathers. Never!

I have met so many wonderful people out there thanks to *Staycation.* It's been surprising and gratifying to talk to you all and hear how much you enjoyed *Staycation,* and my work.

Some of my favorite TikTokers... I'm looking at you: Mickey Tompkins aka irratebass (*poor, poor Justin*), Silent_Twin, JR, Hannah, Cris, Shannon, Ash, Mr. Splatter, Terry H, Amber Gill, Melanie King, Haylie Fry, and Christine Nichole.

THANK YOU for the support. Truly, you are what kept me going on the days the imposter syndrome was raging. **This one's for you.**

Writing, to me, is a lot like what I imagine being possessed feels like. There are times I feel like I am just a receiver, taking dictation, describing what I see. The work and the words come easily. Other days, man... it's like extracting a tooth on your own in the middle of a mosh pit without a mirror or Novocain, using nothing but your knitted mittens. The work and the words are elusive. Masters of hide and seek.

But we made it through with most of our teeth still intact. You're holding the proof in hands. And I would be remiss not to mention a few of the amazing folks who helped birth *Lockdown.*

So, without further ado, a million thank you's to:

My awesome M4L family: Andre and Natasha. Thank you for making my dream come true. Again. And to Melissa Prideaux, for making me sound better than I am.

My "dream team" of early readers: the Melissas, O'Neal and Nelson, and Loralee Janus. Thank you for the encouragement, suggestions, and deciphering my typos!

Loralee, thank you for the ear, the shoulder, and the needed light when the days got dark. As the adage goes, you were right. You told me so.

Friends who are always there when I am in danger of losing myself:

Irin Israel, Rosie Finizio, Ilene Angel, Liz Colabraro, Natasha Squires, Erin Riha, Adam McOmber, David Muniz, Harry Rettino, Patricia Lobosco, Donna Cuccio, Morag MacPherson, Danielle Frangella-Hanily, Heather Edwards, Alex and Gail Repetti, Donna Ingargiola, and Anthony Aloise. Love you!

An extra-special shout out to Pat Lobosco, for helping me become the writer I am today. I would be a lost soul in the world had I not had your encouragement and guidance.

No matter what anyone else says, YOUR TEACHERS MAT-TER.

To my amazing nephew, Kevin Hutchinson, never stop writing!

To my brilliant niece and fellow serial killer/true crime junkie: there's nothing you can't do. Go for it!

And to my equally amazing godson Brian Nelson, remember: you can do anything!

Always, to my partner in crime, Dana DeFrancesco, thank you for giving me space to find the story when the door was closed, and for being there to celebrate when it was opened again.

And finally, this book took probably twice as long to write thanks to my best buddy in the whole world, my Aussillon, Venus, who <u>demanded</u> we play fetch every time the writing was just getting good. Our forced breaks reminded me of the life out there beyond the page. I'll always throw the yellow guy if you're up for fetching him. (She **really** is the cutest thing. Check out my Insta if you don't believe me!)

So, this is where I leave you, for now, Staycationers.

Flo's got a pot of Joe brewing and I have another *Staycation* novel to finish. A saga to bring to an end. I bet you didn't see THAT coming, did you? You have many questions, and I do hope you'll take a ride with me one more time to see how it all ends.

See you on the other side!

RJ Clark
Asbury Park, NJ
Winter 2024

Enjoy this book?

We hope you enjoyed this release from M4L Publishing.

Reviews are the most helpful tools in getting new readers for any books. We don't have the financial backing of a New York publishing house and can't afford to blast our books on billboards or bus stops.

(Not yet!)

That said, your honest review can go a long way in helping us reach new readers. If you've enjoyed this book, we'd be forever grateful if you could spend a couple minutes leaving it a review (it can be as short as you like) on the site you purchased this book from.

Thank you so much!

About the Author

RJ CLARK began his professional career as a child actor and model, following in his famous uncle's footsteps, Stanley Clements. RJ's face was seen nationwide in the U.S. Army "Stay in School" print ad campaign. He also appeared regularly on daytime television, and worked on numerous film and commercial projects before inevitably returning to his first true love, writing.

As a screenwriter, RJ's screenplays won first prize or placed in the top 5 of nearly every major national—and international—competition worth mentioning. His novella, Two for One launched the indie literary magazine "The Instagatorzine," broken into two parts across the magazine's first two issues.

A native New Yorker, RJ attended NYU, holds a BFA and an MFA. He has lived in all five boroughs, but now calls historic Asbury Park, NJ home with his wife and dog, an Aussillon named Venus.

While RJ no longer works in the theatre as an actor, he provides accessibility services for deaf patrons at live performances throughout the country. He is passionate about theatre being for all, and enjoys being able to introduce new shows to deaf or hard of hearing patrons.

When not writing, you're most likely to find RJ either playing guitar along the Jersey Shore, taking photographs of cool dogs and musicians around Asbury Park, voraciously reading new books, working on new music, or traveling the world.

A few of RJ's most favorite things include black coffee, chocolate, Stephen King, peanut butter, Pringle's, Truman Capote, tabletop games, the Universal Studios Monsters, horror movies, and David Tennant.

Follow RJ online:

Facebook: RJ Clark Horror Writer
   Staycation Group (Facebook): Staycationers, Unite!
   TikTok: @rj_clark_writer
   IG: @rj_clark_writer
   Threads: @rj_clark_writer
   Website: www.rjclarkwriter.com

Also from M4L Publishing